THE BEGINNING AND
END OF EVERYTHING

STEVIE J COLE
LAUREN LOVELL

To those we've loved that the darkness has captured.

Chaos is an angel who fell in love with a demon.

— CHRISTOPHER POINDEXTER

1

POPPY

APRIL 2014

There are some moments in life that threaten to rip away a person's soul. Moments where, even years later, the magnitude of the grief is still palpable, and as I wipe my living room window clean, one of those moments is looming.

The very second the black Mercedes pulls into our drive, I know. My heart goes into a pleading gallop, and I brace myself on the wooden frame, praying they have the wrong house.

As the car door swings open, an army officer climbs out. He adjusts the sleeve of his uniform as he stares at my front door. The worried look etched into his features foreshadowed the news he'll soon be sharing.

Closing my eyes, I place a palm to my mouth to cover the sob, and I try to breathe, praying he's come with news other than I'm now a widow. In. Out. But my chest goes tight, robbing my lungs of air when the chimes echo like church bells off the walls of my home, yet now it feels more like a tomb.

I don't recall moving from the window or turning the

latch or even inviting the officer inside. He takes a rigid seat on the edge of the sofa, his spine straight as an arrow and stiff as a board. The host in me offers to put on tea, foolishly clinging to hope that this visit is cordial—that my heart is wrong.

The officer clears his throat and croaks my married name when I'm halfway to the kitchen. The slow turn I make doesn't stop the hands of time. And when I face him, he stands, gripping his hat in front of him. "I'm sorry, ma'am." My name is scribbled in messy handwriting across the front of the envelope he hands me—a grave letter. The man forces himself to make eye contact to convey his painful message. "Your husband was a good soldier. He served his country well."

With a solemn expression, he places a gentle hand to my arm. That touch makes it all too real.

I've lost him.

And *that* was the beginning and end of everything.

PART 1

THE PAST. THE BEGINNING

POPPY

OCTOBER 1999

My mother passed away when I was nine. An age where I would always remember her, but where time would steal away most of the memories, no matter how hard I clung to them. At that point, I understood that death was final, and losing my mother took a chunk of my heart that I believed no one else would ever fill.

That October marked a year since her passing and exactly one month since my father had moved us from America to Ireland for a job that would help cover the debt he owed the hospitals.

He promised I'd make friends, that I would love Ireland just as much as I had loved Georgia, but over the last few weeks, I'd been laughed at more than spoken to. In fact, the only kid in the class who'd even said so much as hello to me was Connor Blaine, the chubby, blond-headed boy who sat beside me. He got picked on for being overweight just as much as I did for talking funny. Connor's best friend, Brandon—at the very least—didn't make fun of me, even if it was painfully obvious that he didn't really like me.

Miss Brown finished our cursive lesson then turned from the chalkboard, dusting her hands before taking heavy strides toward the corner where Brandon stood with his nose to the wall. In the few weeks I'd been there, he'd spent more time in the corner than he had at his seat.

Exhaling, she took him by the shoulders, spun him around, and crouched eye level with him before pointing a stern finger in his face. "Next time you throw a toad at a girl, it's to the head master's office with ya."

"Yes, Miss." Brandon straightened his back and gave a single curt nod like he meant to behave from then on. Even *I* knew that was far from the truth. A subtle smirk curled one corner of his lips before he sank into the seat on the other side of Connor.

The day crept along, and when Miss Brown called on people to read *James and the Giant Peach*, I slouched in my chair, not wanting her to choose me. Two paragraphs in, she called my name with a sweet grin. I took a deep breath, placed both elbows onto the table, pushing myself up to hunch over my book, hoping my hair would hide my face from the rest of the class while I read.

Davie Logan snickered. Miss Brown clapped her hands, and I kept reading until my turn was over. Then the next child stuttered through the first few lines.

Brandon leaned in front of Connor, eyes narrowed. "Why *do* you talk so funny?" he whispered.

I had already explained to Brandon that I wasn't Irish, but for whatever reason, he thought being *in* Ireland meant I should talk in the same sing-song accent everyone else did.

Connor punched him in the arm, and Brandon scowled before he redirected his attention to the notebook in front of him. He scribbled until his pencil ripped the paper. I blocked out the sound of the other kids reading passages, attuned to the incessant ticking of the clock. Finally, the bell rang, followed by the bustle of kids putting books away.

Connor was almost to the door when he glanced over his shoulder at me, then knelt, pretending to tie an already knotted shoelace. Brandon stopped beside him. "You coming to my place?"

"Yeah." Connor pushed to his feet. "Want to come to the Gypo camp with us, Poppy?"

"Gypo camp?" I asked on our way through the hallway. "What's a Gypo camp?"

"It's a place with a bunch of caravans. Brandon lives there."

"Okay."

Brandon tossed his head back on a groan. He didn't want me coming, but I didn't care. I liked Connor.

———

THE GATE into the campsite hung at an angle, chained on both sides. Brandon said it was to stop people from "nicking" their caravans while they slept. I nodded when he nimbly jumped the fence, even though I had no idea what it meant to nick something.

Connor struggled to hoist himself over, then tumbled to the dry ground with an oomph. I slipped between the posts and gave him my hand to help him to his feet, his cheeks blushing.

We followed Brandon across the field to where a messy collection of travel trailers sat, some silver, some white, and some with fabric awnings pitched over the entrance. I took in my surroundings, thinking about how much it reminded me of a traveling circus while the boys rounded a rusted truck a few feet ahead. Weeds and tall grass covered most of the fender, but I didn't stop to linger. I followed them between the trailers—or caravans, as Connor had called them—until Brandon started up a set of steps.

A white dog, covered in dirt and grease, shot out from the underpinning, yapping. He made it a few feet before the frayed piece of rope tethering him to the trailer caught, yanking him back.

"Shut up, Sean!" Brandon said, reaching for the door, but Sean kept barking. When Brandon opened the door, it dropped on its hinges with a thump, and the dog howled.

"Brandon?" a woman shouted.

"Yeah, I'm here." He stepped inside, then stopped, leaving Connor and me on the steps. "Where's Dad?"

"At the pub."

Brandon's shoulders sagged—the same way they did when he was blamed for something in class—before he moved inside. Connor went straight to a plastic-covered, floral couch and flopped down, looking right at home. But I lingered in the doorway. A woman I assumed was Brandon's mother stood in front of a tiny sink, her hands in dishwater. Her dark hair was pulled into a messy bun, and an apron was tied around her cinched waist. If I squinted just enough, she could have looked like my mom. I rubbed at the dull ache in my chest, hoping Brandon knew how lucky he was.

"You and Connor want a snack?" She wiped her hands on her apron and grabbed a plate of cookies. The second she turned, her gaze landed on me, and her steps faltered. She smiled the kind of smile that I'd only seen my mother give. One that caused tiny dimples to pop in her cheeks. She held out the plate of cookies, and both boys snatched two. "Who's this?"

Brandon shoved the treat into his mouth, then yanked

his shirt over his head and tossed it onto the sofa. "Poppy. Connor likes her, but I think she talks funny."

His mother's eyes strayed from me to the crumpled shirt on the plastic-covered couch before she dug her fists into her hips and pointed across the small room. "Boy, that shirt was clean this morning! What did you do? Roll around in the mulch?" She swatted his head, then gave me a smile. "Don't mind him. Boy thinks he was raised in a barn."

After our snack, his mom sent us outside to play. Brandon took off through the maze of caravans while Connor straggled behind, next to me. "His ma's nice."

"Yeah." I nodded. As much as the jealousy that coursed through me made a knot of guilt settle in my stomach, I couldn't help it.

"I'm sure yours is, too," he said. A simple, casual comment, but it hurt.

The kind of pain that stops a child dead in their tracks. I swatted at the tears stinging my eyes, and Connor's brow furrowed. Before he could say a word, I huffed.

"Stupid gnat."

"Yeah. They're bad this time of year."

I lied. I didn't want Connor to feel sorry for me, but most importantly, I didn't want to think about it.

I forced my thoughts elsewhere and followed Connor around a white trailer. It had fallen off three of its wheels, which meant one end sat higher than the others. An old man sat in front of it, slumped over in a ratty lawn chair. A hat covered half of his face, and an empty bottle of whiskey laid propped in his lap.

"That's Old Man McGinty," Connor leaned in to whisper, thumbing back at the sleeping man. "My ma says he's a drunk."

Eventually, the caravans opened to a field where, unlike

most of Ireland, the grass was brown and dead. A black pony stood tied to a metal post, munching on what little green was left. The horse lifted its head, snorting when we approached.

"Hey, Shegar." Brandon patted the pony's mane, then unfastened the harness from the rope before glancing at me. "Wanna ride him?"

The only pony I had ever ridden had been one at the Georgia State Fair. The kind someone led around in a circle. My gaze shifted from the pony to Brandon

"Come on." He jerked his chin toward the horse and smiled.

My gut instinct was not to trust Brandon.

On a huff, he rolled his eyes. "What's the matter? You scared?"

"No." I was terrified I might fall off, but I would never admit it. For whatever reason, I wanted Brandon to like me. Which was why I stepped beside the pony with my racing heart and swatted the gnats buzzing by his face.

"Grab him like this." He fisted Shegar's mane. "Then lift up your leg."

I hesitated before threading my fingers through the horse's coarse hair.

"On three—One. Two." Brandon grabbed my leg and pushed me up. "Three."

The horse lifted its head with a snort when I sprawled out on its back. I shifted, sitting upright and gripping the mane for dear life. "Now, what do I do?"

Brandon tossed his head back, swiping a hand down his face on a groan. "How do you not know how to ride a horse?"

"I don't think they have horses in America," Connor whispered.

"We do, too!"

"Well, riding a pony is kinda like swimming." Brandon fiddled with the collar around the pony's neck, and a smirk danced over his lips just as his eyes locked on mine. "You just jump in and figure it out."

"What?" I panicked. "No, you don't. You drown!"

"Bran," Connor started. "Don't..."

The collar dropped to the dry grass. Brandon smacked the horse on its hindquarter, and he trotted off with another snort, all while I flopped from side to side like a ragdoll. It jumped a small ditch, and I toppled to the hard ground, a cloud of dust billowing around me. My butt throbbed, and my palms ached from where I'd tried to brace my fall. Brandon was bent over at the waist, cackling.

"Bran, you're an arse." Connor took off across the field but stopped halfway to lean over his knees and gasp for breath.

I stood, dusted the dirt from my knees, and stomped across the dead field—right past Connor and right up to Brandon. He wiped tears from his eyes, still laughing.

My cheeks heated. I wasn't sure what hurt more my fall or my pride.

I crossed my arms over my chest, hoping I came off as angry and not hurt. "What's so funny?"

"You should've seen yourself." He imitated a terrorized scream before chuckling some more.

I gritted my teeth. "You're a meany butt!"

His laughter fell silent. He folded his arms over his chest, and I almost wanted to shrink away from him. "That *isn't* a bad word, Poppy."

"Bran," Connor ran up beside me, winded. "Leave her alone."

"Fine." I inched closer. "Butthole."

There was a pause, a slight tic to his jaw. A moment

where I thought maybe I'd won. Then Brandon narrowed his eyes. "Bitch."

I'd never heard that word used outside of the movies, and, at the tender age of ten, having it directed at me from a boy I wished would accept me, it felt like a hot poker driving right through my heart. I fought the quiver in my lip. I tried to keep my nostrils from flaring, but all that did was force the tears out faster than I'd wanted.

Connor's arm came around my shoulders. "You're an arse, Bran!"

Brandon's hardened gaze moved from me to Connor, then back. I shrugged out of Connor's hold, wiped my face with my sleeve, then kicked Brandon right in the shin.

3

POPPY

NOVEMBER 1999

Most days after school, I went to Connor's house until Daddy's shift at the factory ended. And of course, Brandon came, too, because he went wherever Connor did.

As soon as we walked in, Connor's mom checked that we didn't have any unfinished homework. She placed a plate full of fresh-from-the-oven cookies on the table, followed by three small glasses of milk. Connor's mom was nice, like the moms on every sitcom TV show. All smiley, with a sweet, soothing voice.

The warm chocolate chips melted on my tongue when I took a bite. I stuffed the rest of the first cookie into my mouth as I plopped down onto the floor and dumped my Barbies from my backpack. They scattered the carpet, limbs twisted at awkward angles and hair tangled.

I chose one from the pile, fixing her pink tutu while looking at Connor. "Wanna play with me?"

He shrugged and grabbed the lone Ken doll. "Sure."

As expected, Brandon groaned. He was always throwing

his head back and groaning when it came to me. "Can't we play video games?" he asked around a mouthful of cookie. "Barbies suck."

"Video games rot your brain." I combed through my doll's hair while Connor busied himself by cramming Ken's foot into a plastic loafer.

"Says who?" Brandon flopped down onto the sofa, swatting one of the throw pillows to the floor.

"My daddy."

Connor scooted closer to me. He frowned when he pushed Ken's arms above its head. "What do you do with dolls?"

"Run them over with your monster truck." Brandon leaned off the couch and reached for the Barbie in my hand, but I yanked it away. "Like *Grand Theft Auto*."

A slight wrinkle formed on the ridge of Connor's brow. "*Grand Theft Auto*?"

"The video game?" With a roll of his eyes, Brandon rummaged through his ratty backpack for something, then trudged across the room and shoved a disc into the game console. He took the controllers and tossed one to Connor. "I got it from Uncle Darren's caravan. It's awesome!" Brandon's attention narrowed on me. "Girls can't play." Then he turned back to the TV.

I focused on making Barbie's hair silky smooth, pretending I didn't care that the boys didn't include me. But I did. For whatever reason, since the first day I'd met Brandon, I wanted to mean something to him, even though he was terrible.

A myriad of noises: gunshots and screams, sirens, and roaring engines, filled the room. "What do I do?" Connor sounded panicked, so I glanced at the screen. One of the players darted past a rundown building before whacking someone with a baseball bat.

"Just..." Brandon jabbed at his controller. "Drive around and rob stuff—and kill people that get in your way."

"Kill them? With what?"

"Your gun. And—" Brandon yanked his controller to the left—"Your car."

The game looked too chaotic. Most definitely for boys. And I happily went back to dressing my doll, although every few seconds, I would steal a glance at the TV.

"Oh! Run over that hooker." Brandon's fingers went crazy on the controller. "Run her over, Con! Get her!"

Connor moved his player a few steps, then turned to look at Brandon. "What's a hooker?"

A pan clattered in the kitchen.

"Old Man McGinty said it's a lady in a short dress."

Tires screeched on the TV, and a car crashed against a light post, coming to a stop beside a woman whom I had just learned was a hooker.

"Aw, shit!"

Mrs. Blaine rushed into the living room with a mixing spoon covered in whipped potatoes still in her hand. The color drained from her cheeks when she glanced at the TV. A hand covered her heart as she gasped. "What on God's blessed earth? Oh my..." She moved in front of the screen, blocking the image with her wide hips while she reached behind her to fiddle with the buttons.

The screen went blank, and Brandon tossed his controller to the thick carpet. "Aw, Mrs. Blaine. I was about to kill me a hooker."

"Give me strength, Father," she mumbled while she crossed her chest. "Where did you get such filth?"

Brandon's gaze drifted from Mrs. Blaine to Connor, then

back. He scratched his head, tangling his messy, brown hair even more. "Nicked it from Uncle Darren."

"Stealing and hookers..." Mrs. Blaine's nostrils flared as she shook her head. "I shall be talkin' to ya ma."

"Aw, Mrs. Blaine. She'll smack my arse."

"Someone needs to, boy," she said on her way back to the kitchen.

I smiled at Brandon. "Told you video games are bad for you."

With a glare, he grabbed the brunette Barbie my mother had given me on my eighth birthday.

"Be careful with her," I said, but he was too busy trying to undress her to listen.

"Does she have boobs?"

The Velcro ripped, and the sparkly dress dropped to the floor. Brandon wrinkled his nose when he glanced down at the nude plastic. "Gross."

Enraged, I shoved to my feet. Brandon held the unclothed doll above his head, laughing as he waved it around.

"Stop." I jumped to grab the toy, but he dangled it out of reach.

A wicked grin—one that warned something awful was brewing in Brandon's head—tugged at the corner of his lips. Then he ripped off the doll's head and tossed it to the floor. It bounced over the carpet before rolling to a stop beside my foot.

A storm of emotions swirled inside me when I bent to retrieve the decapitated head. I stared at the doll's bright smile, her pretty brown waves, remembering how soft my mother's voice had been when she told me she thought the doll looked like me.

Of course, I would have been angry had Brandon ripped

the head off any of my other dolls, but I wouldn't have been hurt. He'd just unknowingly destroyed the last present my mother had given me. Clenching my fists, I focused on how much I hated him to keep from crying.

"I can fix it, Poppy," Connor started, stepping to my side while Brandon doubled over in laughter.

But what I wanted more than my doll fixed, at least at that moment, was retribution. I wanted Brandon O'Kieffe in trouble. In major, butt-spanking trouble.

I gritted my teeth, sucking air deep into my lungs, then I belted out a scream so shrill it felt like sandpaper in my throat.

Connor and Brandon's hands flew to their ears. In point five seconds, Mrs. Blaine darted around the corner. "What's going on now?" She knelt in front of me, placing her soft hands on my arms. "Poppy? What's wrong?"

"Brandon..." I sniffed back tears and forced my lip to quiver because that always worked on my father. "He tore off my doll's head, then threw it at me! Because he..." I gulped in air for dramatic effect, and then I let the tears fall. "He hates me!" I buried my face in Mrs. Blaine's shoulder, inhaling the delicate scent of fabric softener.

"He doesn't hate you." She hugged me tightly, swept my hair from my face, then kissed my forehead. On a jilted breath, she pushed to her feet and grabbed Brandon by the ear.

Connor stood wide-eyed in the background while his mother marched a wincing Brandon right in front of me.

"Give Poppy her doll back."

He held out the headless Barbie, glaring at me like he wished he could rip off my head instead.

"And tell her you're sorry."

"Aw, Mrs. Blaine, I was just playing. I didn't—"

She tugged harder on his ear to make her point. "Sorry, Brandon. Tell her you're sorry."

"Ow." His nostrils flared. "Sorry."

Shaking her head, she mumbled "heathen" on her way from the room.

Connor scrubbed a hand through his hair and took the doll from my hands, while I glared at Brandon, hoping he felt my anger burn through his skin.

"There." Connor gave a proud, ear-to-ear grin when he handed back the Barbie, her head turned the wrong way around and shoved to her shoulders.

"Thanks."

An awkward silence settled over us while I pulled Barbie's head back into place and smoothed out her hair. From the corner of my eye, I noticed Connor rock from his heels to his toes, hands clasped behind his back. Brandon was still in full self-pity mode on the couch. I hoped he would stay there and leave us alone for the rest of the day.

"Want to go swing?" Connor asked.

"Sure."

Brandon immediately snapped, "No."

Connor shrugged and grabbed another cookie on our way to the backdoor. I couldn't understand why Connor, who was always smiling and sweet, would choose to be best friends with a grouch like Brandon.

Outside, a thick blanket of gray clouds covered the sky, making the day seem as dreary as I felt, and the chilly breeze didn't help. Quietly, I followed Connor to the corner of the yard where he plopped down on the swing set, causing the rusted chains to creak. I took the swing next to him and grabbed the cold, metal links, using my shoe to draw a line through the patch of dirt when I took a seat.

"Why are you even friends with him?"

"Dunno. Just am."

I picked up my feet to swing. "He's a butthole."

"Yeah, sometimes. But he can be nice, too."

I almost laughed at the thought of Brandon O'Kieffe being nice.

Connor pushed back, trying to match my rhythm. "He doesn't like girls. He says they have cooties."

That was the dumbest thing I had ever heard. If anyone in the whole of Ireland had cooties, it was Brandon. Half of the time, he didn't even look like he bathed. "I don't have cooties!"

"I know." His sneakers scuffed the grass to slow down a bit, and a plume of dust flew up in front of us. "I like you, though."

"Well, *you're* nice. He's not." I glanced toward the house.

Brandon stood at the screened door, watching us with a frown. He crossed his arms over his chest, and his unhappiness deepened. Sometimes, I wondered if he worried that I was stealing Connor. After all, Connor was the only kid that didn't call Brandon a gypo or a pikey, the only boy who never made fun of Brandon's clothes that were sometimes too small or riddled with holes. Sure, Brandon was mean, but everyone outside of Connor treated him terribly. I thought, maybe he expected me to be like them, too... Maybe that's why he didn't like me.

On a hard huff, I dragged the toes of my shoes across the grass, slowing myself down to jump from the swing.

A single dandelion had sprouted from one of the cracked paving stones, and I snatched it on my way to the porch. I knew that girls liked flowers, and maybe Brandon might think it was sissy. But really, a dandelion was a weed. Surely, a boy could appreciate a weed.

Brandon backed away from the screen door when I opened it and handed him the weed.

"I picked it for you. Thought it might make you happy."

My mother had always taught me that sometimes people just need someone to be nice to them. She thought kindness was the elixir for most pain. Naively, I truly believed that was all it was...

4

BRANDON

I t had been three days since I'd ripped the head off Poppy's dumb Barbie. That was the first time I understood what it meant to feel guilty. I checked my pocket to make sure the wilted dandelion was still there while I waited outside Connor's.

"Ma? I'm going out with Brandon."

"Be back for tea!" Mrs. Blaine shouted before the door banged shut behind him.

"Wanna swing?" he asked.

I headed through the gate at the front of his house. "Nah."

"Wanna go to the pikey camp?"

"We're going into town."

Behind me, I could hear the rattle of Connor fighting with the gate latch before he came jogging up beside me, already winded. "Town?"

"Yeah. I gotta get something."

The bus stop at the end of the road was empty. Connor frowned when I took a seat inside the little wooden shelter, tearing at one of the advertisements plastered to the wall. "You gotta pay to ride the bus."

I held up a fiver, and Connor's eyes bulged. "Where'd you get that?"

"Dad was asleep. So, I borrowed it."

Connor smacked a hand to his forehead. I inhaled, preparing myself for a lecture on all the ways that stealing was a sin, but thankfully, the low hum of an engine interrupted him before he got past commandment number three. The bus sputtered to a stop in front of us, expelling a toxic cloud of exhaust that made me cough as the doors creaked open. I handed our fare to the driver, then we took seats at the back.

Connor fidgeted in his seat the whole way into town, continuously mumbling about getting into trouble. By the time we stepped off the bus, I was ready to find a Milkybar and cram it down his throat to make him hush. That's all that kid worried about, trouble—and food. And that's all I seemed to stay in.

The bus disappeared around the corner, and my attention went right to the bright red and yellow awning of Callaghan's Toy Shoppe. It reminded me of a circus tent with its tiny flags waving in the breeze from the top of the canopy.

Just before we reached the toy shop door, I held out my arm, and Connor's plump chest bumped into it. The last thing I wanted to do was get him into trouble. I gave him a stern look while thumbing behind me. "You have to wait around the corner, okay?"

"Why?" Connor frowned. "I want to come in and look at the new lightsaber."

"No. You have to stay here. Wait around the corner from

McDonald's." I pointed to the half-lit golden arches a few stores down.

"Fine." He rolled his eyes. Even at that early stage in our friendship, Connor had realized sometimes it was best not to ask questions. "But you owe me a Big Mac," he mumbled and started down the sidewalk.

The bell over the door tinkered when I stepped inside the shop. The older man behind the counter glanced up from his newspaper when I approached the Star Wars display spread out at the front of the store. My pulse raced when I picked up a box with Darth Vader wielding a lightsaber. I didn't care about Darth Vader, but I had to look normal. A woman at the back of the store got his attention, and I watched from the corner of my eye as the man folded the paper, placed it on the counter, and disappeared around the corner. That was my chance. I took off down the aisles, stopping at the one where the shelves were stuffed full of obnoxious pink boxes. Blond Barbies. Brunette Barbies. Pageant Queen Barbie and Scuba Diver Barbie...

I quickly glanced over the shiny packages, snatching one with a doll that had brown hair like Poppy's. I shoved it under my arm and walked back through the shop with my heart in my throat. When I neared the till, I took one good look around, then bolted straight out the door.

"Hey!" a man shouted behind me. "Hey, kid. Stop!"

I glanced over my shoulder at the hefty security guard weaving between people on the sidewalk. That made me kick up my run to a full-blown sprint. I zoomed around the corner, already shouting for Connor to run.

His eyes went wide, and he started down the street with the speed of a sloth.

"Run!" I shouted again. Catching up to him, I grabbed his

arm and yanked him around a building and into an alley where we ducked behind a rusted Volvo.

Connor sidled beside me and coughed. I slammed my hand over his mouth. "Do you want us to get caught?" I whispered.

"Caught?" He panted for a second, swallowed, then shoved me, knocking me against the brick wall. "What did you do? Why are we running and hiding?"

I proudly held up the crumpled Barbie box. "For Poppy." The guard rushed past, blowing his whistle.

Groaning, he covered his face and dropped his chin to his chest. "My ma's going to kill me when she finds out."

His ma would never find out if he didn't tell her, but knowing Connor, he would go home and confess his sins the second she offered him tea.

I grabbed his hands and yanked them from his face, tossing them to his sides. "Don't tell, or I'll break all your video games."

"You play them, too!"

"I'll still do it." I jerked my chin toward the street. "Come on. I think they're gone."

My ma would have smacked me with her slipper if she'd found out I nicked that doll, but I had broken Poppy's Barbie and made her cry.

I didn't want her to be sad, even if she was a girl.

———

When Connor went home for tea, I went to Poppy's.

Nerves churned my stomach when I knocked on the door, and when it swung open, I nearly lost my lunch. I had to crane my neck to stare up at Mr. Turner. His thick beard and impressive height made him look like a lumberjack, and suddenly, I was dwarfed.

"Hey, Mr. Turner." I swallowed nervously. "Can Poppy come out to play?"

His gaze drifted to the box I had clutched in my hand, and a smile curled his lips. "Sure."

I hid the unwrapped present behind my back when he turned to call for Poppy.

Her pigtails bounced behind her when she skipped to the door. She grinned at her dad, and I wished she would grin at me like that. He ruffled her head when she stepped onto the porch.

I swung the box back and forth behind my back. "I got you something," I said, then shoved the package into her arms, hoping I would get one of those smiles.

She ran a finger over the white print, and when she looked up, she gave me a smile—one that was better than the one she'd given her Dad—then she hugged me. "Thank you."

My knees locked, and my arms went stiff at my sides while I fought the urge to shove her off.

"Maybe you aren't a meanybutt." She giggled, clutching the present to her chest. "Where's Connor?"

All of the warm, tingling feelings inside me turned to smoke. Then I did push her away. "I didn't get him a Big Mac, so he went home for tea."

"Daddy's making spaghetti with the sauce out of the can. You want to stay for dinner?"

I really liked spaghetti from the can, so I nodded. When Poppy turned to grab the door, one of the ribbons in her hair fell out, and I picked it up, tucking it into the same pocket as the dandelion for safekeeping. Nobody had ever given me anything before, apart from my ma when she knitted me a Christmas jumper every year. But it was different, and I valued that yellow weed as though it were worth more than gold. I don't know why I took her ribbon, but maybe I just wanted something else from her. Something that wouldn't shrivel up and die.

―――――

THE NEXT DAY AT SCHOOL, Poppy smiled at me before she smiled at Connor, and pride filled my chest that I'd made her happy. It carried me through the morning until the door to the hallway opened.

Halfway through the school day, the headteacher, Mr. Peterson, interrupted class. He apologized to Miss Brown before his beady eyes locked on me through thick, bottle-top glasses. "Brandon O'Kieffe, come with me, please."

I groaned under my breath before reluctantly following him into the hall.

Being in the headteacher's office was nothing new to me —it was just that I couldn't figure out what I'd done this time. I hadn't been sent to the corner once that day, but despite how hard I thought, I didn't come up with anything even by the time we entered Peterson's office.

The sunshine-yellow walls and the tiled ceiling were almost as familiar to me as my own cupboard bedroom in the caravan. I wasn't surprised to see my mum sitting in the chair on the other side of his desk when he led me through the doorway, the policeman, though—well, that was a shock. So much of one, I nearly shat my pants when I saw his fluorescent jacket and flat cap.

"Sit, Brandon." Peterson nodded toward the empty chair

beside my ma, who wouldn't even look at me as I took a seat —that's when I knew it was bad. "This is PC Coombes."

"Mr. O'Kieffe." The middle-aged officer nodded, then folded his arms over his vest. "You were caught on camera stealing from Callaghan's Toy Shoppe yesterday."

I folded my arms over my chest. "Mistaken identity," I said, quoting from that program, CSI. My ma loved it.

"Several people identified you."

Damn small town. Everyone knew everyone, and well, I didn't exactly keep my head down. In the current situation, I determined it was best to remain silent—seeing as how anything I said may be given in evidence and all that.

"Do you have anything to say for yourself?" Mr. Peterson demanded, his face turning beet red.

"No," I mumbled. I didn't regret stealing that Barbie, but I did wish I'd at least thought about the cameras in the shop. I figured that part was best left unsaid.

Mr. Peterson looked at me the way most adults did— with regret. "This is extremely disappointing behavior." He shook his head. "Given your record, I see no option but to expel you."

Expel me? For stealing a Barbie on a *Saturday*? But that would mean I'd have to find a different school, away from Connor and Poppy. I clenched my fist at my sides, fighting the tightness in my chest.

"Please," my ma begged. "I know Brandon can be difficult, but he's a good boy. Really. How is expelling him from school going to help anything?"

"Mrs. O'Kieffe," the policeman interrupted. "Your son could be given a criminal caution for this."

I looked at my ma, hoping she could get me out of this.

"He's just a child."

Coombes inhaled a deep breath and looked down his nose at me. "Which is why the shop owner has decided to be lenient. *And* why this has been brought to the school's attention."

The headteacher pushed to his feet and shook the policeman's hand, thanking him for bringing the matter to his attention.

After the officer left, Mr. Peterson resumed his place behind his desk, folding his hands in front of him.

"I'll suspend you for one week. This is your last chance, Brandon O'Kieffe." His gaze swung to my ma. "I suggest you discipline your son."

Ma gave Mr. Peterson a curt nod, her lips set in a firm line so straight it could've been used as a ruler. There wasn't a word said between us as I was practically dragged to her rusted Nissan with the bumper duct-taped on. The driver's door slammed so hard my ears rung, and I thought yelling would be better. She gripped the steering wheel and dropped her head forward with closed eyes.

"Dammit, Brandon. How could you be so stupid?" Her voice trembled.

I hated disappointing her more than anything. Ma was the most important person in the world to me. The only one who thought I was good, and I'd let her down. "I..."

"I know I can't afford to buy you toys." She looked at me with tears in her eyes. "I'm sorry."

I didn't care that I could never have the new lightsaber or a video game, but it didn't seem fair since Dad could afford to go to the pub every day. As I grew, I came to realize he was selfish. But at that moment, all I could think of was how I couldn't bear to see Ma cry, thinking I stole toys for myself.

"It was for Poppy," I blurted. "I broke her Barbie, and I

wanted to get her a new one." I knotted my fingers in my lap, staring down at them.

Her palm brushed over my cheek, soft and warm. "Oh, Brandon." Her tone was as gentle as her touch. "You're a good boy at heart."

"Are you disappointed?" I asked, my voice cracking with the words.

"No."

I looked up from my wringing hands, and a fleeting smile pulled at her lips.

"Brandon." She paused, and a deep wrinkle formed on her forehead before she clasped my hand. "Poppy Turner. She's a sweet girl, but do you want to go to prison for her?"

The realization washed over me. Cold and heavy. "No. But she's my friend, and I broke her doll and made her sad."

Ma let out a long breath, then stroked her fingers over my cheek. "*Now*. She's your friend *now* because you're children." She tilted her head, and a sad smile touched her lips. "But one day, she'll grow up. Girls like Poppy Turner don't socialize with people like us, sweetheart. Trust me, she isn't worth the suffering. Do you understand?" Her hand left my cheek, and she cranked the engine.

Her words confused me. Poppy *was* my friend, but I nodded anyway to make my ma happy.

"Good. Now, try to behave yourself. For me. That snobby headteacher thinks I'm raising you in a barn."

No, just a caravan, I thought, but I didn't say it. The truth was, I think my ma knew she could never rein me in, but she always stood by me. No matter how much trouble I got into, she defended me. Now I look back, I think she probably felt guilty because my childhood was so messed up, and she compensated as best she could.

"I love you, Ma."

She leaned forward and kissed my forehead. Her strong perfume got right into the back of my throat, and when she pulled away, I knew there would be a pink lipstick mark on my skin.

"I love you, too, Brandon. More than the whole wide world." The engine grated when she shifted the gear into drive. "Now, come on. You and I have a whole week together without your Da." She flashed a rare, mischievous smile.

WHEN WE GOT HOME, Dad was sprawled on the sofa, half-drunk with a bottle of whiskey dangling from his hand.

"Wheruva you been?" He struggled to lift his head, and his eyes crossed when he tried to focus on Ma.

Her nervous gaze darted to me, and she placed a hand on my back. "Go to your room, Brandon. Lock the door."

I hurried to my room and closed the flimsy door, sliding the bolt into place just as the shouting started. I knew the drill well by this point. The deep timbre of my father's voice traveled through the caravan.

"No, Des," Ma pleaded.

"That little shit got caught stealing?"

The thud of footsteps approaching made me shrink back against the wall. My heart hammered against my ribs so hard, I could hardly breathe. I hugged my arms around me to stop myself from shaking. The bang of his fist over my door made me jump out of my skin.

"Bringing trouble to our fecking door!"

"Leave him alone!"

Then came the distinctive, all-too-familiar crack of flesh meeting flesh, followed by the thud of Ma hitting the floor. I put my hands over my ears and fought tears. Most times, my dad hit her because he was drunk and in a bad mood, but this was different. I had done this. For the first time, it was my fault my ma had been beaten.

That broke something in me.

It took a sliver from the ball of fear that sat in my gut, and it replaced it with cold, festering anger that, in truth, stayed with me from that moment on.

5

POPPY

MARCH 2000

Kids darted between the monkey bars and slides, squealing with delighted laughter. I scooped up a handful of sand, then let it sift through my fingers. Connor nudged me, nodding at Brandon.

His tongue darted between his lips while his eyes focused on the magnifying glass in his hand. A pleased grin shaped his face when a little swirl of smoke rose from the wooden border to the sandbox.

"What are you doing?" I asked.

"Burning ants."

Frowning, I grabbed a pebble and tossed it. It landed a few feet to his side. "That's mean."

"Is not. They bite."

With a shake of my head, I sidled over beside Connor, using my finger to draw a kitten and a rainbow beside his stick-figure army men. I had just finished sketching a crown on the kitten's head when a shadow fell over the sandbox.

"Go away, Davie," Brandon said, still focused on the ant squirming underneath the heat of his magnifying glass.

Davie kicked at the dirt, sending a cloud of dust and tiny pebbles toward Brandon. "What are you two twats doing with a girl? Girls are gross." His dark eyes narrowed on me. "Especially her. My ma says I can't play with her because she's a measch." Davie laughed. He was a good foot taller than anyone else in our grade, and even though he got sent to the principal's office more than Brandon, I still glared at him.

Connor hurled his drawing stick at Davie but missed. "Leave her alone!" The twig snapped in two when it smacked the trunk of a nearby tree.

"Or what?" Davie leaned over and jabbed a finger into Connor's chest. "You'll throw a candy bar at me?" He side-stepped Connor, grabbed my hair, and yanked back my head.

I snatched my ponytail away, sucking in breath after breath to keep from crying.

"All right! That's it." Brandon chucked the magnifying glass to the ground and shoved to his feet with his fists balled. Within a millisecond, he'd cocked his arm back and thrown a punch.

Davie grabbed his face on a groan, and I watched as a trail of blood trickled through his fingers and down his forearm.

"Don't mess with her." Brandon lunged toward him, another fist ready and raised, and Davie scampered off boohooing.

Connor paced the sandbox, shaking his head and mumbling about Brandon getting into trouble, while I stared at Brandon's busted knuckles. My stomach kinked and knotted in a way that *didn't* make me want to throw up —in a warm way I'd never felt before. I fought the smile that tugged at my lips because, as much as I liked what Brandon had done, a part of me knew I shouldn't.

"Brandon O'Kieffe!" Mrs. Brown's voice echoed over the playground, and all the children fell silent. Even the creak of the swing set slowed to an abrupt halt. Mrs. Brown stood across the yard, her arm wrapped around a sniffling Davie's shoulder. Her face turned an unbelievable shade of red. "Get over here." She pointed at Brandon. "This instant!"

Brandon's triumphant grin crumpled to a frown. He shoved both hands into his pockets and headed toward the teacher.

"He's gonna get in trouble," I whispered, guilt settling in my chest.

Connor half-way shrugged. "It's Brandon. He's always in trouble."

THAT AFTERNOON, the school decided that Brandon was, in fact, *too much* trouble, because Mr. Peterson had him expelled. I went straight to my room after school, grabbing the Barbie Brandon had given me and holding her in my lap while guilt settled over me, heavy and hard. Deep down, I knew it was my fault Brandon had been kicked out of school. No, I hadn't made him punch Davie Logan, just like I hadn't forced him to hide toads and lizards in Neive Kirkpatrick's desk. But I was the reason he had done those things, because Davie had hurt me, and Neive had made fun of me. And one thing Brandon didn't tolerate was anyone making Connor or me feel bad.

I worried, not that I wouldn't ever see Brandon again, but that I wouldn't see him enough. I wanted Brandon with Connor and me always, and when he wasn't close by, it felt like something important was missing.

Those two boys had somehow made that chunk of my heart that felt so empty when my mother had died, seem a little bit smaller, a tad bit fuller. It wasn't fair that Brandon had been expelled and Davie seemed like the helpless victim. And that evening, over supper, my daddy agreed it wasn't fair at all, and he promised he'd have a talk with Mr. Peterson.

THE NEXT AFTERNOON, Daddy called up the stairs that my friends were waiting outside. I shoved my feet into my shoes, expecting only Connor since Brandon was grounded. However, I was pleasantly surprised to find Brandon on my doorstep, hair scruffy, and his T-shirt crumpled like it had been plucked from his bedroom floor. His chin was tucked to his chest while he scuffed his beat-up sneakers back and forth.

"Come on." Connor disappeared through the gate.

When I started down the steps, Brandon grabbed my arm, then quickly snatched it back.

"Hey, uh— Thanks," he mumbled, finally making eye contact with me.

"For?"

"I know you got your dad to tell on Davie. Thanks."

My cheeks heated. Brandon bolted down the steps and grabbed his rusted bike from where it had been dumped on the pavement. Connor had already lifted the kickstand to his bright green bike and sat waiting on us. I'd gotten a flat tire earlier in the week, and Daddy had worked overtime, which meant he hadn't fixed it yet.

Sighing, I said, "I can't ride. My tire's still flat."

"It's fine. I'll give you a backy." Brandon patted his ripped seat.

I eyed the mangled wires that once served as brakes. Brandon's Mom always gave him grief for wearing holes in the toes of his sneakers, but that was the only way he had to slow down. He patted the seat again, and I took a step back with a slight shake of my head.

"You don't have brakes, Brandon."

"I'll go slow." Slow wasn't in that boy's vocabulary.

Connor slid off the seat and straddled the bar. "I'll take you, Poppy."

My gaze strayed between him and Brandon, then I shrugged before climbing onto the seat and wrapping my arms around Connor's plump middle. He started pedaling, and we inched along the sidewalk. Of course, Brandon took off as fast as he could. He zoomed around the corner before we were even halfway down the street. We circled in front of Mrs. O'Murray's house, and the bike's wheel struck a root protruding from the pavement. The front tire wobbled, and Connor lost his balance, sending both of us toppling to the ground. Connor landed with an oomph, and my knee cracked against the jagged piece of concrete jutted up by the root. Pain shot through my leg, and I hissed in a breath.

"I'm sorry, Poppy." He groaned and pushed to his hands and knees, starting toward me in a crawl. "Are you—"

"Shit, Con!" Brandon shouted. His rusted bike clattered to the pavement, and his shoes scuffed the sidewalk when he skidded to a stop, then crouched beside me with narrowed eyes. "You okay?"

A steady stream of blood trickled down my leg, and my knee throbbed with pain. I'd seen Brandon take falls like this and never cry, and I didn't want him to think I was some wussy girl. "I'm fine," I managed through gritted teeth.

Connor's gaze dropped to my knee. His eyes went wide,

and he scrambled to his feet. "I think she needs stitches." He was already halfway to Mrs. O'Murray's gate. "I'll get help."

Brandon snatched a twig from the sidewalk and chucked it at Connor's back, missing, most likely on purpose. "Shut up, Con. She's fine." He brushed the dirt from my skinned flesh. "It's just a scratch."

"Ow!" Flinching, I yanked my leg away with a scowl. "Don't touch it."

"I'm getting Mrs. O'Murray." The hinges to the gate creaked when Connor opened it.

I didn't want Mrs. O'Murray coming out and making a fuss. Plus, the longer I stayed there, the closer I came to giving in to the sob lodged and waiting in the back of my throat.

"I'm fine, Connor." I forced a smile. "I'm just gonna go home and get a bandage." But when I stood and placed my full weight on my leg, my knee buckled.

Brandon steadied me. With a shake of his head, he turned around, placed his hands on his knees, and squatted. "Come on. I'll carry you."

I didn't hesitate one second. I hopped onto Brandon's back and wrapped my arms around his sweaty neck. Pain lanced through my leg when I bent my knee, but I ignored it.

"Hold on." He hooked his arms underneath my legs, then stood, and started down the sidewalk.

Connor jogged up beside us, eyebrows drawn together and a soft frown on his lips. "Don't drop her."

Brandon sighed. "I'm not gonna. God, Con." Halfway down the street, Brandon chuckled. "You're just like a little possum clinging to me."

"I don't want to be a possum. Those things are ugly."

"Ah, nah. They're well cute... Just like you."

My cheeks warmed, and I clung to him a little tighter, the scent of soap and boy swirling around me. Brandon O'Kieffe had just called me cute.

My weight shifted when he nudged Connor, laughing. "Doesn't she look like one, holding onto me for dear life? Huh, Con?"

But Connor didn't say a word.

6

BRANDON

MARCH 2000

I swung my legs back and forth as rain droplets fell on me from the canopy of leaves above our heads. We were only about five feet off the ground, but Connor's legs were wrapped around the branch so tightly, and he clung to the trunk of the tree like he was terrified he was going to slip on the wet bark and fall. If anything, the branch was more likely to snap from his fat arse.

"You aren't going to fall, Con."

"I shouldn't have come up here," he mumbled.

"Even Poppy would get up here. And she's a girl."

His spine stiffened, and he slowly released his death hold on the tree trunk. "Yeah, if you carried her."

"Why would I carry Poppy up a tree?"

"Why would you carry her on your back the other day?" He snatched a leaf from a limb and shredded it. Tiny, green crumbs drifted to the ground before he grabbed another leaf and tore it to bits.

I studied him, sensing something was wrong. "She hurt her knee," I said, slowly. "If it didn't get you out of breath, you would carry her." I laughed, but Connor stared at the ground, frowning.

The wind rustled through the trees, and after moments of silence, Connor finally huffed. "You like her."

"You *wanted* me to like her! You told me to be nice to her." I shrugged. "Now I am."

"Well. You're *too* nice to her." He crossed his arms over his chest and sank against the trunk. "You're supposed to be *my* best friend."

Guilt tightened my chest. He thought I wasn't his best friend? "Con, I am. We'll always be best friends." He was more like a brother to me than a friend. We were bonded in ways that most people could never understand.

"Promise?"

I spat on my palm and held it out. "Promise."

He did the same, and we shook. A small smile pulled at his lips, and the hostility from only moments before disappeared.

"Connor!" His ma yelled from the house. "Tea."

I jumped down, and Connor landed beside me before he slipped on the damp grass and fell on his arse. I hid my laugh with my hand and hurried through the rain, beating him to the back door.

"You staying for tea?" Connor yanked off his wet hoody then kicked his shoes to the side.

"I can't. My dad's taking me to watch a fight tonight."

"Why would you want to watch a fight?"

"My dad said it's time." After he had smacked me one the week before and I'd gotten right back up, he said I was ready. "He says next year, I'll be fighting. It's a gypsy tradition. Uncle Darren used to be a bare-knuckle champion, you know?"

"I thought you didn't like your dad?"

I hated my dad. I had told myself I only wanted to learn to fight so I could hit him back when he hurt Ma, but the truth was, like any kid, I wanted his approval. Despite the things he did, I craved his attention because I'd never had it. Not once. At twelve years old, I didn't understand why he hated me, and it was that hatred that made me feel like there was something wrong with me. If I learned to fight—especially if I were good at it—then maybe things would change, but that was the foolish hope of an innocent mind. I found myself spinning in a never-ending tornado of anger and hate. For him, for myself, for the crappy hand I'd been dealt. "I don't, but I want to be able to fight."

I didn't want to explain it to Connor. He and Poppy didn't have a dad who beat on them or their mum. Their lives were perfect. And that was exactly why I needed them, so I could pretend like mine wasn't messed up.

By the time I got back to the camp, my stomach felt like a pit of snakes, slipping and coiling around each other. Dad was usually down at the pub by this time on a Sunday afternoon, but today, I knew he would be waiting for me.

Sean barked the same way he always did whenever anyone approached the caravan, growling and snipping until he realized it was me. My lungs filled on a deep breath as I pulled open the door, the unoiled hinges squealing when I stepped into the dreary darkness of the caravan.

A thick haze of cigarette smoke hung in the air, along with the stale scent of cheap whiskey. Dad sat on the couch, a beer bottle hanging lazily from his hand while the Sunday races commentary buzzed from the TV. No doubt, he had money on the race.

Ma poked her head around the corner. Her eyes darted between the back of my dad's head and me. The black eye he'd given her the week before had faded to a mottled green and yellow. The tension pulsing in the room made the tiny caravan feel even smaller.

"Go wash up and get changed, Brandon," she said, her voice tense.

By the time I came out of my room, the TV was off, and Dad was waiting for me by the door. When his bloodshot eyes met mine, I knew he was drunk. Though in truth, I couldn't recall what he looked like sober. My shoulders grew tense, and I released a shaky breath.

"Let's go." He jerked his head toward the door, and I followed him outside.

His beaten-up Transit van was parked out back, the wheel arches crumbling beneath rust and the locks hanging off from being jimmied with a screwdriver one too many times. Most of the white paint had peeled away, leaving behind rust, and every panel was dented. The door opened with a strained creek before he dragged himself into the driving seat.

With a cough, the engine ticked over, and I hopped in.

We drove the few miles down the road to the neighboring camp. It was a miracle my dad had never been pulled over by the cops, but he was so used to being drunk, I guessed he drove better than most people did sober.

We pulled up to a gate where an old man nodded and let us in. Far too soon, I was out of the van and taking in the space around me.

The McKinnley brothers' camp was bigger than ours. Vehicles littered the field along with a janky swing set, an abandoned mattress, and a tattered sofa. Dogs barked at us, tugging on the chains that bound them to the caravans as we wound our way through the camp until we finally reached a clearing.

A blazing fire crackled from an oil barrel where a large

group of men had gathered. Some stood, others laid sprawled out in garden chairs—all with buckets of beer bottles dotted between them. My father guided me toward a cluster of men leaning against the side of a shiny, new caravan. There was even fancy decking by the front door. My ma would have loved a caravan like that.

"Jonny," Dad greeted one of them.

"Des." The man shoved away and pulled my dad into a bear hug. "This your boy?"

I looked up at the grey-haired man and his smile full of crooked teeth.

"Ay. He'll be in the ring next year."

The man laughed. "He got a swing on him?"

My dad squeezed my shoulder.

I wanted to shrug away from him, but I didn't.

"Of course. He's cut from the same cloth as his old man."

My stomach sank, fast and hard. I didn't want to be the same as my dad. In the blink of an eye, my whole future flashed before me, and it looked like days and nights in the pub, a shitty caravan, and hopelessness.

"Nah," Uncle Darren strolled toward us, "He's like his uncle." His massive frame strained against the faded hoody he wore. His red hair was combed, and for Uncle Darren, he almost looked smart. He clapped a hand on my back as he came to stand beside me, dwarfing everyone around him. "He's gonna be a champ. Aren't ya, Brandon?"

I gave a meek nod.

The men talked a while before heading over to a ramshackle-looking barn at the back of the site. Inside, a layer of straw covered the dirt floor, and several wooden pallets had been tied together with bailing twine to form a pen.

People gathered around all four sides, from the way they

swayed and stumbled, I didn't think there was a sober one here, including the woman across the pen who leaned over the pallets, her boobs nearly falling out of her top. Then an older, bearded man stepped into the pen, tugging his jeans over his gut. Something about him carried a frenzied, infectious excitement across the crowd.

"We have a treat for you tonight." He spread his arms wide and turned in a slow circle. "These two have been waiting to go at it since the championship last year."

I didn't see anyone other than more men that looked just like my dad until the announcer stepped aside.

"Thomas O'Leary and Jimmy Gregor."

Cheers and applause erupted when the two men marched into the pen, wearing only their jeans. They couldn't have been much older than me, but as soon as the first punch landed, I could tell they were every bit men. The violence that unfolded before me was captivating. With every blow, blood decorated the straw at their feet, and their faces and knuckles split until the pair of them were streaked in crimson. It terrified me as much as it thrilled me.

Dad hit me, and I feared him. But these men, they were fighting back, and even though I was a kid, I was tempted by that power.

I glanced at my father, his teeth snarled and fist raised as he encouraged the blood bath. I decided then and there that I wanted to be like those two boys. I wanted the respect that I didn't have from my dad, but more than anything, I wanted to be able to protect my ma.

7

CONNOR

SEPTEMBER 2000

The sky was still tinted with slight purples and pinks from the setting sun, although the nearly full moon was out.

Brandon and I had pitched an army green tent five feet from the back door. It was my first outdoor sleepover, and Ma was worried.

The sleepover wasn't the only reason nervous energy fired through me at lightning speed. It was Poppy's birthday, and I wanted to make sure it was special. Even at twelve, I wanted to make sure I did things to ensure Poppy would never forget me.

Brandon swatted at the fairy lights we'd tied from the tree to the tent. "These lights are dumb."

"Are not."

Poppy had fairy lights on her bed, so I knew she liked them, which is why I'd insisted Brandon and I hang them. Of course, Brandon griped about it.

He cocked a brow, thumping another bulb. "They're girly."

The back door creaked, drawing my attention away from

the lights. Poppy stood on the back stoop, fiddling with the skirt of her purple dress. One look at her and my palms grew sweaty. My chest went tight. Poppy was the first girl I ever thought was pretty—but that night, she was beautiful.

"Fairy lights!" She clapped before running toward the tent with a huge smile.

I glanced at Brandon and smirked while he just rolled his eyes on a groan. I bent and lifted the flap. "Come in."

Once Poppy had crawled inside, I hurried around the back to grab her present from its hiding spot before ducking inside myself.

Poppy sat in the middle of the mounds of blankets and torches and snacks. Her eyes locked with mine. "You did all this for me?"

"Yeah." I shrugged like it wasn't a big deal, even though I hoped to God it was, and her face lit up with a smile.

Her gaze finally dropped to the pink, glittery box in my hand, and I fought to keep my voice from cracking. "Happy birthday," I said, handing her the present.

She lifted it to her ear and shook it gently before tearing off the paper, tossing it to the ground. Her finger slipped underneath the side of the white cardboard box. Sweat beaded on my forehead.

"Oh. Connor." She held up the framed photo of me, her, and Brandon—the picture my ma had taken a few weeks before, prior to Brandon getting sent home for pulling out a nudey magazine. "I love it," she said. "It's the best present." She wrapped her arms around me, pressing her body tight to mine, and I took a deep whiff of her strawberry-scented hair—I couldn't help myself.

Seconds later, the tent flap lifted, and Brandon tumbled inside, sprawling over the blankets with a huff. I frowned at his Iron Man T-shirt and ripped jeans. He was supposed to dress up for Poppy's birthday. I'd told him at least three times.

He grabbed one of the flashlights and flipped the switch, holding it under his chin before he sat up and folded his legs. The white light shined over his face, highlighting the nasty, purple and black bruise on his cheek.

"Con." He flicked the light on and off. "Why are you wearing your church clothes?" His brow creased when he glanced at Poppy. "And possum, why do you have on a dress?"

I stopped myself from frowning; I hated that he had that stupid pet name for her.

Poppy smoothed out her skirt. "You were supposed to dress nice, Brandon. It's supposed to be a tea party."

Brandon let out a snort and thumbed in my direction. "He looks like an idiot. I'm not wearing a tie."

I swatted at the top of the tent, trying to ignore him. I liked my tie. He was the one who looked like an idiot with his rat's nest hair and dirty clothes.

"Not only did you not dress up," Poppy shoved Brandon, and he almost fell over on the pile of tattered blankets, "But you look filthy."

"Yeah? Well, you look clean. I managed to get out of shower night on Tuesday." A smug grin worked over his face.

Already annoyed, I nudged Brandon in the ribs, then jerked my head toward Poppy while glaring at him. "Have something you want to say to her, Bran?"

"I didn't forget." He waved a dismissive hand through the air, then pushed onto his knees, biting at his lip while he dug around in the pocket of his jeans. "Happy birthday, poss." He placed a little knot of bailing twine into her palm. "Made you a friendship bracelet." He sniffed, then thumbed under his nose. "Ma showed me how to make it. I told her you'd rather have a puppy, but she wouldn't let me give ya one."

Poppy smiled—bigger than she had at my present—and then she hugged Brandon so hard that she nearly knocked him over. Now he was smelling her strawberry hair, and the first taste of jealousy danced over my tongue.

"I love it. Thank you, Brandon." Poppy looped the tatty thread around her wrist, looking up at him with big eyes while he tied the knot. She twisted it, smiling even bigger. "I'll wear it forever."

Brandon's gaze went to the floor, and his shoulder hiked in an awkward shrug. "Okay."

Poppy kept staring at that bracelet, and Brandon kept stealing glances at her. The only noise in the tent was the soft chirp of the crickets, hiding in the thick grass outside. I wanted whatever moment was passing between them to end, so I cleared my throat, then clasped my hands together, and stretched them out. "So, what do you want to do now?"

"We could tell ghost stories." A twisted grin formed on Brandon's face.

Poppy crept closer to me, pulling one of the blankets into her lap. "I don't like scary stories."

"Aw, come on, poss." Brandon thumped her knee, and she slapped his hand away. "Don't be a baby. It's just a story."

"Yeah," I said, nudging Poppy's shoulder. I didn't like those stupid stories either, but I spotted a chance to put my arm around her, so I went with it. And she let me and settled into my side. "It's just a story, Poppy."

She huffed but didn't protest again, and I guessed Brandon saw that as his go-ahead. His eyes gleamed, and he rubbed his palms together like some greedy swindler preparing to rightfully screw someone over.

"So, there was this girl..." His gaze strayed to Poppy, and

his smirk deepened. "Her parents left her all alone one night." Brandon paused, placing an inquisitive finger to his chin before locking eyes with me. "Now that I think of it, it was Blaire O'Brian. You remember her, right, Connor? The girl that lived in Poppy's house before it was Poppy's house?"

Blaire O'Brian had lived in Poppy's house, so I nodded.

"Anyway, she was all alone"—he held up a finger—"Mind you, Blaire told me this herself. Anyway, that night, she kept hearing a dripping noise. *Drip. Drip.*" He leaned in close to Poppy, and she shrunk back. "*Drip!*"

She got up and checked in all the rooms, but she didn't find anything that could be causing the noise. When she laid back down, she felt her dog, Spunky ..." Brandon nodded. "Yeah, *Spunky,* the dachshund—Blaire felt ole' Spunky lick her hand, so she knew everything was okay. Only thing, it wasn't. Because that dripping kept going."

By then, Poppy clutched my arm so hard, my skin burned. That was why I kind of wanted Brandon to keep going—even though I felt bad that Poppy was obviously scared.

"She finally got up and looked in the wardrobe, and there was Spunky, hung." Brandon stuck his tongue out and made a choking sound as he clutched his neck. "And that dripping was poor Spunky's blood falling on the floor."

Poppy whimpered.

"And there's a note that says, 'Humans can lick, too.'"

Poppy screamed, and Brandon laughed so hard he toppled over.

"That's not true!" she said.

"Is, too."

"Is not."

"I mean, I never heard that," I said.

Brandon glared at me. "Blaire told me herself."

"Blaire was a liar."

Brandon shrugs. "Don't know, but *I* sure wouldn't want to sleep in the room Spunky was hung in."

"I hate you, Brandon," she huddled against my side.

He laughed. "It's just a story, Poppy."

Something rustled in the bushes behind the tent, and she jumped. "What was that?" she whispered.

"It's the crazy man from your wardrobe. He's gonna lick you, possum."

She screamed again, and I hugged her. "Stop it, Bran!"

Tears clung to the corners of Brandon's eyes from how hard he was laughing. Part of me wanted to punch him for scaring her. Part of me wanted to thank him because I had my arms wrapped around her.

Poppy wiggled out of my hold and, placing her palms flat on Brandon's chest, she pushed him over. He toppled to his side, cackling.

"It's not funny, and now I need to go to the bathroom." She glanced nervously at the flap of the tent.

I opened my mouth, ready to offer to walk her through the dark backyard and to the safety of the house.

Her gaze went right past me to Brandon. "Brandon, will you take me?"

Brandon's laughter quieted.

I didn't want him walking Poppy to the door. I wanted to be the knight in shining armor. "I will," I blurted, but Brandon was already outside, holding the flap for her.

"No, offense, Con." Poppy crawled through the opening and glanced over her shoulder. "But Brandon makes me feel safe." The flap fell at the same time I felt the slight smile on my face drop.

Why did Brandon get to scare her, and then be the one to walk her inside? And why did I even care? I snatched a

Milkybar from the pile of snacks, tore off the wrapper, then crammed it into my mouth.

Brandon was mean to Poppy while I was nice. He was trouble. I went to church and prayed every day. Good girls were supposed to like good boys, at least that's what Ma had always told me. But Poppy—I was pretty certain she liked Brandon more than me. I hated that almost as much as I hated that it made me angry at my best friend. At twelve years old, I didn't understand why I wanted her to like me more than him. All I knew was that I did.

I tossed the crumpled up Milkybar wrapper to the ground, then tugged off my tie, and rubbed a furious hand over the top of my head until I was certain my hair had to actually look like more of a mess than Brandon's.

Whatever it was about him that Poppy liked more, I'd figure it out.

8

POPPY

SEPTEMBER 2001

Pretty soon, the memories of American highways and suburbs were replaced by rolling hills and afternoons spent darting between run-down caravans, playing hide and seek with Brandon and Connor. For two years, it had been just the three of us.

It didn't matter that most of the girls teased me, or that the other boys made fun of Brandon and Connor for hanging out with a girl. All that mattered was that, no matter what, we were always there for one another.

The night before the first day of secondary school—middle school in America—I couldn't sleep. My fingers constantly twiddled while my mind refused to go quiet. Tomorrow would be the first time the three of us had been in different classes. We'd be in a bigger school with a lot of people we didn't know. And I hated that.

Exhaling, I rolled onto my side and forced my eyes shut for the hundredth time. Just when I reached the fuzzy, borderline realm between the conscious and unconscious, something tapped my window.

Once.

Twice.

Followed by a knock that forced me upright in bed. A scream threatened my throat when I saw a silhouette at my window, but I slapped a hand over my mouth when it was Brandon's face plastered to the glass and not some stranger's.

"Open up, poss."

Swallowing hard, I crawled out of bed and quietly shut my door, then locked it before tiptoeing to the window. The worn springs creaked when I lifted it, and I prayed the noise didn't wake my dad. The window was barely halfway open before Brandon threw one leg over the ledge, followed by the other.

A nervous heat washed throughout me when he hopped into my room, and I took an unsteady step back. Boys had no business in a girl's room at night. I knew that, but it was Brandon.

The soft glow from my nightlight was just enough that I could make out the dried blood caked to his swollen lip. I knew that split lip was compliments of Mr. O'Kieffe. Tears welled in my eyes, and I spun around because I didn't want the wounded to console the able.

Brandon tucked his chin to his chest while rubbing a hand over his arm. "Connor was already asleep..."

"It's okay," I said, although I knew my daddy would kill me if he found out Brandon was in here. Forcing a smile to hide my worry, I sank to my bed. "Are you okay?"

He gave a curt nod. One that caused a crumpled feeling to travel through my chest. Brandon always tried so hard to come across as tough. To act like nothing bothered him. But I didn't want him to feel like he had to be tough around me.

I wiggled down beneath the covers, pulling the

comforter over my chest, then flattening it out. "You can tell me anything, Brandon. You know that, right?"

"Yeah, poss. I know."

Silence passed between us. Eventually, he lifted his head, and I could just make out the glisten of tears that begged to fall. Tears I knew he never would set free. Everything I had been taught about right and wrong flew straight out the same window Brandon had crawled through.

I patted the mattress, knowing that boys and girls shouldn't be in the same bed but also knowing that friends took care of one another. Brandon took a single step, then hesitated.

"There's nowhere else for you to sleep if you're going to stay here." I had a pink sleeping bag in my closet that Daddy had bought for my last birthday, but that lie slipped through my lips easily. I couldn't stand the thought of Brandon sleeping all alone on the floor when I was certain he already felt alone enough.

I tossed the comforter back, and he shuffled out of his shoes, then crawled in beside me. His head hit the pillow. I didn't understand why, but it felt exciting to have him so close in the dark quiet.

"Thanks, poss."

"Yep."

We laid rigid and unnaturally still like we were afraid to brush against one another as though something about this bed made it worse. The covers shifted when Brandon moved an arm behind his head.

"Brandon..." I turned onto my side, and he rolled to face me. I touched a gentle finger to his swollen cheek because I couldn't force the next words out: Why does your father hit you? So, I settled with a simple, "Why?"

A small line sunk between his brows. "My dad just gets

mad." He shrugged one shoulder like that was a good enough reason, and for the first time, I realized just how broken Brandon's life was. "And I can't let him hit Ma all the time."

Something in my chest twisted like a rubber band winding tighter and tighter. "It's not right."

"It is what it is, poss."

I shook my head, and the tears I'd been holding back broke free, soaking my pillowcase. "I don't want him to hurt you, Brandon."

"Hey." He swiped a thumb beneath my eye. "Don't cry, poss."

"I just..." I sucked in a ragged breath. "My daddy could help you. If you needed to live here for a little while I'm sure—"

"No. It won't change anything. And I can't leave my ma."

"Just let me tell—"

"It'll make it worse."

I gnawed at my lip for a second, knowing deep down that I should tell my father. Brandon held out his pinky, and his eyes narrowed. "Promise me you won't."

I reluctantly hooked my finger around his in a solemn oath not to tell. A promise that broke my heart.

Minutes of silence passed between us. "I won't be a kid forever, Poppy." It was like that simple fact offered him relief.

Most kids wanted to grow up so they could be a fireman or a teacher. Brandon—he wanted to grow up so he wouldn't get beat on anymore.

"I'm going to learn how to fight. Then he won't be able to hurt Ma or me again."

I studied him, noting the way his jaw ticced as he stared at the ceiling. The deep swells his chest made every time he drew in a hard breath. He was hurting, that much was obvious, so I did what my mother always did that made my world right. I threw my arms around him and hugged him, holding him tight. The smell of soap and dirt filled my nose —a smell that was so undeniably Brandon O'Kieffe. I held that scent deep in my lungs until I drifted off to sleep.

———

THE ANNOYING BUZZ of my alarm woke me. Grumbling, I swatted the snooze and turned on my side with every intention of going back to sleep until I remembered I wasn't alone. My eyes shot open, and I sat straight up, ready to shake Brandon awake and get him out before my dad came in. But the bed was empty.

A gust of wind fluttered the curtains, and a folded piece of paper skipped across the worn, wood floors. I leaned over and snatched it, opening it with a smile when I saw the note from Brandon: SEE YOU AT SCHOOL. A tiny, round blob, I assumed, was meant to be a possum, was drawn in glittery pink pen. A heart beside it.

I pulled on a T-shirt and jeans, then shoved the note into my pocket for safekeeping.

After a dry piece of toast and a hug from my dad, I grabbed my backpack and met Connor at the street corner. He nudged me. "Are you scared?"

"Yeah. You?"

"Not really." But I could tell he was nervous from the way he rocked back and forth on his heels. Connor checked his shiny new watch. "He's gonna be late."

Just then, Brandon strutted around Mrs. O'Malley's overgrown rose bush, whistling. Connor mumbled, "What in the..."

Not only had Brandon combed his hair, but his *clean* shirt was *tucked* into his jeans. The bruise on his jaw gave him a certain bad boy vibe I knew the girls at school would find appealing—because, at that very moment, I found it appealing.

He whacked Connor on the back, then glanced at me with a wry smirk. "Why are you looking at me all funny, poss?"

A sting of heat swept over my cheeks and chest, and I swallowed. I hated that my best friend could fluster me in ways a best friend shouldn't, and it seemed to be becoming a regular occurrence.

BRANDON TALKED about the new Star Wars movie on the way to school while I barely managed three words before we reached the schoolyard and stopped. Older kids brushed passed us with confident strides and backpacks slung over their shoulders while we stared at the massive, red-brick building looming in front of us.

Connor touched a hand to my shoulder, ducking his chin to come eye level with me; I hated that they were both getting taller than me. "It'll be okay, Poppy," he said.

"Yeah, poss. It'll be grand just like..." Brandon's voice trailed off. His gaze honed in on a group of girls in short skirts prancing past.

The thing was, their eyes were on Brandon, too. They grinned, then giggled with blushing cheeks before they walked off. The way they kept glancing over their shoulders to catch another glimpse of him made me mad.

"Told you, Con." Brandon nudged Connor with a grin. "Short skirts."

"Gross," I muttered under my breath.

"Hey! I'm not wearing a skirt. Don't mind looking up them, though." He laughed and strolled backward toward the building. "Have a good first day, possum. I gotta go see cousin Billy, but I'll see you at lunch."

Something inside my chest crumpled when Brandon turned and disappear among the other students. I was nervous—or maybe scared of what new friends may mean for the three of us.

Connor walked me to my class, promising everything would be fine and that I would see him and Brandon at lunch.

I took a seat at the front of the classroom and pulled a notebook from my bag, placing it on the desk. The kids in the class were already grouped in their clichés, whispering and talking, and I slouched a little in my chair.

I'd just scribbled the date at the top of my paper when a girl walked past. All I could see was a bare leg. Davie Logan whistled, and I glanced up from my paper just in time to catch the leggy redhead shoot an angry glare at Davie. She dumped her bag onto the desk a few seats over from me, then rolled the waist of her skirt over once more, making the skirt dangerously short.

Her gaze met mine, and I instantly looked away. Girls like that—I'd learned not to mess with.

Other kids entered. Some I knew, others I'd never seen. Then, Neive Kirkpatrick and her minions of friends strutted in. She stopped beside my desk and cocked her hip. "If it isn't the mankie measch."

"Go to hell, Neive." I glared at her, a little swell of pride rising in my chest at the thought of how proud Brandon would be at me for cussing at Neive.

Her jaw dropped for a second before her shocked expression was replaced with a nasty smirk. She swatted my notebook to the floor, stomping on it before she pranced to her desk.

I snatched it with a grumble. The redhead pushed her chair back, the metal legs screeching across the tile when she rose to her feet. She smoothed a hand over her skirt, then made a beeline toward the back of the room.

"I don't believe we've met," she said. "I'm Hope McGrath."

Of course, she was. I almost rolled my eyes. An heiress to McGrath Whiskey, the girl was every bit as loaded as she looked, which meant her and Neive would most likely join forces in ruining the lives of those of us who weren't as fortunate.

"I know who you are," Neive said, and Hope laughed.

"You may have been Queen Bee at whatever crappy little school you went to before, but you sure as shit aren't now. Don't make me ruin your life." I found the certain cheer to her tone more than amusing. "And, I'm taking this, cunt."

The class gasped at her crass choice of words.

Seconds later, Hope dropped into the chair beside me, and a glittery, purple notebook skidded across the desk. "For you. Since yours has cheap shoe prints on it." She turned in her seat, glaring back in Neive's direction.

I stared at her, eventually mumbling a very confused thanks. Hope wore expensive-looking clothes. Her hair was perfectly styled, her nails manicured, and her face caked in more make-up than I would ever be allowed to wear. Which meant, she was the kind of girl I would expect to befriend Neive, not me.

Brandon, Connor, and I had always been the outcasts, but for whatever reason, Hope had picked me—the measch —over the popular girl.

Later in the day, Hope and I trudged into the crowded,

noisy cafeteria and fell into line with the other students. She shot death glares at Neive while we made our way through the line.

"Do you have some personal vendetta against Neive or something?" I asked Hope, taking my tray from the cafeteria worker.

"No. I just don't like girls like her."

We found an empty table and set down our food. Hope dropped into the seat across from me, grabbing her apple and taking a bite. "So, do football players really shove kids into lockers in America?"

I shrugged a shoulder. "I guess."

A tray clattered to the table. "Hey, poss." Brandon sank to the stool beside me, his eyes locked on Hope, and a smile crossed his face that made it hard to breathe. Connor plopped down on the other side of me, already shoving half a slice of pizza into his mouth.

Hope paid no attention to Connor, she was too busy giving Brandon a once over. Her nose wrinkled. "I can smell pikey a mile away."

Brandon thumbed at Hope. "Who's this bitch?"

"Hope." I swallowed down her last name because I knew Brandon would lose it if he figured out who she really was, but an arrogant grin had already twisted Hope's glossed lips.

"McGrath," she finished the introduction, and Brandon's eyes rolled back in his head on a hard huff.

"Hey." Connor paused to lick grease from his fingers. "Doesn't your family own McGrath Whiskey?"

"Yeah."

He flashed an innocent, wholesome smile that marked him as the good boy. "Nice to meet you. I'm Connor." He held out a grease-covered hand, but Hope just eyed it until he finally dropped it to the table and went back to his food with a hint of a shrug.

"Tell me you aren't trying to be friends with her, poss." Brandon nudged my shoulder. "She's a redheaded, rich snot."

I shoved him, and he nearly toppled off the stool. "She's nice."

"She's a bitch."

Hope's eyes narrowed. "Only to pikeys."

Brandon's stare hardened on her. It was almost like watching two dogs circling a bone, foaming at the mouth. Then Brandon scooped mashed potatoes onto his fork and turned the utensil around. A deep smirk settled on his face.

"Brandon." I grabbed at his arm, but he yanked away. "Don't you—"

The fork pinged back, and a glob of food hurdled toward Hope, splattering her shirt. On a gasp, she scraped off the potato with her fingers, then hurled an entire apple at Brandon. It made a distinct crack when it nailed him on the forehead, and a hush fell over the cafeteria—except for the slurp from Connor's downing his milkshake, eyes trained on the catastrophe at hand.

"Oh, that's it." Brandon snatched up his tray, nostrils flaring.

I wasn't sure whether he intended to throw the whole tray at her or just sling every scrape of food off.

"Brandon," I shouted. "Stop!"

The tray was still raised by his head when he faced me, brows knitted together. "You're defending her? She's a soulless ginger, poss." He pointed an accusing finger at her with his free hand. "She's not one of us."

But I wanted her to be. Which meant I needed to play at

Brandon's weaknesses, and the only weakness I'd ever seen him have was for me...

"Neive called me a mankie measch this morning." I tugged at his sleeve, and he dropped the tray a little, his attention directed at me. "She knocked my notebook to the floor, then stepped on it. Hope called her names, snatched Neive's notebook, and gave it to me."

Brandon tossed the tray to the table, sending mashed potatoes and peas into the air. He huffed before dropping into his seat. "Still soulless," he mumbled under his breath.

9

POPPY

DECEMBER 2001

I t had been three months since we'd started secondary school, and Brandon and Hope still had a battle of wills going. Like there was some unspoken law that wouldn't allow them to be civil to one another, but I figured, given enough time, they would eventually warm up to each other. Which is one of the many reasons why I didn't tell Hope whose house—or rather caravan—we were going to.

We stopped outside the gate, our breath turning to puffs of fog the second it met the cold air. I climbed over the rickety metal, but Hope stayed on the other side. Her gaze drifted over the caravans dotted haphazardly around the overgrown field. "You brought me to a Gypo camp?"

I hated the term Gypo. "It's a gypsy camp. And yeah"

"And why, exactly, are we here?" Her arms folded over her chest.

"Brandon lives here."

"Of course, he does." She gave a flippant roll of her eyes before she hoisted herself over the gate and fell in step behind me.

We wove through the maze of make-shift homes, right past Old Man bundled up in wool blankets and passed out in his tattered lawn chair.

"Is he dead?" Hope nudged his foot with the toe of her shoe like he was an animal left on the side of the road.

"He's just drunk."

She shrugged and followed me to Brandon's door. As soon as I knocked, Brandon peeked out from the side of the curtain. The lock clicked, and the door swung open. Brandon's ever-growing frame blocked most of the doorway. His gaze darted over my shoulder, and he tossed his head back on a groan. "Ah, poss. What'd you bring her for?"

"Because I like her." I placed my palms against his chest to shove him out of the way, letting them linger a touch too long before I shouldered past him with Hope in tow.

Connor greeted us from the plastic-covered couch, never looking up from the smoldering cigarette gripped between his fingers. Over the past year and a half, Connor had begun untucking his shirts, swearing—doing little things that emulated Brandon, so I wasn't as shocked by the cigarette as Hope seemed to be. She gasped, clutching a dramatic hand to her chest. "Milkybar. Don't let the pikey taint you."

"It's just a cigarette." He grinned when his gaze trailed to me.

"Want one, poss?" Brandon stepped between us, already handing over one of the thin sticks.

In my gut, I knew it was a bad idea, but... Brandon handed one to Hope, then took one for himself and placed it to his mouth, drawing my attention to his lips. His eyes locked on me when he lit it.

As much as I hated it, I liked the way my stomach kinked when smoke crawled between his lips. Something about

Brandon had always made my heart do a stupid tap dance in my chest. Always.

"I don't know," I sighed and rolled the white cylinder between my fingers. "What's the point?" The point, at least to me, was to impress Brandon. To show him, I could be just as bad as he was.

His gaze lifted to mine on a shrug. "Because it's what grown-ups do." He passed the lighter to Hope. "It's just badass, poss."

"Yeah." Hope pointed at Connor and snort-laughed under her breath. "Milkybar looks like a real badass."

After a hesitant second, Connor halfway lifted a middle finger. "Shut it, McGrath." His eyes watered the instant he took another puff, and the attempt he made to hold his breath lasted less than two seconds before he went into a coughing fit.

Hope nudged my shoulder. "Total badass," she mumbled, then lit hers before handing the lighter to me.

I stared at the black piece of plastic with a picture of a girl in a bikini, thinking that Brandon must have nicked it from his Uncle Darren...

Hope blew out a cloud of smoke on a hard wheeze. "It's not that bad."

Not that bad. I wanted to roll my eyes because the disgusted look on Hope's face when she glanced back at the cigarette told me it was nothing short of awful. But, at our age, we wanted nothing more than to be grown. To be taken seriously and not told what we should and shouldn't do, so she took another drag, visibly fighting the urge to cough.

"I swear, Poppy. It kind of makes you tingly."

"Come on, poss." Brandon stepped closer to me and dipped his head so that his eyes were level with mine. "Do it."

The tiny lighter felt like a lead weight in my damp palm. Brandon inched closer, his nose almost touching mine. The scent of soap and something absolutely Brandon almost swallowed me whole. I wanted him to stay right there, and maybe that was why I pressed my thumb to the striker and paused, holding his gaze. So he'd stay close to me like that. Just a little longer.

"You don't have to do it," Connor managed between coughs.

Brandon's gaze tore from mine, and he took a sudden step back, running a hand over his messy hair.

"I know I don't have to, Connor," I snipped, angry he'd distracted Brandon.

Connor held up his hands, palms out while directing his attention to an invisible, loose thread on the sleeve of his shirt. He mouthed sorry, then grabbed his cigarette and took a small puff.

Guilt twisted my insides. I was tired of Connor attempting to be the angel on my shoulder while it was so painfully obvious that all he wanted to do was wear Brandon's horns.

I pressed my thumb over the wheel. A flame sparked to life, and I inhaled, watching in horror when the end of the cigarette went from white to orange to bright red, and a taste similar to burnt popcorn coated my tongue. I blew out a thick stream of smoke, triumphantly, because I—Poppy Turner—wasn't coughing like everyone else in the caravan. "Not that bad." I shot the smuggest grin I could muster to Brandon, while I took another drag like a champ.

He shook his head on a cough-laced laugh.

"What?"

"Poss, you ain't even inhaling."

"What? Am too!"

He kept laughing, Hope was fighting a laugh, and Connor was staring down at the table. Brandon moved toward me, placing his cigarette to his mouth. He inhaled a deep breath and held it before allowing the smoke to slowly creep between his lips like fog rolling through a cemetery. "Act like you're about to go under water. Take a breath like that, poss."

I took a hefty drag, sucking the smoke deep inside my lungs. My throat and chest burned, my stomach rolled, and the smoke came out in a fit of coughs that had me bent at the waist and desperate to drag in fresh air.

Howling, Brandon slapped his hand on his thigh, then wiped tears from his face. Heat stung my cheeks. All that, and he would still see me as the good girl.

Still choking on the smoke, I dropped the cigarette into a soda can in front of Connor. The ember hissed, and I flopped down onto the floor beside the table topper Christmas tree, dejected and angry at myself for even trying to do something so stupid to impress Brandon.

"Do you have things to do in this..." Hope glanced around, a slight snarl of disgust on her lips. "Caravan."

Brandon grabbed a box from the corner and dumped a pile of DVDs out on the seat beside Connor. Several of the plastic cases clattered to the floor.

Hope and Connor sifted through the pile while I sulked. "*Die Hard. Monty Python.* Oh!" She held one up. "*Titanic.*"

"Oh, that's my favorite!"

Brandon snatched the DVD from her hand and hurled it across the room. "I'm not watching anything with Leonardo DiCaprio in it. Even if he does die at the end." Gripping the cigarette between his lips, he grabbed a case. "*Die Hard*, it is."

Hope crossed her arms over her chest with a roll of her eyes, and we both groaned in unison.

Brandon was already crouched in front of the ancient box TV when Connor took a movie and flipped it over in his hands. "*Deep Throat?*" His brows pinched together. "What's that?"

"Don't know. It's my dad's. He says not to touch it." Brandon tossed *Die Hard* down reached across the table to snatch the one from Connor's hand. "Which means it's probably something we should watch."

Brandon switched on the TV, then shoved the disc into the DVD player, and took a seat next to Connor.

Hope crouched beside me, pressing a hand to the carpet before inspected her palm. "Is it safe to sit?" she whispered.

I grabbed her arm and yanked her down.

The beginning of the movie was full of permed hair and men with thick mustaches. Brandon had already popped open *Die Hard* and started to the TV but stopped midstride when some weird 80s music started, and the woman on the screen slowly pulled her shirt over her head. Brandon inched closer to the screen. Connor pulled a Milkybar from his pocket, peeled back the wrapper, and took a bite, his eyes glued to the movie. Brandon raked his teeth over his lip, and all I could think about was how I wanted him to look at me with that same intensity.

The woman stripped down to nothing, then the man touched her in ways that brought a strange, fluttering sensation to my stomach and between my legs. I wanted to look away, but as ashamed as I was to think it, I liked it. I liked watching Brandon's reaction to it until he turned and glanced at me. Then embarrassment bled through me, and I slammed a hand over my face.

A long moan came from the screen, and I peeked through the slit in my fingers.

Hope was right beside Brandon, and she'd lit another cigarette. "Your dad's a pervert," she said, taking a puff.

"You're watching it, too."

She shrugged, then whacked him on the back. "So I am, pikey. So I am…"

10

BRANDON

JANUARY 2002

It was almost five, and Uncle Darren said he'd be here by a quarter to four. He was always late.

Sighing, I picked a wide blade of grass and held it to my lips, blowing it until it sounded like a mini trumpet, then leaned against the side of Uncle Darren's caravan. From here, I could see the whole camp and Old Man passed out in his lawn chair. A rare glimpse of sunshine peeked through the trees, bathing the leaf-strewn grass in golden light. When I was seven, I asked Uncle Darren why his caravan was out in the middle of the field, well away from the others. He said it was so he didn't wake everyone up when he brought his lady friends back.

Old Man's goat came bleating around the side of the caravan, followed by Uncle Darren's heavy footfalls. Excitement darted through me like an electrical current. I had been waiting for this for what seemed like an eternity. Ever since Dad took me to my first fight, I had been counting down the days, waiting for my first lesson with Uncle Darren.

He finally stumbled around the corner of the caravan,

then slumped sideways against it with a thud. His jeans weren't even done up properly, and his bright, ginger hair stuck up in every direction. The stout smell of Guinness permeated the air when he exhaled a hard breath.

"First thing you need to know..." He placed his feet a shoulders width apart and twisted his body. His stained, white vest strained over the bulging muscles of his chest. Unlike my dad, Uncle Darren still fought. "You need to stand like this." He raised his fists in front of his face, swaying on the spot. When he flexed his biceps, the tattoos that covered his skin stretched and bulged.

I mimicked his stance, and a crooked smile worked over his lips.

"Good. Now punch me." He tapped his jaw. "Right here."

"But—"

"Hit me, you little pussy!"

I swung. My fist smacked against his face. Though a painful crack radiated through my knuckles, Uncle Darren didn't even flinch.

A deep belly laugh rumbled from his chest. His hands clapped together like a performing seal as he threw his head back. "Again. This time, don't hit like a girl." He stared right at me, one ginger eyebrow arching high over mischievous eyes.

I must have hit him a hundred times while he drank three more tins of Guinness. By the time I threw my last punch, the sun had all but sank below the horizon. Uncle Darren's cheeks and jaw were bright red—not that he seemed to care—and my hand was swollen and throbbing.

I held up my fist, barely able to open my fingers. "I think I broke my hand."

"Good. It'll heal stronger."

"But, I can't straighten my fingers."

"What do you need to be doing that for?" He burped. "You need fists, lad." He tipped up the last of his can.

I glanced at the marks on his face. "Doesn't that hurt?"

Through a snort, he choked on his mouthful of Guinness, then finally wheezed out a breath. "I once fought Billy Big Bollocks. Got my nose, my eye socket, and my jaw broken. And then we went out in Dublin, partied until the wee hours. The trick is..." He tapped his temple, and I waited with bated breath, expecting some revolutionary tactic worthy of the Dalai Lama to be revealed. "To get shit faced. Then you can't feel a damn thing."

I wanted to learn how to fight, but at the same time, something uncomfortable sat in my gut at the thought of being like Uncle Darren. Like my Dad.

"Right, off with ya. I have a pool game to get to." Uncle Darren turned and strolled back toward the gate, hefting himself up and teetering dangerously at the top, finally descending the gate on the other side before he staggered out of sight. I'd probably find him passed out outside his caravan the next day. He never seemed to quite make it inside.

I walked back across the field, toward the other caravans. The closer I got to home, the more acid burned up the back of my throat. It was Saturday, and the sun was down, which meant Dad would be drunk.

My hand trembled as I reached for the door. I stepped inside to Dad holding Ma against the wall, his hand around her throat. My flight or fight response kicked in, the problem was I wanted to both run *and* fight. Anger washed over me, tightening my chest. Red tinted my vision, and before I knew what I was doing, I balled my fist the same way Uncle Darren had taught me. I threw one, solid punch at Dad's kidney, and his hand unwound from Ma's neck. For one amazing moment, I felt triumphant. I didn't feel power-less—then came the blow.

His knuckles collided with my face with a harsh smack. I went from standing to sprawled out, flat on my back with no in-between.

"Des!"

My vision cleared enough to see Ma standing between Dad and her back in my direction.

"Leave him alone!" There was a strength in her voice I'd never heard.

Dad peeked around Ma, pointing a finger. "Try to hit me, you little shit. You get the feck out of my house."

I scrambled to my feet and dove for the door while Ma's cries blended and mixed with the ruckus shout of my father. He would hurt her, but I couldn't do a damn thing to save her, and it seemed I only made things worse. That internal battle of a child who could do nothing in an adult situation had been a constant in my life. I asked her once why she stayed with him. Her answer: my Dad was a complicated man. He had demons, but she loved him. In the same breath, she told me that we don't give up on people.

She needed to, though, because my dad was a lost cause and a horrible person. Let the Devil have him.

A sea of anger and worry swam inside me while I made my way from the camp into town. Before long, I was outside Connor's bedroom window, banging. He hurried across the room and shoved up the pane of glass, his gaze darting over his shoulder. The second his eyes met mine, they bugged wide. "Bran! Are you okay?"

I threw my leg through the gap, climbing over the ledge and dropping to his carpet. "Yeah, I'm fine." My words were thick and awkward, even to my own ears.

Frowning, he said, "Your face doesn't look fine," on his

way out of the room. He rushed back with a mirror and held it up to reveal my father's handiwork. The left side of my face was swollen like a chipmunk storing nuts, and the bruise was already setting in. Even I was shocked at how bad it appeared. Dad had never hit me that hard before.

"Can I stay here tonight?"

"Sure. I'll go get you some ice." Connor retrieved some frozen peas, then made up a bed on the floor for me from a bundle of old blankets.

I was happy that he was right there next to me, but as darkness engulfed us, I realized how utterly alone I felt. Connor was like a brother to me, but he was a good boy from a good family. When I told him I was fine, he believed me, and even if he hadn't, he couldn't have done anything to change it.

While he was my best friend, he wasn't the friend I needed—not at that moment. His breaths finally evened out into a deep sleep, and I silently crept to the window and left.

It was well past midnight by the time I made it to Poppy's, but when I knocked on her window, she got up immediately. In her half-asleep state, she slid the glass up and let me in. She didn't say a word, simply crawled back into bed and lifted the duvet, waiting for me to climb in beside her.

As soon as my head hit the pillow, her arms came around me, and that peace I only felt with her washed over me. Poppy gave me a sense of safety that no one else could.

I would never admit it, but she made me feel loved. That simple fact instilled in me the belief that I could take on this shitty world for one more day.

CONNOR

MARCH 2002

Sighing, I plopped onto the empty park swing between Poppy and Hope. The chains creaked and groaned when I pushed back, then stopped.

I was in the purgatory between childhood and adolescence. The time of life where I sometimes didn't do things I wanted to—like swing—for the simple fact that I felt too old.

Brandon came from the tree line, zipping his pants before he took a seat in the grass. No sooner had his butt hit the ground than Poppy hopped from the swing and went straight to him, sitting down behind him and picking a dandelion. I kicked up a cloud of dust with the toe of my shoe and exhaled.

"He's such a pikey." Hope spun in circles, knotting the chain until her toes barely touched the dirt. When she lifted her feet, the swing whirled around like a carnival ride. Her red hair fanned out behind her like a soft flame.

I dug into my pocket for my candy bar, holding the smooshed, melted bar in my palm while watching Poppy stick a field's worth of yellow weeds in Brandon's hair. It bothered me that she did things like that with him. That she gave him all those little touches... Jealousy swelled in my chest, and I chucked the stupid candy bar across the playground, then gripped the chain until it dug into my palm.

"What gives, Milkybar?" Hope had already twisted up the swing again.

"Nothing."

"If you like her, you should just tell her."

Embarrassment heated my cheeks. "I don't *like* her."

"Whatever." The swing spun again, and when it stopped, Hope jumped down and went to sit beside Poppy. Which, I guessed, was why Brandon shot right to his feet. He said the sound of her voice made him want to bang his head against a rock.

He swatted the flowers from his hair on his way toward the swing set, stopping to pick up my melted Milkybar and cram it into his pocket.

He took the swing that Hope had vacated. The chains creaked under his weight when he gently swayed back and forth. "So, I heard that Suzie Brady'll show you her girly bits for two quid."

I'd seen plenty of girly bits in nudey magazines, thanks to Brandon. And I'd gone to plenty of confessions for it, too. But taking a peek at a naked girl in real life had a certain... sinful allure to it. "No way?"

There was a good chance Brandon was lying. And I hoped for my soul's sake that he was.

"Yeah." His eyes gleamed with mischief. "For a fiver, she'll show you that *and* her titties. And she's fifteen, Con. She's got *real* ones." Brandon smiled before he fished five quid from one of his pockets, eyebrows waggling. "Fancy a walk over to ole' Suzie's house?" He clicked his tongue.

My gaze drifted to Poppy, who, of course, was watching

Brandon. Hope was watching her watch Brandon with a displeased snarl.

Deep down, I felt that Poppy liked him the same way Neive did, and it bothered me. Even though I prayed time and time again for it not to, it did, and something inside of me snapped. Having Suzie give us a peek for money was nothing short of adolescent prostitution, and while I knew it would send me straight to hell, I didn't care.

Poppy liked Brandon.

The rebel.

The pikey.

The guy who nicked "shit" and wanted to hand over five quid to stare at a pair of boobs he couldn't even touch. Maybe if I toughened up...

I slid out of the swing, yanked my nice, clean shirt out from the waist of my trousers, and ran a hand through my hair, hoping it looked half as disheveled as Brandon's. "Let's go to Suzie's," I said, glaring at the girls.

"Our lives are about to change, Con." Brandon slapped a hand on my back. "We're about to cross over into manhood."

"Right."

We crossed the playground with determined strides. Brandon went on and on about some speech his Uncle Darren had given him about becoming a man, but I couldn't listen. I was too busy convincing myself all sins were equal in the eyes of God, and that this would be no worse than the time I held Davie Logan's dog while Brandon spray painted it. Three hail Mary's and I should be good.

"Hey, guys! Wait up." Poppy shouted from the playground, her and Hope already jogging to catch up to us on the sidewalk.

Before they reached us, I held up my hand. "Not now, Poppy," I said. "We're going to become men."

We continued walking, and Brandon draped an arm around my shoulder. "That's right, poss. You're gonna have to sit this one out. No girls allowed."

Poppy shoved him. "You're acting weird."

"They're dumb boys. Of course, they're acting weird." Hope crossed her arms over her chest. "It's okay. We'll just follow you."

With a smile, Poppy looped her arm through Brandon's, then he stopped walking, which meant I stopped walking. Hope bumped right into me.

"You can't go." Brandon's tone left no real room for argument.

Her face crumpled a little when he moved her arm. "I can go wherever I want."

Brandon shook his head, and we started down the sidewalk just as Darryl O'Sheehan and his two dumb friends, Matt and Jimmy, trotted around the corner.

"Aw," Darryl halted, nudging Matt in the ribs while pointing our direction. "Look, it's the little pikey snot and his fat friend."

Hope shoved between Brandon me, then dug her fists into her hips. "What do you want, Darryl?"

His attention swung to Hope, his gaze dropping below her chin for a second before a slight smirk settled on his face. "My brother says that ginger lasses have ginger pubes." He laughed. "That true?"

"Wouldn't you want to know." She flipped her hair behind her shoulder, flaunting the air of complete arrogance Hope carried so well. "My sister says your brothers are prize twats, and my dad says your family's a joke."

Darryl edged closer to Hope, jaw tensed.

Then Poppy stepped between them. She jabbed him in the chest. "Leave her alone, Darryl."

"If it isn't Measch." He flicked a strand of Poppy's hair while his friends laughed.

Brandon moved closer to Poppy—just like I knew he would.

I wanted to be the one to help her for once. So I shouted, "You need to leave!" my voice cracking right on cue.

Darryl's attention shifted to me. "Did you say something, fatso?"

A lump lodged in my throat when he stepped closer. "Y —yeah." I sucked in a breath to keep from passing out. "I said." I had to clear my throat to get the word "leave" out.

"Or what? You'll sit on me with your fat arse?" He laughed, his friends joining in. "Or maybe you'll chase me? Can you run as far as the swing set with all that blubber?" Now they were cackling, but I pretended like I didn't care, even though I did.

Brandon squared his shoulders and clenched his fist. "Darryl O'Sheehan, you shut your feckin' mouth. Or I'm gonna punch it."

"Shut up, pikey. I was talking to fatso."

"Ah, that's it. No one calls my best friend, fat." Brandon threw a jab that landed squarely on Darryl's mouth and busted his lip wide open.

"You little..." Darryl stumbled back, cupping his face while Matt and Jimmy stepped in and grabbed Brandon by the shirt, everyone exchanging punches while I stood there in shock.

This wasn't just a fight; this was a brawl. A feral part of me wanted to snatch one of those guys by the collar and throw them to the ground, my feet remained cemented to the spot. Brandon elbowed Matt in the face with such force that he dropped to his knees.

Poppy screamed for everyone to stop while Hope kneed

Darryl in the crotch, and Brandon staggered over to Matt to help him to his feet while the boys took off.

"Better run," Brandon started after them. "Or I'm gonna come burn your house down!"

Brandon wiped his bloodied mouth with the sleeve of his shirt, and I hung my head. I'd stood there and let my best friend take a beating to defend me.

Poppy threw her arms around Brandon's neck. "Oh, Brandon...are you okay?" And the adrenaline pumping through me slowed, quickly replaced by dejection. Like always, Brandon was the hero.

I followed Bran back to the pikey camp, hardly saying a word.

We'd barely set foot inside the caravan before his ma swatted him with her dishcloth. "Brandon Patrick O'Kieffe, you been fighting again?"

He sighed when she grabbed his face and inspected his battered jaw. "He hit me first, Ma."

"Doesn't matter." She let go of his cheeks with a slight shove. Then planted her fists onto her hips, looking down at him with the kind of stern look that made even me want to shrink away. "That boy's mother called me. You told him you'd burn his house to the ground?" She shook her head. "What do ya think it makes me look like? Like you were raised by dogs. Stealing. Fighting—suspended from school." She exhaled, disappointment obvious with her frown. "You're grounded for a week."

"That's so fecking unfair!"

"Boy!"

The flimsy door to the bedroom at the back of the caravan flung open. Brandon and I both flinched.

"Talk to your mother like that again..." His dad's shoulder bumped the doorway as he stumbled out in nothing but a pair of boxers. "And you'll feel my belt on your arse."

"You talk to her worse," Brandon mumbled, and I cringed.

I was too afraid to even make eye contact with the man, much less mumble under my breath.

Mr. O'Kieffe stormed toward us, face red and jaw twitching. Instead of cowering away, Brandon pushed back his shoulders, making himself as tall as he could. Then Mr. O'Kieffe smacked Brandon's jaw with such force that it knocked him to the floor. My breath stilled. And fear seized my muscles when his dad reared back to strike him again.

Mrs. O'Kieffe grabbed his arm. "Des! Connor's here," she said quietly.

His dad's bloodshot eyes cut over to me, and I scrambled back against the wall, reaching for the door. I thought maybe if I could run to his Uncle Darren's or grab Old Man McGinty, I could help him, but before I could turn the knob, Mr. O'Kieffe shoved his foot against Brandon's side. "Get on out of here, boy."

I threw open the door while Brandon stumbled to his feet, and then we both fell out of the caravan. When the door slammed shut behind us, a weak, sinking sensation flooded my body. Brandon started across the field, and I followed, uncertain of what to say or do.

Guilt festered in my gut. The only reason Brandon got into that fight was to stick up for me. Which made me feel as though it were my fault he'd just been hit.

He stopped in front of Old Man's caravan and kicked a rock before he sat on an upturned wheelbarrow with the wheel missing. He put his head in his hands. "I hate my dad."

"He's horrible." I nodded, scraping my trainer over the

edge of the wheelbarrow. "Look, I'm sorry you got in trouble for fighting. But thanks for sticking up for me."

He shrugged. "I'm not gonna let them say shit to you."

"Yeah, I wish I could punch them."

"You can."

"Nah," I let out a sigh. "I'm too scared. And they're right; I am fat."

Brandon pushed off the wheelbarrow, slapping a hand on my shoulder. "I'll always have your back."

I didn't want him to help me all the time, though. I wanted to *be* like him, have Poppy hug me, and the bullies stop picking on me because they were scared of me—not Brandon. And besides, who was gonna have Brandon's back?

More than anything, I wanted to be the kind of friend to Brandon that he was to me. "Can you teach me how to punch?" I asked.

A slow grin worked over his lips. "Sure."

"And then we can have each other's backs," I said.

He nodded. "Friends forever, remember?"

"Always."

12

BRANDON

SEPTEMBER 2003

Two boys circled each other in the pen, dishing out punches that left the straw spattered with blood. With each blow, drunken cheers rang out from the crowd. Any second, I'd be in that very ring, and the thought of it made my stomach a jittery ball of nerves.

A hand landed on my shoulder, and I jumped.

"Easy, lad," Uncle Darren said. "Here. Drink this." He thrust his hip flask in my face, and I tipped it back. "It'll help steady ya."

The whiskey burned my throat, but that didn't keep me from chugging several more gulps before he snatched the flask from my hand.

"Easy. I want you confident. Not shitfaced."

"You said you used to fight drunk."

He snorted. "Lad, I can handle my liquor. You?" He squeezed my small bulge of a bicep. "Not so much."

The roar of the crowd grew louder, dragging my attention to the pen. One of the fighters stood in the center with both fists raised above his head while a group of men dragged the other, unconscious guy between the pallets.

The whiskey churned in my gut, and that sensation summed up my feelings on the whole situation.

Uncle Darren grabbed both of my shoulders hard, bringing his lips close to my ear. "Now, remember what I said. He's a chunky little bastard, so dance around him. When you hit, make it hard and fast." He slapped me on the back, and I stumbled forward.

The few people in front of the haphazard gate stepped aside, letting me into the pen just as the old man in the center cupped his hands to his mouth and shouted, "Welcome, Brandon O'Kieffe!" A mixture of cheers, wolf whistles, and shouts rang out, and that churn in my gut turned to fear in my chest.

My opponent stepped across from me. He was bigger, chubby, and although my head spun under the rush of adrenaline, I was scared.

"And he'll be fighting, Billy Richards!"

Fear laced worry crackled through my veins. I didn't want to be a disappointment to Uncle Darren or my dad. I didn't want to lose in front of all these people. With a heavy swallow, I forced myself to calm down and do everything Uncle Darren had taught me.

The bell pinged, and for a second, I froze. Billy moved toward me, bouncing from side to side. When he went for a right hook, I ducked. Then popped up and drove my fist into his jaw as hard as I could.

There was a second where everything slowed.

The cheers of the crowd faded into muted background noise, and it was just Billy Richards and me. He staggered a step and went down, hitting the ground like a felled tree. Much to my shock, I'd knocked him out. All I could do was stand and stare in disbelief.

Someone grabbed me. I was thrown into the air, hoisted

onto Uncle Darren's shoulders. All the noise filtered back in, the cheering, the praise. *Next Champion. Better than Darren.*

One punch. That was all it took for everything I knew to change. One punch both saved and doomed me.

News of the fight spread from Billy's school to mine, until it was all anyone talked about. I reveled in the new-found power. The bullies, who for years, had called me a pikey and Connor fat, now stayed out of my way. And the girls...well, the girls couldn't get enough of me.

Which is what had led me to this moment. The moment where all of me needed to cross the line from boy to man in one fell swoop.

It was past time. I was a fighter now, and I needed to become a man in every sense of the word. Now I just had to figure out how to make that happen. But I had a plan.

I scanned the length of the aisle at the One Stop. The bright, fluorescent bulbs felt like a spotlight, a beacon for any passersby, alerting them to what I was doing. My attention turned back to the shelves, skimming the boxes of johnnies: Thin. Ribbed. Magnum. Glow in the dark. I didn't know where the hell to start. Although, I guessed glow in the dark might be helpful...

An old lady shuffled around the corner with her walker, and I panicked, grabbing a box of the glow in the dark rubbers and shoving them inside my jacket before heading to the exit.

"Hey!"

"Ah, shit." I rushed out of the store, taking off in the direction of the camp. But when I chanced a look over my shoulder, a guy in a One Stop vest was chasing after me, which meant I couldn't go back to the camp. I hooked it around a corner and darted down an alley, changing course and booking it to Poppy's. I vaulted the gate and climbed the trellis, tumbling in through her open window, completely out of breath.

"Do you ever use a door?" Poppy asked.

When I glanced up, I was shocked to see Connor sitting on the floor next to her. A math book laid open between them, but they were close enough that their knees touched.

"You two look cozy." I forced a mask over the sinking feeling in the pit of my stomach.

Honestly, I wanted to sit close to Poppy like that, but I couldn't. Not without wanting to run my fingers through her soft hair, or inhale the sweet smell of her perfume. I'd much rather have been planning to lose my virginity to Poppy rather than Lisa, but Connor liked her. No. He *loved* her. That boy had always looked at Poppy Turner as if she hung the moon, and I understood why. I really did. She was kind and good; she was everything lacking in my life and everything I craved. Everything. And I cherished her far too much to ever pull her down to my level. My dad said I was good for nothing, and Poppy, well, she needed someone good for something. Connor was good, and I saw how happy it made him when Poppy smiled at him. So I swallowed my own feelings and teased them both like I didn't care, even though seeing them like that made my insides twist.

"Shut it, Brandon." Poppy shoved me. "What did you nick this time?"

Connor arched a brow. "A nudey magazine?"

I flashed them a wide smile. Despite the situation, they were both my best friends, and I was about to make what was potentially the biggest step in a man's life. "Check this shit out." I pulled out the box from under my jacket and threw it at Connor. "Glow in the dark johnnies. I'm gonna pop Lisa's cherry with a lightsaber dick."

The smile on Poppy's face fell clean off. She looked away, but I pretended not to notice.

"What?" Con snatched them off the carpet. "Glow in the dark johnnies? Who would've thought?" He tossed them back. "You know you have to date her if you pop her cherry. It's a rule.."

"I do not! I bought her flowers for Christ's sake. Jesus and me talked about it."

"Lisa? Really, Brandon. She's not even cute." Poppy's arms were crossed, her gaze glued to the wall.

Poppy was jealous, but I remained in blissful denial. She was my friend. That was it. I refused to acknowledge the fact that I thought she was the most beautiful girl I'd ever seen, because, apart from Con, she was my best friend. And although I was ruled by hormones, when it came to Poppy, I was determined not to let those desires win.

"You could do better," she said.

"Yeah, but she has massive boobs. That's the most important thing about a girl. Everyone knows that."

It was obvious from the way Connor's lips rolled in that he was trying his best not to laugh.

Poppy's gaze dropped to her chest, and a deep frown etched across her face. "Nice to know. I don't have big boobs."

"Ah, poss. You don't count. You're my best friend."

"I like your boobs, Poppy." Connor's eyes went wide like he had shocked himself.

I doubled over in laughter, Poppy shoved him, and he toppled over on the floor, his cheeks cherry red.

I stuffed the condoms inside my jacket pocket on my way to the window. After I threw my leg over the ledge, I paused. "Next time you see me, I'll be a changed man." Then

I climbed down from Poppy's window, feeling a lot less confident than I pretended to be.

LISA'S HOUSE was on the nice side of town, where rows of three-story brick townhomes sat nestled among shiny new cars. A few years ago, girls from this side of town wouldn't have given me a second glance...

Crickets chirped in the bushes, silencing when I walked up the empty driveway to the dark townhome. I knocked on the door and waited, unable to find a good place for my hands—my pockets, my sides. When no one answered, I almost sighed in relief. Just as I turned to leave, a light inside cut on, spilling through the small semi-circle of glass in the front door. Lisa pulled it open, and we stood in awkward silence the way only two virginal teenagers could.

She invited me in to watch a movie. The whole time, I was on edge. My gaze kept darting to the doorway, waiting for her parents to storm in and kick me out. If I were going to do this, I needed to get it done before they came back.

I placed my hand, with a little too much force, on her thigh. That was the teenage code for "I want to have sex with you." She faced me, and I swallowed hard, telling myself I just had to be a man and go for it. So, I kissed her.

One thing led to another, and before I knew it, Lisa was in nothing but her pink underwear, and I was scrambling for my lightsaber johnnie.

They say that losing your virginity should be meaningful, but I'm sure most people would recall it as nothing more than a fumble and a poke. The only reason I remembered losing mine was that all I could think of the entire time was Poppy.

With every brush of Lisa's lips, each touch of her bare skin against mine, I imagined it was Poppy, pretending to have the girl that I never would. The girl I loved too much to ever dare try to touch like that. I felt guilty for fantasizing about her and guilty that the person I was losing it to wasn't her.

I pictured the disappointment I would see on Poppy's face when she found out I'd slept with Lisa—and she would find out. Because I'd tell her. Then she'd see what everyone else did, and she'd stop looking at me like I was someone worth saving.

My ma thought she could save my dad, and look where that got her.

When I stumbled out of Lisa's house that night, I felt hollow. I didn't know it then, but that empty feeling would stay with me.

13

CONNOR

The blue haze from the TV was the only light in Poppy's living room.

I'd watched movies with Poppy countless times, but thanks to Brandon being at Lisa's, this was the first time it was just the two of us. And God was I nervous. I wanted to reach over and hold her hand. Maybe kiss her, but I knew better, so I settled for having her snuggled close to me on the couch while we watched *Titanic*.

Brandon never would watch that movie; he said it was the longest chick flick of all time. I didn't mind, though, because Poppy liked it. And I would do anything to make her happy.

By the time the blond guy was dead and sinking to the bottom of the ocean, Poppy was balling. She buried her face in my shoulder, and I took the opportunity to put my arm around her. "It's okay," I said. "It's just a movie."

"But ...that ship really sank." Her head popped up, and tear-filled eyes met mine. "People died on that ship."

"Well. Yeah." I shifted uncomfortably in the seat. "But there wasn't a Jack and Rose."

"Maybe there was."

"Maybe."

The screen faded to black, plunging us into darkness while the end credits rolled. My heart banged out an uneven rhythm. She hadn't pulled away from me yet, which meant my arm was still around her. It also meant I couldn't concentrate on anything but whether she would push me away if I did try to kiss her.

For the past month, I'd practiced telling Poppy how much I cared about her, and it always sounded poetic, like Wadsworth or Hemingway, but sitting in this dark room with her body touching mine; the thought terrified me. Swallowing, I wet my lips. "I would have given up the door for you," I said, hoping she would read between those lines.

She pulled away and smiled through her tears. "You would?"

"Always."

Then she pressed a kiss to my cheek. I closed my eyes, savoring how soft her lips were. The gesture was completely innocent, but it felt like she had just offered me the world.

Our eyes met before my gaze drifted to her lips. I leaned in, and when she didn't move back, I closed my eyes. This was it. I was going to kiss Poppy Turner. But when the living room door banged against the wall, we both jumped away from each other.

Brandon strutted in with a stupid grin on his face. "Behold." He spread his arms wide. "I am no longer a virgin!"

I could have punched him for ruining the moment I'd fantasized about for four years. Poppy hopped up with a huff and shoved past Brandon. She was upset, obviously at Brandon, but I wasn't sure whether it was because he had ruined our moment, or because he'd had sex with Lisa.

Anyone with half a brain could see the way Poppy

looked at Brandon—the same way I'm sure I looked at her most of the time— even though he never gave her the same attention. My chest went hot and tight, and I clenched my fist in my lap when I looked at him. Pots and pans banged around in the kitchen.

"Bran. Get out."

Brandon's confused gaze slowly drifted between me and the kitchen. "Were you? Was that?" He pointed at me, then hiked a thumb over his shoulder toward the doorway.

"I don't know. You're the non-virgin now. You tell me."

"Well, she seems pissed I came in."

"Yeah, so get your arse out, would you? Geez."

He scratched a hand through his hair, then rolled his eyes. "You're my best friends. It's like a code. When one of us loses our virginity, we tell the others. It's a thing."

That was the first I'd heard of that. Of course, Brandon was the first of us to lose his..."Okay. Well, leave, and I'll tell you all about it." For a second, I smiled, but the teenage male comradery I reveled in was quickly smothered by guilt for talking about Poppy like that.

Brandon tensed for a moment like someone had just knocked the wind from him. "You're not supposed to lose it with Poppy. You've gotta practice with somebody else."

"Why would I want to stick my willy in some girl I don't like?"

"Oh." He gave a slight nod, accompanied by a grin. "You'll like it."

"Would you get out of here already?"

He held up his hands and went to turn around but stopped to dig around in his pocket. He chucked something at me. "Don't be silly. Cover that willy."

"Leave!" I quickly shoved the condom into my pocket, my

face burning all the way to my hairline while Brandon laughed his way down the hall.

I listened for the front door, but instead, heard the bang of a cabinet. "What do you want?" Poppy said, and if I had to guess, she had her arms crossed, her hip cocked.

"Don't be mad, poss. I just needed to see Con. It's a guy thing."

"Yeah. Whatever."

"I'm sorry. I know you love *Titanic*." Brandon paused, and I shifted on the couch. "I'm going now, so you and Connor can get right back to it."

The hinges to the back door squealed before the lock clicked shut. There was a moment of silence where I wondered if maybe Poppy had followed him outside, but after a few seconds, her footsteps stomped down the hall.

"He's so annoying." She moved around me and flopped down on the couch.

And there we sat.

Next to each other.

In the dark.

I wanted to put my arm back around her but couldn't find the nerve to do it when she wasn't crying.

She leaned into me, resting her head on my shoulder. "Why does everything have to change, Con, huh?"

"What's changed?"

"Brandon's gonna get a girlfriend. Then you'll get one. And we won't be best friends anymore."

"Aw, come on now. We'll always be best friends."

She shook her head against my shoulder. "I just wish we could stay here forever."

I did too.

She traced her finger over my arm, leaving a trail of chill

bumps behind her soft touch. "If I tell you something, do you promise not to tell Brandon?"

I nodded, even though I wasn't sure I wanted to hear what she was about to say.

"I think he'll end up leaving us, and one day, it will just be you and me."

"Why would you think that?"

"I don't know." She shrugged. "I just feel it. Just promise me you'll never leave me, Con, okay?"

Then I did put my arm around her. "I'll never leave you, Poppy. I promise."

That was the easiest promise I had made in my life. I never intended to leave that girl. Ever.

14

POPPY

Not long after Brandon made his triumphant entrance, Connor left. We exchanged an awkward hug, followed by an even more awkward pause where his gaze dropped to my lips.

I shut the front door and pressed my back to it while guilt weighed my shoulders down.

I'd almost kissed Connor.

And the more concerning thing was: I'd *wanted* to kiss him. Because he was sweet and kind, and, when he started inching his way toward me, it had felt so very right—at least, until Brandon stormed in all victorious.

That changed everything.

My emotions jumbled and tangled, tightening my chest as I climbed the stairs to my room. As far as my adolescent self could tell, I was in love with Brandon, and yet, part of me was beginning to fall for Connor. What kind of person was I? Falling for not one, but both of my best friends.

I slammed my bedroom door, then paced at the foot of my bed. Something had to be wrong with me. Even Hope wouldn't pull some stunt like this. If I weren't careful, I'd ruin everything.

On a huff, I wiggled out of my jeans and shirt and pulled on one of Brandon's old T-shirts he'd left at my house. A familiar knock sounded at my window, and I took a deep breath. When I didn't go to the window, he tapped the glass again. Brandon knew I left it unlocked—specifically for him. Knocking was nothing but a curtesy.

I spun around, shot him the nastiest glare I could manage, then flipped him the bird before I fell back onto my bed. He was still at the window when I took the book from my nightstand and turned to the dog-eared page. It was harder than I thought it would be to focus on the print while trying to ignore the subtle ache in my chest.

The glass juddered against the frame, followed by the rustle of Brandon's crawling through the gap. His feet hit the carpet with a thud, but I kept my gaze locked onto the words, pretending to be invested even though I wasn't comprehending a single line.

"Possum?"

On a sigh, I flipped the page, smoothing the crease in the paper. I was angry at him, but the thing that made it worse: I had no right to be.

"You're mad at me for interrupting your thing with Connor."

My face went fire-hot. I tossed the book to the foot of my bed, then crossed my arms over my chest on a hard stare. "It wasn't a *thing* with Connor, Brandon." It almost was, but there was no way I'd ever admit that.

"*O*-kay..." He shoved his hands into his pockets and scraped a heel over the carpet.

It was all different now. One night and everything had

changed. He'd kissed Lisa—done *other* things with Lisa, and I despised that she now had parts of Brandon I never would.

"What do you want?" My voice caught in the back of my throat.

"Poss, you know I hate it when you're mad at me."

When I didn't say anything, he face-planted on my bed, grabbing fistfuls of the comforter and groaning. "Girls are so confusing!"

I studied the way his biceps flexed while he gripped the covers, the tangles in his hair that I was certain Lisa had caused. Anger bubbled inside, popping and fizzing, heating my core until I wanted to explode. And I did.

"Why don't you go crawl through Lisa's window then. She doesn't seem to confuse you." The second those words left my mouth, I regretted them. They made me sound jealous, but as much as I hated it, I was.

He lifted his head, then rolled onto his side and propped his head on his hand. "Because I don't like Lisa. And the last time I checked, you're my best friend."

"You had sex with her. What do you mean you don't like her?"

He rolled his eyes. "Poss, you don't have to like a girl to, you know..." He swept an invisible crumb from my bed. "I just didn't want to be a virgin anymore."

And he thought girls were confusing. Groaning, I grabbed the book from the end of my bed, reopened it, and leaned against the headboard. "Whatever, Brandon."

Brandon sat up and scooted beside me. His warm breath touched my shoulder. "Whatcha reading?" The smell of soap and sweat that was all Brandon invaded my space just before I caught a subtle hint of vanilla body spray.

I swallowed while my stomach turned. Lisa had even ruined the way he smelled. *"Frankenstein,"* I managed.

"Cool." He reclined back on the pillow next to me. "You know I'm not going anywhere until you forgive me for whatever I did. Then, if you want me to go home, I will." There was a trace of disappointment in his voice, and it didn't belong there. No matter how much it felt like we were more than friends, we weren't. I wasn't Lisa McAdams.

I placed the book on my nightstand, then got out of bed to lock the bedroom door before slipping beneath the covers. "You didn't do anything to me, Brandon. I'm just..." I reached over and switched off the lamp, settling into the darkness.

I couldn't tell him I was hurt because I didn't want him to know how I felt. As hurt as I may have been, I refused to ruin what Brandon and I did have. "Don't pay attention to me. It's just a girl thing, I guess. And you don't have to leave."

"Okay. Just so you know, I'll never like any other girl more than you. Love you, poss."

A dizzying heat washed over my body, a tsunami I would have gladly drowned in. A notebook was tucked away in my nightstand drawer, *I love Brandon* scribbled over most of the pages.

Out of the thousand ways I'd daydreamed he'd tell me he loved me, I never imagined it would be like this. Right after he'd given himself to someone else, after I'd almost kissed his best friend.

But as much as it broke my heart, I'd take that boy loving me any way I could, so I whispered, "I love you, too," before I closed my eyes to sleep.

15

BRANDON

APRIL 2004

With the press of a button, I shot Connor's avatar in the head. "Too slow," I said with a triumphant grin when digital blood splattered across Connor's TV screen.

Connor threw his controller and sank back into the sofa cushions. "I thought you were coming here last night."

"Nah. Went to Poppy's." I always went to Poppy's, because —and I never told Con this since, at the time, it felt stupid— she made me feel safe. I swiped the bottle of Mountain Dew from the coffee table and took a swig.

"Huh." He fidgeted with the remote. "You like her or something?"

"What?" My chest squeezed with something akin to panic. "No! Gross. It's Poppy." So much dishonesty lingered between us, but I kept my secrets close for two reasons: Connor and Poppy.

My loyalty to him was the only thing strong enough to stop my raging teenage hormones dead in their tracks.

The memory of the two of them snuggled up on her couch watching *Titanic* popped to mind, and jealousy sunk its claws in deep. "I always stay at her house," I said. "You know that. She's like my sister." The lies continued to pour in a desperate bid to cover the truth.

"Yeah ..."

"Jesus, Mary, and Joseph. You pine after that girl more than a pisshead with a bottle of whiskey." I took the pack of cigarettes from my back pocket and dabbed one out, but he snatched it from me.

"Not in the house. Ma will have my arse."

"Worried she'll think you're smokin', Golden Balls?"

"Piss off."

I fell back against the cushions, combating the ugly feeling that tightened my chest. "Seriously, though, you're my best friend. Poppy's my best friend. You two...are best friends. You can't be looking at her like *that*."

"Why not?"

"Look. I get it. Poppy *is* pretty, but it would ruin everything. It's perfect exactly how it is."

I didn't want anything to change, but I could sense it on the horizon. We were on the precipice between adolescents and young adults. Part of me wished I could hit pause. The tumultuous emotions were already proving to be a confusing push and pull, and the situation between Poppy, Connor, and me—one wrong decision could destroy everything. I needed them both too much to risk it.

Connor's brows pulled together. "Yeah. I guess you're right."

"You don't really want Poppy. She's just the only girl who talks to you."

"Maybe."

"Feckin' hell. Come on." I grabbed his arm, dragging him from the couch as I stood.

"Where?"

"We're going to see Slutty Suzie."

"Bran. Come on." He started to pull away, but my grip just tightened. This was for his own good.

"No. We're going. She showed me her pussy last year and changed my whole world. Look, you took me to confession when we were kids, now it's time for me to help you sin. You won't even talk to a girl because you're so hung up on Poppy." I shook my head. "It's just getting sad now."

He pulled against me again. I was always the devil on Connor's shoulder, but he needed a push. Without me, he would be a virgin until he found some girl to marry.

I grinned on our way to the door. "I'm not asking you to sleep with her. Just kiss the girl—anything to get a little experience." I stared at Connor and the uncertainty on his face. "Look, I'll take ya to confession right after."

"The entire church would go up in smoke the second your arse walked through the doors."

"I happen to be baptized, thank you very much."

We were halfway through his yard before he stopped resisting. Then he shoved me. "I swear to God, Bran. You tell anyone about this, and I will let everyone know about that time we had that farting contest and you strained so hard you shit yourself."

"You'd never prove it."

"Might would."

"Fine. I won't tell." I spat on my palm and held out my hand. He did the same, and we shook. "I swear if you ask me to pinky swear ..."

He let out a sigh. "Come on, let's get this over with. It's just a kiss, right?"

16

BRANDON

MAY 2004

Ma flopped down on the couch with a hand to her head. "Can you get me the paracetamol?"

I grabbed it from the cupboard, filled a glass with water, and handed both to her. "You've been having a lot of headaches."

She tossed the pill back, then laid back down. "It's just the weather. Are you going to Connor's?"

"Yeah. I'll be home for dinner."

"Okay, sweetheart. I love you." She smiled up at me, and I leaned down to press a kiss to her cheek.

"Love you too, Ma," I said on my way out the door.

———

I SPENT the afternoon and most of the early evening playing video games with Connor, just like most days, but when I stepped into the caravan that evening, the aroma of hash and cabbage wasn't there.

But my dad was, and with him being home instead of at

the pub, I knew something was wrong. He sat on the couch, his elbows rested on his spread knees. His head hung forward.

No TV. No beer in his lap.

I craned my neck, trying to locate Ma, and the floor creaked. Dad's head lifted slowly, his tear-filled gaze meeting mine.

"Where's Ma?"

He swiped a hand over his face before patting the couch. "Come here."

Panic crept around my throat, strangling me like a boa constrictor when I perched on the edge of the sofa. Every muscle in my body tensed, but for once, it wasn't because I was scared of my dad, just what he was going to say.

"Your ma is gone." He paused. He ducked his head, and his fists balled on his thighs. "She's gone, Brandon." The slight vulnerability in his words crashed over me with startling reality.

Gone? My jaw tensed. She wouldn't leave me.

"A brain aneurysm."

She'd been getting headaches and having to nap a lot, but she was okay. She had to be.

"I called the medics," Dad breathed. "They took her, but there was nothing they could do."

A numbness settled over me.

He just let them take her, without even coming to find me. And I hated him for it. A world without my ma in it— my world imploded until I was left standing alone in the dark, sucked into a dark void where nothing good existed. Without her, ebbing loneliness would consume me. She was all I had.

I couldn't bear to look at the empty caravan, at my

worthless father, pretending to mourn a woman that he did nothing but hurt. So I left.

I needed something. Something I'd never turned to before, so I went to Connor's.

As soon as he opened the door and looked at me, his face fell. He pulled me into a bear hug, and I let him, but I was numb.

"I need to go to the church," I whispered.

Without question, he pulled away from me and grabbed his coat. I don't know why I wanted Connor to go with me. Partly, I thought God wouldn't listen to me, but Connor was good. If I went with him, maybe I stood more of a chance. The entire way there, silent tears continued to track down my cheeks, but I didn't feel the despair that went with them, not really. I just felt lost, like I was watching someone else navigate the ever-harder path that was my life.

When we stepped inside, I headed straight for the statue of the Virgin Mary. The closer I got, the more intimidating she seemed, though her face was kind, forgiving. It just made me think of Ma. I fell to my knees in front of her and closed my eyes. I thought about my ma, and I begged Jesus to let her into heaven. As I knelt there, I realized it was too late. Too late for prayers, or help. She was gone. It felt so utterly final. She just...no longer existed.

I didn't know why I went there. Perhaps I was looking for some kind of redemption or peace. Part of me felt like I deserved this because I wasn't good. I stole and sinned. But God was supposed to forgive all sins, and Ma...she never sinned. Where was her forgiveness? In a cold, dark hole in the ground. That's where.

It was there in front of the statue of the virgin that I finally felt it all, every sharp, jagged edge of my pain sliced through me until I simply sobbed. I broke down crying until I could cry no more, and then I went back to Connor's house too fractured and scared to go home. My ma was dead, and I'd never really had a father.

I was an orphan.

17

POPPY

Cathedrals in Ireland are a stark contrast to the churches in America. They're cold and solemn. The slightest of whispers sound loud, echoing from the vaulted ceilings, but what doesn't differ is the thick fog of dread that clings to the air during a funeral.

The wooden pew creaked when I shifted my weight, crossing and uncrossing my legs. My gaze drifted from Connor to the stained-glass window to the wrought iron chandelier. I looked everywhere but to the front where Mrs. O'Kieffe's casket sat.

The slight rustle of people moving, the intermittent cough—all silenced when soft footsteps fell over the stone floor. Brandon pulled a crumpled piece of paper from his pocket as he made his way to the pulpit. Clearing his throat, he exhaled and smoothed the note over the podium. "My ma was the best person I knew ..." Brandon's words were lost on a choked sob.

Each beat of my heart felt like a thunderclap. I just wanted to hold his hand, to make sure he knew he wasn't alone, but when I flattened my feet on the floor and gripped the edge of the pew to rise, my father placed a gentle hand on my knee, subtly shaking his head.

"She was kind," Brandon continued, his voice wavering. "And nice to everyone. It didn't matter how bad I was or what I did. She always loved me. Always stood up for me." His chin dropped to his chest on a ragged breath. "And now she's gone." Moments passed before he lifted his tear-streaked face to look out over the crowd. He looked so lost, like someone left without anyone to fight for them. "My ma would have said that this isn't goodbye, just see you later. And I really hope there's a heaven because I can't wait to see her again."

Glancing at the coffin, he wiped his face and stepped down, stopping beside his mother's body. His fingers clutched the side of the casket when the clergyman came to close it, and I had to look away. I couldn't bear to watch him break.

Connor grabbed my hand, threading his fingers through mine.

Footsteps echoed into the ceiling as several men from the camp—Old Man and Uncle Darren included—walked to the front of the cathedral. They each grabbed one of the coffin's handles and hoisted it onto their shoulders, carting it through the open doors at the side of the church.

Connor and I didn't say a word as we followed the masses outside, weaving through the moss-covered crosses and tombstones. My father squeezed my arm before stepping to the side to stand with Mr. and Mrs. Blaine.

Brandon stood right at the edge of her grave, a lily in his hand. He held it over the grave and hesitated, and I knew this was the hardest part—knowing that any minute, the person who means the most will be covered with dirt and left. Leaving the dead feels wrong and leaves us empty.

After a hard breath, Brandon dropped the lily into the grave.

Mr. O'Kieffe moved beside him. He pulled a hip flask from his pocket and took a hefty swig before he scooped a handful of fresh dirt from the ground and sprinkled it over the coffin. He choked back a sob and stumbled off with the flask to his lips, leaving Brandon alone at the edge of the grave.

Brandon's jaw ticced. His nostrils flared. His fist clenched and unclenched, and just when I thought he would turn around and come over to Connor and me, he collapsed on his knees.

And I crumpled right along with him.

In a heartbeat, I was him, and he was me. I recalled being exactly where he now was, buried under a mountain of indescribable loss, unable to see how the world could keep turning when mine had been taken away.

I rushed toward him, kneeling and wrapping my arms around his neck. "I love you," I whispered into his messy hair, clutching him harder while his chest heaved. The gut-felt sob that followed sent a poison-laced dagger straight through my chest. As much as I wanted to take all his pain away, I couldn't. I couldn't do anything to change what had happened.

All I could do was make sure he knew that I would never leave him.

———

BY THE TIME people left the cemetery, Mr. O'Kieffe was staggering drunk, and Connor's parents took Brandon home with them, which made me feel better. The last place I wanted Brandon was in that caravan with his dad.

Daddy and I sat down to a dinner neither of us touched. The day dredged up feelings—memories that were never easy for either of us to address. Life had a million wonderful moments, but man, those crappy ones could take a toll. My chest went tight at the thought of death. At how final it was. How cruel it was to those it left behind.

Knotting the friendship bracelet Brandon had given me on my eleventh birthday, and I wondered how bad it would be if I broke that promise I made to him not to tell. I'd always worried about Brandon, but now, I was terrified for him. His mother protected him as best she could, and I just wanted him to be safe.

Daddy looked up from his plate of spaghetti. "Not hungry, either, huh?"

Shaking my head, I took both our plates to the sink and rinsed them. By the time I dried my hands, I'd almost convinced myself Brandon would forgive me if I broke my promise. I turned around, but when Daddy's eyes met mine, all I asked was to be excused.

It shouldn't have shocked me when I walked in and found Brandon sprawled out on top of my comforter, his hands behind his head, and gaze aimed at the ceiling. But it did.

"Hey, possum," he whispered.

"Hey." I locked the door, then moved toward the bed. "I'm glad you're here." I wanted to say so much more.

"Nowhere else to go."

I sank to the mattress beside him. The words, "I'm sorry" were on the tip of my tongue, but I swallowed those down like a bitter pill. Nothing I could say would make things better, and I knew that.

Brandon rolled onto his side with a heavy sigh before he laid his head in my lap. His eyes closed, and he grabbed my hand, placing my fingers in his unruly hair. "Make it go away," he whispered, fighting tears.

Pieces of my soul splintered apart while I scratched through his hair. I hoped he realized that I would always love him.

"I wish I could," I said, my voice thick.

He grabbed my thigh and squeezed until it hurt, and I took it. Brandon needed something to hold onto, and I was glad it was me.

I wanted it to always be me.

18

BRANDON

APRIL 2006

Weeks changed to months. Months changed to years. Life went on, and yet it didn't. I put on a face. Pretended I was okay when I wasn't. I'd become so good at perfecting the image of a bad boy who didn't give a shit, I'm not sure even Poppy or Connor knew just how much I wasn't okay.

DAD DRANK MORE, which led to him throwing more punches. I either took them, for my ma, or I lost my shit and hit him back. And he got up from those blows less often now.

My life was a constant state of chasing anything and everything that would make me forget how pointless my existence was. Every so often, I'd think of Ma, and guilt would make me check in on the old man. Today was just such a day, and the caravan was just as much of a shit hole as it always was.

I threw two empty bottles of whiskey in the bin and began washing the dirty dishes cluttering the tiny kitchen.

"Keep it down, boy." Dad turned up the volume on the TV and cracked opened a new bottle of whiskey.

I'd tried to keep on top of everything, for Ma's sake. I went to school, though my grades were bad. I fought most weekends, and I cleaned up the caravan. After a year with the old man, my patience had worn thin.

I chucked the plate into the overflowing sink and stepped into the narrow hallway. "You know. You could wash your own dishes."

"What did you just say to me?" He heaved himself out of the chair and stumbled toward me.

My shoulders squared. My fists tightened. I thought of what he put Ma through, of how he treated her—how he'd treated me. "You were a piece of shit when Ma was alive, but now—"

"I put food on the table." His nostrils flared. "A roof over your head!"

I laughed. "The only money you make is betting on *my* fights. And a roof?" I gestured around the caravan. "You call *this* a roof?"

"You think you're the big lad now, eh?" He took a threatening step toward me, and I braced myself.

I should just leave this shithole and never come back, but Ma would turn in her grave. And that's the only thing that had me stopping in every few days to stock the fridge and clean up.

"Ma would be disgusted."

The force of his fist when it collided with my face sent me crashing into the kitchen door. He usually stopped at one punch, but this time he went for a second, smacking the other side of my face. When he reared back to throw another, I ducked and swung.

One punch and he fell to the floor with a thud. Out cold.

I left him there, swiping my leather jacket and a bottle of cheap whiskey on my way out. On my way through town, I stopped in front of Poppy's house and stared up at the window I used to climb through. It had almost been a year since I'd climbed that trellis. I saw the way Poppy looked at me sometimes—the same way all the other girls looked at me right before I kissed them. The same way she'd been looking at me since we were eleven years old when neither of us even understood what that look meant.

Ma's words from years ago played on repeat in my head. "Girls like Poppy Turner, they end up with boys like Connor." The concerning thing was, I couldn't trust myself not to ruin Poppy the same way I ruined everything else. And I couldn't lose her. Some days she felt like the only thing that kept me going, so I turned around and headed across town to Lola Steven's house. Because all I needed was a warm body and a bottle of whiskey to forget about my life. Just for a little while.

———

"OH MY GOD. I think my dad's home," Lola gasped, yanking the duvet over her bare chest. She waved a hand through the air in a piss-poor attempt to dissipate the thick cloud of smoke that made it smell like Snoopdog had moved into her bedroom. A roach sat burning on a plate on her bedside table. We were so screwed.

"What? Now?"

"You need to leave." She grabbed my boxers and threw them at me. "Right now!"

I yanked on my underwear and nearly fell flat on my face when I rushed to step into my jeans. The floorboard on the landing groaned. Throwing clothes around in an attempt to find my shirt, I panicked. "Shit. Gotta go." Forgetting about my shirt, I gave her a quick kiss, grabbed the roach and shoved it between my lips, then forced up the window. One of my legs was already over the ledge before I spotted the bottle of whiskey on her dresser. I swiped it and threw my other leg over just in time for her father to throw open her bedroom door. His face was puce red, his eyes aimed right at me.

"Aw, shit." I jumped for the garage roof and hit it hard, my knees landed on the asphalt top. The whiskey flew out of my hands and skittered across the roof before it rolled off, smashing to pieces on the concrete below.

"You get back here, you little fucker!" her dad shouted from her bedroom window.

By the time I got off the roof and made it around the front, he was at the front door, holding a shotgun.

I had never run so fast in my damn life.

I legged it straight to Poppy's house. By the time I threw myself through her bedroom window, I could barely breathe.

Poppy and Connor both glanced up from the books spread out on the bed between them.

The boom of a shotgun rang through the air, and all of us jumped.

Poppy's eyes went wide. "What did you do, Brandon?"

"You come back 'round my girl, and I'll have you castrated!" Mr. Stevens shouted from the street.

"It's not as bad as it looks," I said.

Connor nodded. "It looks like you've been chasing the private school girls again."

Poppy snatched her notebook from the bedspread and

scribbled something on the page. "Let me guess, Lola Stevens?" She shot daggers at me before going back to her writing.

"It's the uniform, poss. What do you want me to say?" I looked to Connor for back up, but he just shrugged. He was too much of a pussy to agree with me in front of Poppy. "Even golden balls there would be tempted if she'd give him a shot."

And Lola would definitely give Con a shot. Captain of the rugby team, Con was no longer the chubby kid cramming Milkybars in his pocket. Most of the girls in school wanted his attention, of course, he never noticed anyone but Poppy.

Poppy directed an inquisitive brow at Connor, tapping her pencil on her notebook. "Would you?"

"No!" His cheeks tinged pink. "Of course not."

Poppy's jaw dropped a little. Then she shoved him so hard he nearly toppled off the bed. "You just blushed! Oh my God. I can't with you two."

"Ah, don't be hard on Con. He doesn't possess balls, despite all evidence to the contrary."

Connor grabbed the stuffed possum I'd given Poppy for her birthday last year and hurled it at my face.

"Well, you two chase after girls like Lola Stevens all you want." Poppy snatched the stuffed animal and placed it back on her bed. "I've got a date next weekend. With a guy who would never go after Lola Stevens."

The muscle in my jaw spasmed. The thought of some guy touching her made my fists clench. "With who?"

Her gaze narrowed while a subtle smirk played at her lips. "I'd prefer to keep my date private, thank you very much."

"You're okay with this?" I asked Connor while thumbing at Poppy.

He shrugged. "I mean…" Then he shrugged again.

"I don't need either of you to be okay with anything."

"I'll find out who it is, Poppy. And then…" I fixed my gaze on her and sighed. "You know what happens."

If looks could kill, the one Poppy shot at me would have put me in my grave. "Don't. You. Dare."

"Tell me who it is." I pushed to my feet. "If he's nice, maybe I won't have to kill him." It was a lie, there was no guy on earth nice enough to date my possum. Well, Connor, but even that thought had me riddled with jealousy.

Poppy swung her legs over the mattress and rounded the foot of her bed, stopping inches in front of my face. The top of her head barely brushed my chin. Her chest bumped up against me and made me all too aware of her curves. My jeans tightened, and I shifted on my feet, fighting my body's natural response to her. It had grown increasingly harder to ignore the way I felt about Poppy and the things I dreamt about doing with her, but it was those very feelings that kept me leashed.

I loved her too much to let her fall for someone like me. And she would.

We both knew she would.

Her storm-grey eyes looked particularly turbulent. "Fuck off, Brandon."

A shocked expression tore across Con's face, but a smile crept over mine. Good girl, Poppy Turner had finally gotten a mouth on her. And it was hot.

"Didn't know you had it in you, poss. Gotta say, I'm a little turned on."

Her nostrils flared on a deep breath. "I'll be sure to use that word on my date then."

I groaned at the thought. This wasn't getting me anywhere. I'd find out exactly who Poppy was dating, and then I'd fill him in, the same way I had every other guy who had looked at her.

19

POPPY

My telling Brandon and Connor that I had a date was the absolute dumbest lie I could have told. If I fessed up, they'd never let me live it down. And while I'd toyed with the idea of pretending that the mystery guy had stood me up, a lie like that, and Brandon would make it his life's goal to find out who the guy was so he could pummel him.

Hope stood in front of my dresser, tugging at the short hem of her dress while shooting a judgmental glare at me through the mirror. "Tell me that's not what you're wearing to the party?"

"I don't know." What I was wearing to the party was the least of my concerns. "So. I did something stupid."

Her chin dropped with a disappointed sigh. "I knew it would happen sooner or later. You banged the pikey, didn't you?"

"What?" I feigned disgust at the suggestion. "No. God, no!"

Her eyes narrowed in accusation. "What other stupid thing is there then?"

"I told the guys I had a date."

"Why?"

I dropped my gaze to my bedspread, tracing my finger over the flower pattern. I wasn't even sure why I had done it.

"Well, you're hot. It can't be that hard to get a date." She grabbed a tube of lipstick from the makeup caddy. "Darryl's always had a thing for you. And Davie."

Darryl and Davie wouldn't do at all. One, Brandon would never believe I chose to go out with either of those creeps and two, there was no way I *would* go anywhere with either of them. I wanted the male version of Lola Stevens. A guy that would make Brandon's blood boil, and one that Brandon wouldn't dare try to start a fight with. "Hope, I need a date. With a hot guy." I chewed at my lip. "A really hot guy that could knock out Brandon."

A short-lived laugh bubbled from her lips. "First of all, no one can knock out Brandon." She pulled a short, black skirt from her backpack and tossed it to me. "Secondly, since when did you stop pining after that dickhead long enough to look at another bloke."

Hope may have been my best friend that was a girl, but the way I felt about Brandon was a secret I hadn't confessed to anyone. I feigned disgust. "I do not pine after him."

"You do, but so does every girl." She shrugged one shoulder. "Hell, I might even give the pikey a crack if he wasn't such a wanker. Probably had the clap more times than the circus."

Heat spread across my chest while I stared down at the skirt in my hands. I hated the way I felt about him. I hated that there was nothing he could do to make me feel differently.

I chucked the miniskirt to my bed. "I'm not wearing that."

Hope snatched it up and threw it at me again. "Yeah, you probably shouldn't. Brandon would hate it because it shows to much skin."

I pulled off the modest skirt I had been wearing and slipped into the flimsy material. It clung to my hips, my butt, and it barely hit midthigh.

"Now, back to this date. You're trying to make the pikey jealous, aren't you?" She tilted her head, her gaze locking with mine in the mirror before she spun around with an excited grin. "Or is it Connor?"

"Hope..."

With a roll of her eyes, she went back to touching up her already made-up face. "I'll ask Silas if he has any friends."

"Silas? As in, Slutty Suzie's older brother? The one that just got back from war? With the tattoos and scars!"

"M-hmm." She wiggled her eyebrows. "Hot, isn't he?"

Silas looked the part of a cartel boss. Intimidating and bad—exactly Hope's cup of tea. "Hope, he's twenty. Twenty!"

"And?"

There was no use debating the likely moral compromise that accompanied a twenty-year-old trying to date a sixteen-year-old. Besides, anything that compromised morals was right up Hope's alley.

"You want to make Brandon O'Kieffe jealous. One of Silas' friends should do the trick."

"I didn't say I wanted to make him jealous!"

"Didn't have to." She eyed the short skirt I'd put on with a smile, then plucked her cell phone from the bed and tapped the buttons. Barely a minute later, the device dinged. "You officially have a date with Liam Malley. You're welcome."

My jaw dropped.

"What?" she said, her gaze meeting mine in the mirror while she fluffed her hair. "He's nineteen. Not twenty."

Brandon would absolutely lose it if, and when, he found out I was going on a date with a womanizer like Liam. But that *was* what I had wanted, wasn't it? Even if I hadn't admitted it to Hope.

"Possuuuum!" Brandon's head popped through the window before he tumbled over the ledge and toppled to the floor with a roll. The smell of whiskey permeated the room.

"Only a pikey would crawl through a window like a stray cat," Hope said.

With a smirk, he sprawled out on his back. "Why are you friends with that ginger bitch? You know they have no souls and eat babies and shit."

"Brandon O'Kieffe, you know you're a cunt!" Hope chucked a hairbrush at him, and he gave a drunken salute.

"That I am."

His jaw was red and swollen. Knuckles bloody. With a sigh, I scooted off the bed and crouched beside him, softly gripping his chin to survey the damage. "What were you doing?"

"Well, I was drinking my whiskey."

"Standard." Hope snickered, and Brandon attempted a glare.

"And then I thought: I should share with my possum. Sharing is caring." He brandished the whiskey bottle. When he waved it around, the hem of his shirt inched up his stomach. On instinct, my gaze went to the deep-cut *V* that dipped below the waist of his jeans. I swallowed before tugging it down.

"He wouldn't use the door," Connor's voice came from the open doorway. "I tried."

Laughing, Brandon guzzled back a few shots worth of whiskey. I snatched away the bottle when amber liquid began to trickle from the corners of his lips. There was no way he could go to a party. He'd either end up in another fight or with alcohol poisoning. Or both.

When Brandon got to this state, he was trying to forget. And trying to forget was a dangerous place to be.

"You two go ahead," I said, brushing a hand over Brandon's jaw. "We'll catch up with you."

Connor rubbed over the back of his neck, his gaze drifting from me to Brandon and back. "We can wait."

"Nope." Hope linked her arm through Connor's. "I'm not waiting around on that drunk twat. Come on, Milkybar, let's get there before all the wine coolers are gone."

"Stop calling me that, would you? I haven't had a damn Milkybar in two years."

Hope grabbed his face, squeezing his cheeks. "But it's *so* cute."

With a roll of his eyes, Connor flashed me a pleading look while she dragged him from the room.

Seconds later, the front door shut, and I managed to sit Brandon up, inspecting his scrapes and bruises again. "How bad this time?"

"Well, I managed to duck. And then—" A lazy, drunk smile crossed his face. "I knocked his arse clean out."

"You knocked your dad out. Again?" I sighed. "Brandon."

He reached for the bottle still in my hand, and I yanked it away. "It's fine, poss." His eyelids lulled shut, but he pulled himself up enough to rest his head in my lap. "It's fine," he said again, moving my hand to his head and forcing my fingers through his thick hair while he fiddled with the hem of my short skirt. His warm skin brushed my mine, the touch creating a pull between my legs only he could.

"I know I'm not good enough for you." He took an uneven breath. "But..."

He was drunk, and when Brandon was drunk, he said all kinds of things. But this...what I thought it might mean that he wanted more—I wanted so badly to believe it did. "Brandon, what are you talking about?"

Seconds passed before his fingers brushed my chin, forcing me to look at him. His jade green eyes touched every inch of my face, as though he were committing me to memory, then his rough fingers trailed my cheekbone, and he smiled. "I love you, possum."

His gaze fixed on my lips, and the air seemed to still. Each heavy beat of my heart counted down the seconds. The pull that danced between us, I wanted it. God, I so desperately wanted to know what his lips would feel like on mine, even if it were just one time. Then his eyes closed and his fingers tightened into fists. "Don't worry..." His chest fell into a heavy rhythm. "Con's good enough."

That night I realized just how hopelessly in love I was with Brandon. I told myself that I would rather be the girl he leaned on than the girl who ended up with him between her legs; I would rather keep his respect than lose it. Still, had Brandon let me, I would have *loved* him and given him every piece of my heart to destroy.

But instead, I was just his possum. Always and forever.

20

BRANDON

I'd spent days trying to find out what bellend Poppy had a date with, but it was none of the guys at our school. Or at the townie school.

Then I realized—girls usually set their friends up with their boyfriend's friends, and Hope was dating Suzie's brother, Silas. Which was why I paid Slutty Suzie twenty quid to nick her brother's phone. And it was worth it. Low and behold, some guy called Liam was going on a date with Poppy tonight at the local Sprinkles.

I sat at the bus stop across the road, watching through the shop window. One of Hope's dresses clung to Poppy's tiny frame, leaving nothing to the imagination, which pissed me off a treat. Not to mention, the arsehole who bought her ice cream looked like a fully-grown man and was clearly a pervert.

She sat across from him, twirling the friendship bracelet I'd given her years ago—fidgeting the way she did whenever she was nervous or uncomfortable. With each passing second, my pulse rose until I was certain I was about to have a heart attack.

After about an hour, they left, and I followed, trying to remain rational while telling myself that I was only making sure she was safe.

Halfway down the block, his hand came around her waist, and he pulled her close. That was all it took.

In an instant, I was right behind them, grabbing Liam and shoving him against the glass front of a shop that was locked up for the night.

A moment of shock flashed over his face before his brows pulled together. His frame tightened, and he swung. He may have been bigger than me—probably stronger—but not faster. I dodged—the movement now second nature—before my fist met his nose. Blood splattered the dark shop window.

"Aw. Shit!" He doubled over and clutched his face.

"Brandon!" Poppy grabbed the back of my shirt and pulled until the fabric ripped. "Stop it!"

"You stay the fuck away from her!" I spat, jabbing a finger into his chest.

He tried to shove me away, but I punched him in the gut, forcing him to double over on a cough. Poppy tugged me harder this time, but I couldn't tear myself from the red mist descending over me. In a fight, it helped, but it wasn't until I took a step back and Liam staggered away, that I realized the damage I'd just done.

"I can't believe you." Poppy's arms came around her body like she was shielding herself from the cold, even though it was sweltering hot outside. A look of disappointment fell over her face, and my shoulders fell. "Just tell me why, Brandon."

"You're sixteen. The guy was a pervert."

She took a step toward me, anger ticing in her jaw. "Lisa Swinson, Slutty Suzie." She jabbed a finger at my chest.

"Brenda O'Malley, Nieve Kirkpatrick. Lola Stevens." Each name was a bullet through my heart, and with each one, her finger dug deeper into my skin. "And you don't date them. You just screw them. So who's the pervert, Brandon? Huh?"

"It's different."

The sarcastic laugh echoed from the vacant buildings cut me deep. "Of course it is." She went to turn, then froze. Her gaze swung right back to me, jaw tense. "I guess you can parade however many girls around in front of me, and I just have to take it. Huh?"

Frustration tightened my chest. Years of unspoken words lingered between us, just waiting to bubble over. "You're good, Poppy. Too good for Liam, and sure as hell too good for someone like me. All those girls. They're just..." I threw my hands into the air.

"Just *what*, Brandon?"

There was a beat of silence, a moment where I almost swallowed the words, but unlike every other time, I didn't.

"Not you," I confessed.

Her expression fell blank. Tears swam in her eyes, and I hated myself for doing this to her, but it was for the best.

"I love you, poss," I said, and her breath hitched. No matter how badly it sucked right now. It was so for the best. I had to kill any chance there was for us to be anything more than we were right now. "You're my best friend."

Her lips parted like she was going to speak, but instead, she shook her head again and walked off.

I fell forward a step, wanting to follow her, but I knew I'd just screwed up. I saw exactly how this would go. It was all mapped out in front of me.

We weren't kids anymore, and one way or another, I was about to lose Poppy. And I knew it. I could choose to be with her and drag her right down to my level. Ruin her. Or I could watch her be with someone else. The idea killed me, but if I kept doing this, she would end up hating me, and I needed her. More than she could ever know.

There was only one person who I could stomach her being with. One person who was good enough for her— Connor, and he was already in love with her.

It was all so simple. They would be happy together, and I would always choose their happiness over mine.

LATER THAT SAME EVENING, I sat at the table with Connor's family, my stomach churning as we ate Mrs. Blaine's bacon and cabbage stew.

After dinner, we went to Connor's room to play video games, but my mind was on other things. The game was nothing but a blur in the background, which meant I kept losing to Con.

"You okay?" Connor finally asked, pausing the game.

With a deep sigh, I put my controller down. "Con, be honest. Do you love Poppy?"

"What?" His brow wrinkled. "Of course, I do. What kind of stupid question is—"

"No, like, do you *love* her?"

He sank into the beanbag and scrubbed a hand over his jaw. "She's Poppy, Brandon. Of course, I do."

"Jesus. Do you want to bang her, Con?"

That got his cheeks red. His gaze fell to his lap, and he pretended to fiddle with an imaginary string. "You don't bang a girl like Poppy, Bran."

"Fine." I clenched my fist and thumped my thigh. "Do you want to marry her and have babies and shit?"

"I'm sixteen..." He was still messing with the imaginary string.

I exhaled a long breath, then closed my eyes because damn, I didn't want to do this, but I had to. "Look, I need you to kiss her."

"What is going on? I can't kiss her. She's our friend and—"

I looked at him. "I punched Poppy's date tonight. Like, beat the shit out of him."

The beanbag rustled when he fell back into it, his palm to his forehead. "Now you've done it, Bran. Now you've really done it."

"And don't give me that bullshit about her being a friend. You've been staring at her like she's a giant Milkybar for years."

He frowned.

"Look, no one is ever going to be good enough for her. Agreed?"

"Yeah..."

"Except you, Con. You're the best person I know. She loves you. You love her..." I spread my hands in a ta-dah motion, forcing a smile while a part of me died.

———

THE NEXT WEEKEND ROLLED AROUND, and Poppy still hadn't talked to me. I guessed I'd finally pushed her too far.

I skipped a fight to go to Hope's party with the sole purpose of talking to Poppy, but instead, when she walked into the room, I just stared at her until I couldn't any longer.

With my head down, sipping beer, I spent the better half of that party in the corner of the room. Then Lola perched on the arm of the chair, I pushed to my feet and walked away without acknowledging her. I grabbed a beer from the cooler, then hopped the gate at the back of the McGrath's property and headed to the lake to clear my head. I didn't even pop the tab on that beer, just chucked the can into the woods surrounding the property. If tossing alcohol didn't say something...

Halfway between the house and lake, my steps faltered. Poppy sat at the end of the pier, her legs dangling over the edge with her back to the party. The clouds parted, letting the silver moonlight slip through. The way it bathed Poppy made her seem otherworldly, untouchable. And really, she was.

She didn't look up when I started down the wooden walkway, and she didn't say a word when I moved her shoes out of the way to take a seat beside her.

"Why you out here all by yourself, possum?" I folded my knees to my chest.

"Don't know." She dipped her toes beneath the dark water. The motion sent ripples across the surface, the movement catching the reflection of the moon. I wanted to tell her I was sorry, but instead, I said, "Connor was looking for you."

"And Lola was looking for you."

As selfish as it made me, I couldn't pretend that her jealousy didn't make me happy. Even though I would never be good enough for Poppy, she thought I was, and that was everything to me simply because I loved her.

"Well, she can keep looking," I said.

A slight smile worked over Poppy's lips, catching my attention before I tore my gaze away. It was getting harder and harder with her.

"Wouldn't be jealous, would you, poss?" I scooted a little closer and wrapped an arm around her, drawing circles over her bare arm with my fingertip. I should drop it, but before I let go of that fantasy completely...

"I hate you," she whispered, and I moved closer.

"Nah, I think you love me."

"You wish."

She was so damned close. Her lips inches from mine. Out of all the times I'd wondered whether Poppy would taste sweet like candy, I'd almost given in a handful. But this time, when she closed her eyes and leaned in ever so slightly, I couldn't talk myself out of wanting her. I just couldn't, so I brushed her thick hair away from her neck. Before I gave her to Connor, before I lost any chance I had, I wanted to know what it was like to kiss her.

Just one time.

I wrapped my hand around the back of her neck. My thumb swept her jaw, and when I so damn slowly pressed my lips to hers, the world stopped. For one second, all the noise and pain subsided.

Our tongues brushed against each other, and I fought back a groan. God, she was everything—every-fucking-thing I would never have, which was why, as difficult as it was, I tore away from her soft lips.

"Shit..." I pushed up, pacing the pier with the taste of her still on my tongue, then, without another word, I turned tail.

B randon had kissed me and walked off.

I stared across the quiet lake, halfway floating, but mostly plummeting.

It was everything I'd imagined—brutal and raw. The taste of his mouth was still on mine, and I pressed my fingers to my lips, trying to savor it to keep from crying.

"Poppy?" Connor's voice echoed over the water, and I quickly blinked away the pathetic tears building in my eyes.

"Down here."

A few seconds later, footsteps sounded over the wooden planks. "Why are you out here by yourself?" The warmth of his jacket draped around my shoulders when he settled behind me and pulled me to his chest. "Just tired, I guess." But I wasn't. I was devastated. Broken-hearted.

"I'll take you home. I'm bored anyway."

THAT NIGHT, I stared at my window, waiting for Brandon to

crawl through, but one o'clock came and went. Then two, and my bed was still empty.

I tried to force sleep, but every time I closed my eyes, all I saw was the look of regret that washed over Brandon's face after he'd kissed me. No matter whether either of us wanted things to change or not, they had. And there was no coming back from that. At a quarter to three, I threw the covers off, slipped into a pair of shorts, and my shoes, then climbed through my window.

I'd always taken him in when he was hurt, and now it was his turn to return the favor.

The roads between my house and the Gypsy camp were empty. The metal gate clanked when I climbed over it to weave my way between the dark trailers.

I stopped outside of Brandon's caravan, forgetting Sean wasn't there to bark anymore.

The blue haze from the TV lit up the living room window. When I raised my hand to knock, I hesitated, wondering if he may have a girl in there. The thought of him going from me to someone else made my skin heat, and I pounded my fist over the door.

A shadow appeared through the glass. "Poss?"

The latch clicked, the door swung open, and I didn't even care that he was in nothing but a pair of low-slung jeans, or that he looked like every bit the bad boy he was. I couldn't take the time to appreciate any of that because he'd hurt me. And that was one thing Brandon was never supposed to do.

He scrubbed a hand through his messy hair, stepping to the side to let me in before he closed the door. "You okay?"

I was anything but okay. But how could I even begin to tell Brandon he was the reason I wasn't when I feared it may end everything we were to each other?

"No." My voice caught, and his brows furrowed. "I'm not."

"Tell me who, and I'll..." His fists clenched at his side. Brandon O'Kieffe, always eager to defend his possum. The only irony was that he couldn't possibly protect me from the pain being in love with him caused. Not when he was so oblivious to it.

"Poss?"

At any given moment, a person has a countless number of decisions to make. Right then, I could have lied, or I could have brushed past Brandon and left. There are so many things I could have said, but words would cheapen things— like the eternal pull I felt between Brandon and me. And it was that gravity-defying push and pull that I was so over— so over being in love with a boy I thought I had no shot with, and I was so goddamn angry at him for giving me hope that I did.

So, despite the unsteady beat of my heart and the sinking feeling in my stomach, I stepped forward, gripped his jaw, and pushed up on my toes. Then I pressed my lips to his. Instead of him tensing the way I expected, Brandon's arm came around my waist.

He may have been the only person I'd kissed, but I was certain there was an infinite difference to that kiss than any I would ever have. Because it felt like the beginning and end of everything all at once.

The heat of his bare chest bled through my shirt when he tugged my body flush against his.

"Poss," he breathed against my lips. "I—"

But I swallowed his words on another kiss. And another. I wasn't going to give him a chance to tell me no again.

His hands went to my hair, tilting back my head to deepen the kiss while he backed me through the living room. We bumped into walls on our way down the hall, and when we fell onto the lumpy mattress in his room, I followed his lead, just like I always had. Honestly, I would have followed that boy into hell if it meant I could have his heart.

We were a mess of lips and teeth, roaming hands, and before long, I was on my back in Brandon's bed with nothing left on but my panties. His mouth traveled the length of my neck while his hand crept along my side, his fingers sweeping my hip before tracing lower. A ball of tension formed between my legs while I fumbled with his jeans. Then his boxers, but Brandon's touch stayed right there, inches away from where I wanted.

"Fuck. I can't..." he breathed against my throat before his teeth raked my lip.

I grabbed his wrist, shoving his hand between my legs, and that touch was enough to make my breath catch.

Brandon's lips froze over mine. "Shit."

The string of touches that followed, though—it had my fingers digging into his biceps and my back bowing away from the bed.

"Promise me you won't hate me," he mumbled into my neck, his hands gliding over my hips while his eyes touched every part of my body.

I kissed him harder than I had all night. "I won't."

The weight of his body shifted between my legs. I closed my eyes when he tore open a condom, fisting the blanket while I waited. His body pressed over mine, and then he hesitated, staring down at me with pinched brows. "I love you."

"And I love you." Then I grabbed his hips and pulled him into me, making the decision for us.

I wanted it to be Brandon. I had never been more sure of

anything in my life, and no amount of meaningless girls would ever change that, because, at the end of the day, I knew Brandon in ways none of them ever would. And he knew me in ways I refused to let anyone else.

————

My naïve heart believed fate had finally taken its course, that Brandon loved me, and that nothing else would matter.

Then, the next morning came.

When I woke, Brandon was sitting on the edge of the mattress with his back to me. I shifted on the bed, and he pushed to his feet, grabbing his shirt from the floor and pulling it on. "I have to train with Uncle Darren," he said, his voice strange and cold. "I'll walk you home."

A palpable tension filled the tiny room, squeezing my heart in a vice. I was another Lola Stevens. The thought made me all too aware of my naked body, and I clutched the sheets to my chest just as Brandon turned to face me.

His gaze swept over me with a hostility I'd never seen before as he scooped my clothes from the floor and dropped them on the bed next to me.

The flimsy door closed behind him with a bang.

As soon as I was dressed, I crept from his room. He herded me to the door, without a word. Without a glance, and shame draped around me like a heavy shawl, one that had me burning up from the inside out.

Brandon marched across the camp, toward the gate with such determination, I had to jog just to keep up, and when I did catch up, he kept space between us. Two houses down from mine, the silence was unbearable. "Are you okay?" I asked.

"Fine."

Whatever I thought it would feel like to be with Brandon, this wasn't it. This is how he treated other girls, but I had foolishly believed I would be different. A storm of emotions churned inside me.

"Fine," I said and took off toward my gate. I didn't need whatever chivalrous bullshit he was trying to pull by walking me home—like that would lessen the pain. I ran up the stairs and into my house, and he never called for me to turn around. When I peeked through the living room window, he was already halfway down the block, his hands shoved deep in his jean pockets.

My breath stuttered, and my jaw tightened. I wanted to cry and scream and curl into a ball on the floor for being so stupid.

When Daddy's car pulled down the street, slowing to park, I rushed out the backdoor. Each step I took jarred loose tears until an endless stream poured down my cheeks. By the time I reached Connor's, I couldn't catch my breath.

He opened the door and pulled me into a hug, one that felt safe. "What's wrong, Poppy?"

I was too embarrassed to tell him, so I shook my head and buried my face in his shoulder. That was when I realized, the bad boys may break a girl's heart, but the good ones will piece it back together.

PART II

THE PRESENT. THE BEGINNING AND THE END.

22

CONNOR

NOVEMBER 2013

"This is feckin stupid." Brandon rips the piece of paper from the notebook and balls it up, tossing it into the bin. "Grave letter... Can't you just sign my name to yours?"

"No."

With a huff, Brandon scrawls something on the new page.

These letters are protocol, and while I know the chances of it ever being sent are slim, it still leaves me unsettled. It brings an uneasy awareness of my own mortality crashing down around me.

I read over the few words I've written, and I hope to God Poppy never gets this.

Poppy,

I hate writing these letters. It's depressing. But if you're reading this

But what do I write? If she ever reads this letter, that means I'm gone. It means we'll never have the life we spent the last seven years planning. And there is not a dictionary's worth of words that I could write to tell her everything I would want to say.

That I was in love with her at nine—as in love as a kid can be, and those feelings only grew. That all of my happiest moments in life have revolved around her. How do I put into words the regret I feel when I think there's a possibility I may leave her?

Poppy was the first girl I kissed. The only girl I had ever dated—we were each other's firsts at everything...

Brandon tears off another page. "There. That'll do."

"You're done?"

"Not much to say." He clears his throat. "Poss, you and Con were always my best friends. Name your first born after me. Even if it's a girl. Sorry I croaked. Love, Brandon."

"Blunt and to the point," I say and pen another line of my letter before glancing back at him. "But I'm not naming my firstborn after you. I love you, but you were a shithead as a kid."

He snorts, then stuffs the letter into an envelope and tosses it to the table. "Afghanistan's going to blow."

"Probably."

Brandon cocks his head to the side, considering something, although I'm not sure what that might be—with Brandon, one never knows. "Do you hate me for making you join yet?"

"You didn't *make* me." He always gives himself too much credit.

Brandon laughs. "Sure thing, Con."

The day Brandon marched in, interrupting mine and Poppy's dinner, to tell us he'd joined the army, it just made sense that I join, too. We promised to stay with each other always. And it does make for a nice career, at least when I'm at home.

"You would've gone AWOL during training," I say, not really giving him much of my attention.

Brandon tips his chair back on two legs, pointing at me with a grin. "True. Those few days in the muddy ditch were enough to do me in."

I nod. It was enough to do anyone in.

"How'd Poppy take the news of deployment?"

I drop the pen to the table and spin it. "Not good."

She cried. Not full out sobbing or anything, but I could hear it in her voice. The strain, the fear. I promised her I'd come back, and I intend to, but writing this letter makes me picture what would happen if she ever received it. And it shatters me.

I never want to hurt her.

I never want to leave her.

This isn't how it was supposed to go. We're supposed to grow old together…

And I had to believe we would.

23

BRANDON

APRIL 2014

I squint against the sunlight pouring through the windscreen. It always seems so much brighter here in Afghanistan, the sun that much hotter sitting amongst endless blue skies. It's nothing but desert over a desert. Sweat trickles down the back of my neck, and not for the first time, I wish I could strip out of my body armor and rig.

"My balls are so sweaty, I think my swimmers have been boiled," I groan.

The other three guys in the Foxhound laugh.

"Three weeks until you're back to the piss-wet rain in Dublin," Connor shouts over the rumble of the engine. "I can't wait to go home."

Home. I should be excited. I'm happy for Con, at least, but truthfully, I no longer have a home, anywhere. Every time I go on leave, I'm itching to get back here, to this hell hole because I fit in here. I crave the chaos, walking on the edge of a knife every day. Back there, I'm nobody, but here... here, I count. Here I have a purpose. Here I have Connor, but when we're home, he has Poppy. They don't need me, though they insist on involving me in their lives. The truth I can't tell them is, sometimes it hurts to witness their happiness. I feel like an intruder.

"Yep. I'm going to drink all the whiskey Ireland has to offer."

My sergeant glances at me briefly, a smile on his lips. "And by 'all the whiskey,' you really mean all the women. Careful your dick doesn't drop off."

"Why would you say such horrible things to me? I thought we were friends."

The sound of laughter blends in with the hum of the engine, then in a fraction of a second, there's a bang so loud that it shatters everything else. A deafening silence follows, and I'm weightless in my seat as the world outside whirls past the windscreen in a blur. It's like I'm watching a nightmare through someone else's eyes. Violent and unstoppable. I don't have a chance to think or react before there's just nothing.

Everything goes dark.

Blinking open my eyes, I try to lift my head, but pain ricochets through my skull, leaving nothing other than a continuous static ring in my ears. I flinch when something drips onto my face. When I lift my hand to wipe it away, my fingers come away crimson. Realization slowly creeps back in, and I lift my head, looking around. The Husky is on its side, and my Sargent limply hangs above me, his body held in place by the seat harness. A thick piece of shrapnel is buried in his neck, the blood dripping on me like a leaky faucet.

I manage to assess the situation with an odd sense of distance, nothing but blood and twisted metal. I release my harness and fall the short distance from the seat to the window grill. Groaning, I push up, shards of glass biting into my palms as I do. The stench of smoke, diesel fuel, and charred flesh hangs heavy in the air, and even though I'm disoriented, that smell sends me into fight mode.

I need to move. I need to get them out of here.

Pushing to my feet, I press my fingers to Serg's neck. He's gone.

Connor.

Panic pulses through me. When I glance into the back seat, I see him slumped against the rear door, lifeless eyes staring straight at me.

No, no, no.

The sight of his mangled face covered with burns and blood makes my chest heave. I choke out an anguished sob, but the sound is lost, falling on my own deaf ears.

I throw myself into the back of the vehicle, landing on him in a heap. With a tug, I lie him as flat as I can against the glass-scattered window grill, then rip open his vest, and start chest compressions.

He will not die.

He will not die.

A rabid kind of desperation falls over me, driving each push until I hear his ribs crack. Still, I keep going. Thirty compressions, two breaths.

Thirty, two.

Over and over, until my arms ache, and my lungs strain from the effort. His skin has now gone pale and waxy, and realization dawns on me like a sledgehammer straight to my heart.

Connor's gone.

My best friend. My brother.

I finally close his eyes and break. My soul is being cleaved in two, and it hurts more than anything I've ever experienced. I just sit there—I don't know how long—holding his hand, living in denial. I don't want to leave him, but the longer I sit here, the more real it becomes, and the more danger I'm in. So I push to my feet and climb over the body of the final soldier before throwing the door open to get out of the vehicle.

The second my boots hit the sand, I start walking, stripping my vest, helmet, and jacket as I go. I don't know where I'm going or why. I don't think I care anymore because my last reason for anything just died.

So I just...walk.

24

BRANDON

JANUARY 2015

The roar of the crowd reaches me from the end of the corridor, their cries echoing along bleak, concrete walls.

Ladies and gentlemen, welcome to the ring: The one. The only. Brandon The Breaker Blaine!

That's my cue, and every time I hear it, my stomach bottoms out. I can't fight under my real name. Brandon O'Kieffe died in Afghanistan, alongside his best friend, Connor Blaine. The Breaker isn't real. He doesn't exist. He's an apparition I became in order to survive.

I pass through the doorway, into the stripped-out basement of Larry's Pub we call The Pit. This is the dark and dirty underbelly of London, where the corrupt and nameless come to trade punches, to draw blood, and to cash in. A place where there are no rules, only a winner and a loser.

The regular drunks and gamblers shout and wave handfuls of cash through the air while chanting: *Breaker, Breaker, Breaker.*

I ignore it.

I ignore *them* as I duck through the ropes and into the pitiful square of bloodstained concrete that serves as a ring.

My opponent bounces on the balls of his feet, then punches the air. He laps up the cheers while I stand with my arms loose at my sides, waiting for the ding of the bell to sound.

This moment, right here, is all I have any more. It's all I'm good at. I tune out the shouting and screaming, the commentator's voice crackling over the microphone until the only sound is the steady pounding of my own heart. In this moment, nothing outside of this ring exists, and that makes it a strange kind of salvation.

The bell rings, and he comes at me like a train, swinging twice. I duck easily before throwing a right hook. My fist makes impact with his cheek with a loud smack. There's one perfect moment where he staggers back and sways for a second. Then it's over. He goes down hard and is out cold.

The room explodes. The referee steps toward me and reaches for my arm, but I turn and walk out of the ring, straight to the exit in the corner that leads into the storage room.

I both love and hate to fight. The power in the moment of a win is always overshadowed by the shame I feel afterward. I was supposed to be better than this rage—my father's rage. I was supposed to be more.

I'm almost done unwrapping the tape from my hands when Larry bursts into the room and slams the door behind him.

"You gotta give the crowd a fight, boy!" His southern drawl booms around the small space.

I glance up without much thought as Larry grabs an aluminum chair from the corner, spins it around, and straddles it. He rests his thick, ink-covered arms along the top, and I stare at the tat of the topless hula girl smoking a joint on his right forearm.

I don't know what more he wants from me besides a win. "I fought, didn't I?" I take off my shorts and pull on a pair of jeans.

"That ain't no fight." His glass eye drifts in the wrong direction, and it makes it hard for me to take him seriously. "It's a fuckin' massacre." He laughs.

Larry is a Vietnam Vet, and at one time in his life, he was a boxer. Which, I guess, is why he owns the pub and the fight ring.

I stumbled in here one day, looking for some whiskey and a brawl. Just so happened, Kyan and Finn, two of Larry's fighters, were both sitting at the bar that night. It didn't take much. One cross look and *wham.* I knocked Kyan's smartass right off the stool. Even with two of them, I still won. Instead of kicking me out or having me arrested, Larry welcomed me into the fold.

I yank a hoody over my head and stuff my fight gear back inside my bag. "I'm not here for a show, Larry. I'm here for the money." I toss my bag over my shoulder. Some days, I want a world of pain, but others, I just want to inflict it. He knows the drill—he's repeated the same charade with countless other vets tormented by their own memories.

"Get your panties out of a wad, you miserable shit," he says. "You should go on out there and grab yourself a lady friend. Something. Every winner has to celebrate. And you won, boy."

No, I lost—a long time ago.

25

POPPY

Poppy,

I hate writing these letters. It's depressing. But if you're reading this, then it means I'm dead, and well, that sucks. Don't let them play shit music at the funeral, okay? I want to go out in a blaze of glory with all the Catholics looking positively scandalized.

This isn't how it was supposed to go. We're supposed to grow old together and annoy our kids because we won't hurry up and die already. I'm destined to be the guy who farts at the family dinner but accidentally shits himself. But seriously…

Poppy, I have been in love with you since I was ten years old when you put gum in my hair before hacking a massive bald patch in my scalp with a pair of safety scissors. My ma went mad and shaved my whole head on pure principle. I looked like a right prick, but I was still like a lovesick puppy for you. You had me by the balls, and everyone knew it.

I'm sorry. I'm sorry I left you when I promised I never would. I can honestly say I have lived with no regrets, until now. Until I'm faced with the idea of leaving you. But you won't be alone. Brandon will always watch out for you because he loves you almost as much as I do.

Look after each other, and make sure he doesn't drown at the bottom of a whiskey bottle.

Life can be shit, but it's also short, and it does go on. The sun will still rise in the east tomorrow and set in the west, so I ask nothing of you except this: Don't die with me. Live. Be happy. Love again because you deserve to experience as much love as this life has to give. I only wish I could have been the one to give it to you.

You are my world, my heart. Whatever lies beyond this life, at least I can rest easy, knowing that all the best pieces of me are right here with you. If you just close your eyes, you'll feel me. I love you in a way that transcends life and death.

This isn't goodbye, only see you later.

Love always,

Connor

I can't breathe...I lean forward and rest my head on the steering wheel, fighting against the pain twisting my chest. I've read these words countless times, and each time, I break all over again.

Ten months later and it's still hard to accept that Connor is never coming home, and Brandon...I glance at the dark-wood facing of the old London pub across the street and anger swallows my grief.

Brandon left Connor in that crumpled Foxhound. He ran off and left him.

Just like he'd left me...

My mobile dings with rapid-fire texts. Exhaling, I fold the letter and slip it back inside my purse, then grab my phone.

Hope: Where are you?

Hope: Poppy!

Hope: I just went by your house, and there's an eviction notice.

Hope: Call me back, or I'll have the MI5 after your arse!

Me: I'm fine. Don't worry…

To say my life has fallen apart over the past ten months would be an understatement. Hope is one of the few people who knows just how far I've fallen, but if she knew I was here for Brandon... That's a fight for another day.

I silence my phone and wait for the string of black taxis to sputter past, then I climb out of the rental and cross the street to The Dog and Bell Pub.

It took months and a PI that cost me most of Connor's life insurance—and my house—to find Brandon. The military assumed he'd died in the explosion or been captured by the enemy, but with no proof of either, Brandon had essentially just vanished. And that wasn't good enough for me.

When the investigator informed me that he'd found Brandon in London, I'd waxed and waned from wanting to hop the ferry from Dublin and come straight over to wanting nothing to do with him. The last person I expected to abandon Connor—the last person I expected to leave when our entire world crashed and burned—was Brandon.

But he did both of those things.

My hand comes to rest on the old, brass door handle, and I hesitate, still unsure how I'll react when I see Brandon.

The tinker of glasses and the low buzz of conversation filter onto the sidewalk when I open the door and step inside. The pub is crowded with men chugging pints and shouting at the football game broadcast on the flat-screen at the back of the room.

I skim the faces while I approach the bar, my stomach knotting.

"Larry, my money's on Breaker." A burly man slaps a wad of cash on the bar top.

"Ah, of course, it is." The gray-headed man's American accent rises above the hustle and bustle of the bar. One of his tattoo-covered arms comes across the counter, and he swipes the money, then shoves it into the pocket of his jeans. "Boy ain't lost a fight yet."

Larry lets the man through a door to the side of the bar, and that kink in my stomach tightens.

I sidle closer to Larry and clear my throat before sliding a crisp twenty-pound note across the wood bar. "My money's on Breaker."

The old man grabs a bar towel and wipes the counter. "Don't know what you're on about, darlin'."

He must take me for an idiot, anyone in the bar can hear the shouting bellow up the stairwell. He pushes the money back toward me.

"I said"—I shove it right back with a firm glare—"I'm here for the fight."

With a grin, he pockets the cash. "A little thing like you don't need to be down there with all them sweaty men. It's awful bloody." He feigns a grimace and shakes his head.

"I don't care."

"All right." Shrugging, he flings the bar towel over his shoulder, opens the door, and then motions me through. "But don't complain if you get blood on your pretty dress there."

The scent of stale cigarettes and beer wafts up the stairwell. Larry closes the door behind me, plunging me into darkness. I use the cold, concrete wall as a guide on my way into the dingy underbelly of the pub.

The stairs open into a room with bare concrete walls and a thin haze of cigarette smoke. Rough and tumble-looking men are packed in like a can of sardines. Shouts and cheers mix with the dull smack of punches being exchanged.

"Knock 'is teeth down, 'is throat, champ!"

"Kick 'em in the nuts."

I slip between the men where I can find space, dodging pints of ale and beer guts, until I reach the tattered ropes that mark the boundaries of the ring. My heart misses a few critical beats before going into a full-on sprint when Brandon dodges a punch.

A quick smile flinches over Brandon's lips before he throws a punch that leaves his opponent dazed. One more jab and the guy falls flat on his face. The men in the room go crazy, shouting and exchanging high fives.

Brandon's effect is completely flat while his gaze drifts

over the crowd, but then his attention freezes on me. His brows pinch together. His stare turns cold.

A man steps in front of me, blocking my view, and by the time he moves away, Brandon is gone.

It's like I don't even exist.

26

BRANDON

A heavy fist collides with my jaw, and I relish in the pain. Spitting a mouthful of blood onto the floor, I slowly lift my gaze to my opponent to see sweat trickle down his brow, still bouncing on the balls of his feet. He grins at the cheering crowd before he comes at me again —mistake. My temper rises with each clumsy step he takes. By the time he lunges, I'm all out of patience. I duck, then drive my fist into the side of his head. Once. Twice. And he goes down hard, his skull cracking against the bloodstained concrete. The crowd roars.

I close my eyes, chest heaving as I attempt to chain the rage pulsing through my every muscle. When I snap open my eyes, and turn toward the ropes, I pause. There, in the middle of all the drunk punters, stands a woman—the only woman who has ever mattered. She's out of place like an angel walking among the cursed—her aura making her stand apart. My gaze glides over the dress that covers everything, yet shows me all the curves I need to see. Long, chocolate waves of hair spill over her shoulders, and when I finally meet her face, my heart seizes in my chest.

Poppy.

Her steel gray eyes, branded in my mind like a familiar scar, meet mine. Her face washes white like she's just seen a ghost, and in a way, she has.

The shattered fragments of my heart pitifully attempt to pull themselves together as a thousand memories flash through my mind—every single one revolving around Connor. And that hurts. It hurts so much. She might as well have doused me in petrol and set me on fire.

Someone cuts between us, blocking my view and breaking the debilitating hold she has over me. I drag in a lungful of air as though surfacing from deep, dark waters. In an instant, I'm past the ropes and shouldering through the packed room until I finally fall into the storeroom.

The door closes with a heavy thud, muting the cries of the basement beyond. And in the silence, the pounding of my pulse against my skull is like a drumbeat I can't stop. I brace my back against the wall and close my eyes, willing calm. *How the hell did she find me?*

The door against the wall opens, and I know it's her without looking, so I keep my eyes closed, a bleak attempt at avoiding this inevitable train wreck.

"Brandon Patrick O'Kieffe!"

My stomach clenches at the sound of her voice. I can't do this with her. I'm not ready. Heels tap over the concrete floor, and as suddenly as it started, the noise stops right in front of me. The familiar, floral scent of her perfume almost brings me to my knees. Maybe, if I don't look at her, if I stay just like this, maybe she'll go away.

"Brandon!" She pokes a finger into my chest, and I react on instinct, swiping her hand away and meeting her startled gaze.

"You..." Her jaw clenches, and she inhales an unsteady breath.

I don't even see her move, but in the next second, her palm meets my cheek. The clap bounces around the room as the sting sets in.

"I thought you were dead!"

I tear my gaze away from the only girl I've ever loved, focusing on the wall behind her. "Well, I'm not."

"You should go, Poppy," I say, feigning indifference I wish I felt. But the truth is, every second that I stand here feels like a sick form of torture.

"I'm not leaving," she whispers.

I don't say anything because, in truth, there's nothing left to say. Poppy and I were once best friends, and now we're strangers.

She grabs my face, her fingers digging into my cheeks as though she could anchor herself to me permanently. "Look at me, Brandon."

Dark circles linger below her eyes, and her face has sunken with weight loss. It's as though everything that made Poppy, Poppy, has withered and faded away. Connor would be rolling in his grave. I promised, should anything ever happen to him, I would take care of her. But I can't even take care of myself. The guy that made that promise—he's long gone.

Tears well in her eyes. "Connor's gone." At the mention of his name, those tears fall. "And you left me."

Guilt eats away at me, though I can't hate myself any more than I already do. If I were a better person, I would try to shoulder her pain, but the fact is, I can't see past my own grief. It's too big, too all-consuming. I'm drowning, slowly suffocating under the weight of it. I can't help her when I can't help myself.

She forces me to look at her again. "Say something."

Pulling out of her hold, I step around her to retrieve my clothes from the storeroom. "You shouldn't have come." My back stays to her while I shove my shorts down my thighs. "Whatever it is you came here looking for, you aren't going to find it."

Long moments pass in unnerving silence. I'm fully dressed before her voice breaks the stifling tension.

"Did he suffer?"

I stiffen and take a deep breath, holding it before air slowly hisses through my teeth. "No."

"What happened, Brandon?"

"He died. I didn't." And isn't that the shitty truth of my existence summed up in four words? I should have offered her more, but what was there to tell that Poppy would understand—she'd never get the truth of war.

Her footfalls cross the room, and she grips my arm in an unforgiving way—the way a widow deserves to hate the last man who saw her husband alive. "Why'd you leave him?"

"I..." The words stick in my throat. I want to punch something until my knuckles rip open and bleed, then drown myself in whiskey, all in the hope that my mind will switch off for just *one* second. "He was dead," I say in a strangled breath. "And I left him because there was nothing to stay for. Just bodies." I pull on my tracksuit bottoms and finally turn to face her. "I'm sorry about Connor."

"Sorry? That's *all* I get? Sorry?"

"I try not to look back. There was nothing left but bodies."

She brings her gaze to mine, the pain I'm causing evident on her face. This *isn't* the part where we heal each other, which is why I shoulder my bag and leave the room without a backward glance. She knows I'm alive, but it would be better if she didn't. Her being here isn't going to help either of us.

If I'm honest with myself, I've thought about contacting her a thousand times, but I just couldn't do it. I knew I would look at her and see everything we've lost, my own pain reflected back at me. Because it was never just Connor and me. It was the three of us. By running and avoiding her, I've let Connor down in the worst way.

I go upstairs and take a seat at the mahogany bar. All I need in life is to drown everything out. Whiskey and meaningless sex are old friends, ones I can rely on and expect nothing in return.

I flag Larry for a drink, downing in one quick gulp.

Larry thumps the empty glass. "What's got you drinking like a goddamn one-flippered goldfish?"

"You told me to drink. Here I am."

"Nah. Something's itching your butt. Wouldn't have anything to do with that classy-looking girl that followed you out, would it?" He blows a long whistle through his teeth. "She's a looker."

Larry places two more drinks onto the counter.

"She's like my sister," I say, disgust lacing my voice.

"Hell, where I came from, girls like that, didn't matter if they *were* your sister." A perverted grin slinks across his face when he slaps me on the back.

"She's Connor's widow," I whisper.

Even breathing his name hurts, like a knife being wedged right in the center of my chest. I haven't opened up to many people, but Larry knows all about Connor. Kyan, Finn, Larry, me, we're all ex-military. All running, still fighting a war we wish we'd never signed up for. I don't like to talk about it, but they understand. They've all seen things they'll never forget, lost friends. Lost part of what essentially makes us human.

"Aw, hell." He hitches his pants back under his gut, and a heavy sigh slips through Larry's lips before he downs his shot.

Thankfully, before memory lane takes us into a shit-storm I can't get out of, a peroxide-blonde steps to the end of the bar and shamelessly stares at me—small waist, a ton of cleavage. She's just what I need right now. Larry follows my gaze and pats me on the shoulder as he stands, and then finds his way behind the bar.

Six glasses of whiskey later, and the guilt is gone. *Everything* is gone. I'm blissfully numb. Blondie is hanging off my arm, her lips leaving a trail of bright red lipstick down my neck.

"Wanna get outta here?" she purrs against my ear, and my gaze drops to her ample chest.

"Sure."

27

POPPY

The street running in front of the pub is deserted, except for the old men loitering by the entrance who let out a whoop of catcalls as a group of girls walks by in short skirts.

For a moment, I wonder why I'm even here. Brandon has always been stubborn. It would be foolish of me to believe I could talk some sense into him. Then I remind myself: Connor would want us to lean on each other. He always said friends carry each other when no one else will. And, right now, Brandon and I both need someone to carry us.

The ruckus of bar noise spills onto the street when the bar door swings open. The group of men cheers when Brandon's stumbles out with a curvy blonde. She presses her lips to his neck and wraps around him like a vine. They are almost to the curb when his gaze lands on me, and he unwinds himself from her hold. She reaches for him again, and he staggers back, saying something I can't make out. Whatever it is, wins him a shove, followed by a middle finger before the blonde heads back into the bar.

He drags a hand through his hair and takes a step toward me, then stops and turns around.

"Brandon?" I start after him, but he keeps walking.

A sportscar's headlights flash, the alarm disarms, and he reaches for the door.

"Brandon O'Kieffe!" I reach the car just as he falls into the driver's seat.

"Go away."

The stout aroma of whiskey wafts up. There is no way he should be driving. He goes to shut the door, but I grab it, then reach over him and take the keys from the ignition.

"What the fuck, Poppy?"

"You are not driving."

He straightens his arms, gripping the steering wheel while his jaw tics. Just as I think he's about to argue, he slides over into the passenger seat, giving me silent permission to take the wheel.

BRANDON DIRECTS me through London's city center. We wind through squares and roundabouts, and all I can think about is how in the world he would have ever made it home. We park in front of a row of townhomes, and he topples out of the passenger side, swaying and bobbing on his way up to the entrance.

He slumps against the door, and I grab him by the elbow to pull him away, so he doesn't fall on his face when I open the door. He stumbles over empty pizza boxes and bottles of whiskey before he falls onto the sofa.

I take a hesitant step inside, and my stomach sinks. This reminds me of his dad—the one person Brandon never wanted to be like.

His stomach rumbles. "Oh, shit," he groans and sits up,

wobbling for a second before he slides to the floor and starts to crawl across the floor.

"*What* are you doing?" I grab his arm and attempt to get him to his feet, but he swats me away.

When he reaches the bathroom, he grabs the door-frame, hoists himself up, and hurls himself inside. A chorus of heaves and coughs, followed by a string of profanities filter through the door, and then, minutes later, the toilet flushes. Brandon stumbles out and slumps against the door-way. His bloodshot eyes meet mine for a moment before he pushes off the frame and heads down the hall.

"Brandon?"

He swipes a hand through the air and grunts before disappearing into another room. By the time I step to the doorway, he's stripped out of his shirt and jeans and lies, sprawled out and face-down on a bare mattress. For a moment, I'm sixteen again, watching him self-destruct after his mother passed away. Only this time he hasn't climbed through my window—he's run away.

Exhaling, I make my way to his bed and sit on the edge. Out of habit, I sweep my fingers through his thick hair, and the memories of who we once were nearly crush me.

"I'm fine," he manages. But he's not, neither of us is.

"No matter how pissed I am at you," I say around the lump lodged in my throat. "I'm just glad you're alive."

"And I didn't—" he hiccups—"I didn't mean it when I said you should go home."

"I know."

"You always know, possum."

He hasn't called me possum since that night at Hope's party—the night that changed everything between us. Tears blur my vision, and I duck my chin, swiping them away.

"You're still my possum." He swats at my hair. "That never changes."

I knot my hands, fighting the emotions, the hurt, the memories of Brandon and Connor, and me. Brandon's breaths fall into a heavy rhythm, and before long, a deep snore cuts through the silence. For a moment, I sit and watch him sleep. There were so many nights growing up just like this. A lifetime of memories, of heartbreak, of promises to never leave each other. I trace a light finger over his bruised jaw. I lay beside him, and all I can think of is Connor.

"Possum..." Brandon mumbles in his sleep.

My chest tightens, placing my lungs in a vice and forcing me out of bed. Grief weighs me down. Learning to accept my life without Connor has been the most difficult thing I've ever done.

It destroyed my soul, and it destroyed Brandon's.

28

BRANDON

I stare down the scope of my rifle. My heart slams against my ribs, no matter how much I will it to slow. The ground trembles as chaos ensues around me. The occasional explosion interrupts the steady pop of gunfire, and my arm shakes but stills when Connor's hand lands on my shoulder.

"Breathe, Bran. Just take a breath."

"I can't do this."

"Those guys," he points toward the derelict factory our unit surrounds, "They'll kill hundreds, if not thousands. They'd blow up kids in the name of their cause. This is war, Bran. And in war, there are always casualties."

It really is that simple to him, right and wrong. Good and bad. I pick up my rifle and stare down the sight before I pull the trigger.

The bullet tears a hole straight through the chest of the elderly woman the enemy is using as a shield. I aimed for her shoulder but missed. I didn't want to kill her, but I did, and that makes me a monster.

I JOLT AWAKE, pitching upright as a ragged breath fills my lungs. The bedsheets are drenched with sweat, the same as always. But this time, something brushes my arm, and it's not until I instinctively lash out that my mind quiets from the memory of war and comes back into focus.

Suddenly, I'm on my knees, straddling Poppy with my forearm pressed to her throat. Her eyes lock with mine as a choking sound slips past her lips, and reality sets in. In a panic, I scramble to the edge of the mattress.

She shouldn't even be here, let alone in my bed.

An all too familiar sinking sensation settles in my gut.

I rise to my feet. "You need to go," I say through clenched teeth. I'm angry at myself—angry at her. I'm angry at the whole world for screwing me so damn hard.

She stares at me like I just punched her.

"Just go, Poppy!" I squeeze my eyes shut and swallow around the lump in my throat. "I can't look at you. I look at you, and all I see is him."

"And when I look at you, all I see is him, too, but I don't want to let that go. I feel him when I'm with you..."

"He's dead." I open my eyes. "I've let go. So should you." And with that, I leave the room.

Hurting Poppy is the only thing I could possibly do that would make Connor hate me, and that thought eats away at me.

"Fuck you, Brandon O'Kieffe!" she shouts from my room.

I can't take this shit—her grief. Mine. The guilt and tragedy of it all. I find myself running for the kitchen and tearing open the cabinet in need of a drink.

The bottle of whiskey sits there like the answer to all my prayers, and I press it to my lips, swallowing gulp after gulp, finding a mild form of relief in the familiar burn.

Poppy moves into the kitchen, but I ignore her, instead,

watching bubbles float their way up the neck of the bottle as I continue to drink.

She snatches the bottle from me, and liquid spills onto my chest before it splashes onto the linoleum floor. "You can be as mean and nasty as you want, but I'm not going anywhere."

I try to grab the bottle, but she smashes it against the wall. Glass and whiskey spray everywhere.

Anger rises like a cobra, hissing and spitting its way to the surface, and I grab her shoulder, backing her into the whiskey-soaked wall while glass cuts into the soles of my bare feet. "What the hell do you want from me?" I shout. "You want me to save you? Huh, Poppy?" I laugh as my grip on her shoulder tightens.

Tears cling to her lashes before spilling down her cheeks. "I think I'm the one who needs to save you."

"I don't need saving." I shove away from her. "The devil looks after his own. And I'm beyond redemption."

I just want her to leave—having her here is too painful. Too real. I'd almost convinced myself that Connor never existed, that everything before the fight ring in London was nothing more than a dream.

Almost...

Poppy rubs at the finger marks on her arms. "Then take me down with you." She slides to the floor and buries her face in her hands. The diamonds of her wedding ring glint in the light, and that's just another knife in my heart because she hasn't let him go. Not one bit.

"You're all I have, Brandon," she whispers. Her tired gaze meets mine. "So if you want to drink yourself to death, fine. Push me away. But I'm not going anywhere."

I drop next to her, and she leans her head on my

shoulder like nothing has changed. And we sit in silence, allowing the pain and heartbreak to fester between us.

They say the people left behind are the ones who suffer the most—isn't that the truth? I'd give anything to swap places with Connor. *Anything.* Poppy didn't deserve this. And now, I'm all she has.

If there is a God, he has a sick sense of humor.

29

POPPY

I tossed and turned on the couch last night, and finally, around four am, I gave up and started cleaning the grime from the coffee table. I picked up beer bottles and half-smoked joints, socks, and condom wrappers, thanking God Brandon was at least safe. Around seven am, I pulled the cushions from the couch and found a crumpled photo of Brandon perched on the hood of a tank, Connor against the side with an AK-47 saddled on his hip. The sight of the two of them at war tore my heart right in two, and I sank onto the couch with a half-filled trash bin at my feet. It's true.; life is ever-changing—it's unfair. But that knowledge doesn't make any of it easier.

"My head." Brandon stumbles down the hall with his hands to his head, his shirt off.

My gaze skims the tattoos peppering his bare chest, ones I've never seen, and then my gaze lingers on the one both Connor and Brandon had. Connor regretted it, thinking it looked more like a rat than a possum, but Brandon had worn it with pride, insisting it wasn't a rodent. *Possum.*

Brandon places a hand over the tattoo and scowls at me. "Don't start."

I realize, instead of two rat tattoos, there is now only one. My chest tightens, but I fight against it and manage, "It's a rat," hoping to pick a fight and change the somber mood that's settled between us.

"It's a possum," he says and shoulders past me on his way to the kitchen.

With his back to me, I notice the raised scar that zigzags along his side. A multitude of tiny blemishes accompany that one. *Shrapnel.* He disappears into the kitchen, and I sink back against the cushion, closing my eyes and trying not to think of Connor.

Cabinets open and shut, and Brandon comes back, shoveling dry Coco Pops into his mouth. "Why does my flat look like Mary fuckin' Poppins has been in here?"

"Because it was disgusting. I'm worried I've caught something from sitting in here for too long."

He cocks a brow and smirks before sticking his hand back into the cereal box. "You might from that couch."

"That cereal is crap. You need better than that for breakfast, Brandon."

He frowns. "Don't you have a life or something?"

The sad thing is, no, I don't. Not without Connor. Not without Brandon.

"You should go home, Poppy. This is no place for you."

I take a breath and let the shame drown me. "They'll have repossessed the house by the time I get back."

He crouches in front of me, and I nearly jump when his knuckles trail across my cheek. My gaze meets his, and there's nothing but pain.

"It's not that I don't want *you*," he whispers. "I just can't handle the memories. We were happy once, and now—look at us. We're nothing more than empty shells. You remind me of everything I've lost, and every time I look at you, it breaks me all over again."

My gaze drops to the floor, then his fingers grip my chin, forcing me to look at him. "Did you hear me?" he says. "It's not that I don't want you."

His arms wrap around me, holding me tight, and I cling to him. I cling to the familiar safety I thought I'd lost.

"You can stay here. I'll sleep on the sofa," Brandon murmurs, his warm breath blowing through the strands of my hair. "But, you can't be throwing my Coco Pops away."

30

BRANDON

I hold the lighter to the small glass pipe until the green ignites in the bowl and fizzles to embers. The pungent smoke fills my lungs, and I can feel Poppy's judgment from across the room—I ignore her.

"Really, Brandon?" She huffs. "Weed?"

I hold the smoldering pipe out towards her. "Want some?"

"No."

There's a moment of silence while I take another drag. I wait desperately for that numb feeling to kick in. "This will make you forget *all* your troubles," I offer.

She shakes her head, and, for a split second, a hint of shame crosses my mind, but I quickly brush it off. Poppy always did have this way of making me feel guilty. But in the grand scheme of things, smoking weed ranks pretty low on my guilt scale. And that's exactly why I do it, to try to forget all that shit.

I'm blissfully numb when the front door clicks open, and Kyan, one of the guys from the fight ring, walks in. I frown at him. "You could knock, prick."

His dirty-blond hair is dragged into a haphazard man bun, and his eyes are bloodshot. I'd put money on the fact that he rolled out of bed sometime in the last half hour.

"You're normally too pissed to get up and answer, so why bother?" His eyes stray to the burning pipe, and he holds his hand out.

I pass it to him, and heavily tattooed fingers clasp the glass as he brings it to his lips. Poppy makes some noise in the kitchen, and his gaze darts across the room, sliding over her body.

He coughs, waving the smoke away from his face. "Well, hello there." He stares at her with all the subtlety of a brick.

Kyan is a dog. Pussy, booze, blow, and fighting are all he knows. We don't talk all that much, other than when Larry sends him over here to sober me up for a fight.

"I'm Kyan." He reaches for her hand, but she yanks it away. "You down for seconds? I'll take you out for dinner and everything." He glances in my direction with a smirk. "And I'll do you better than that one and his permanent weed dick."

"As charming as that sounds," Poppy's gaze strays to me. "I think I'll have to pass."

"Ah, you're breaking my heart." He hands me the smoldering pipe and clutches at his chest.

"Poppy doesn't want your STI's, Kyan."

I shake my head.

A wrinkle forms on Kyan's brow. "If you know her name, does that mean you *didn't* bang her?"

"Oh my God." Poppy wrinkles her nose.

"No bang zone," I say, pointing at Poppy while eyeing Kyan. I don't miss the way he's dragging his eyes all over her, and I don't like it. "Repeat after me: no bang zone."

"Yeah, yeah." He sighs. "Just checking you're alive. I'm

going down to the pub. One-eyed Larry wants you there in a half-hour." He gives Poppy another quick once over. "You should come down and watch the fight. I'll introduce you to Madame Wrinkles."

"I'm sorry, who?"

I toss my head back on a groan.

"Madame Wrinkles," he says again. "She's the bald pussy Larry keeps behind the bar."

"Dear God..." Poppy tosses her hands up in the air.

"All right," I point at the door. "Out. Fuck off." I set down the pipe, get up, and open the door, shoving him through and locking the deadbolt behind him.

I reach for the pipe on the table again, but Poppy snatches it away, tucking it behind her back. It's enough to make my temper spike, and I rise to my feet, towering over her

"I didn't ask you to come here. You want to stay, stay, but I'm not looking for a mother. And you're not coming to my fight."

"You don't get to order me around."

I smirk, leaning closer to her until I'm in her face. "You won't last five minutes in there, *princess*."

"I was just fine the other night. Besides, Kyan asked me to come. Not you. I'll go to see him." She looks pleased with herself as she pops her hip to the side.

"You're *not* going!" I shout, and she flinches away.

My fists clench and release as I try to get ahold of my temper. The weed usually numbs it, keeps it locked down, but damn, if she doesn't bring it right to the surface again.

She turns around, storming to the front door and slamming it shut behind her.

"Shit!" I pick up a beer bottle from the table and throw it

at the now-closed door. It smashes, bits of glass firing in every direction.

She can go to that fight, but I'm not helping her when some guy decides to cop a feel. She's on her own.

I stand up and head to the bathroom, pulling my shirt over my head as I go.

Poppy can judge me all she likes. I don't care. We both know this is exactly where I would have been all along without Connor.

It's almost fitting that, in his absence, I should become everything he tried so hard to save me from.

31

POPPY

The bar is more crowded with men than last time—if that's even possible. A few keep smiling and shooting glances at me, but I ignore them.

"Ah, treacle." Someone brushes my hair from my shoulder, before resting their hand on me. "Was it the lure of the ball bag cat, or just my dashing good looks?"

I turn just as Kyan steps up beside me. He's cleaned up from earlier. His blond hair is twisted into a messy bun, the scruff on his face shaved into clean lines.

"It was most definitely the cat." I've dealt with enough guys like Kyan to know I can't give him an inch.

"Right." He hops over the counter and squats in front of a cooler, shoving his hand between it and the wall. "Come on now, you little scroate."

There's a hiss, and a tiny, flesh-colored paw swats at him from the crevice. He yanks his arm back and bites down on his lip. "You little shithead." He reaches in again, this time dragging the ugliest cat I have ever seen out by the nape of its neck. It's hairless, with pink, wrinkled skin, and bulging blue eyes, and to top it off, someone had put a pink rhine-stone collar around its neck.

He cradles it in his arms and leans over the counter, so I can pet it. Kyan may seem rough around the edges, but there's something endearing about him.

Larry struts out from the back, hitching his pants underneath his bulging gut, and his gaze pings between Kyan and me. "Word of advice," he says, thumbing toward Kyan. "He ain't worth a pile of shit. You're more likely to get a three-legged midget to win 'Strictly Come Dancing' than get that boy to fall in love with you."

"Oh, bug off, old man."

Larry swats his hand through the air. "You bug off. Now, you gonna be a proper gentleman and introduce me to this lovely girl or not?"

"This is Poppy. She's Brandon's..." His brow scrunches. "*Something.*"

Larry smiles and scratches a hand over his stubble like he's thinking.

"Here's your pussy." Kyan dumps the cat—who I assume is Madam Wrinkles—into Larry's arms, grabs a beer from the cooler, and opens the door leading to the basement. "We've got a fight to watch."

I follow him down, right to the front of the ring, and the crowd behind us grows thicker by the second. Brandon appears in the exit, his eyes glued on me. He starts across the room, shoving people out of the way, and the closer he gets, I realize his gaze is locked on Kyan, not me.

He grabs the front of Kyan's shirt and yanks him up, bringing their faces inches apart. "You brought her into the middle of The Pit?" Anger swirls in Brandon's eyes, but Kyan looks unfazed by any of it.

"She wanted to come."

"If she gets hurt, I'm going to personally tear you a new arsehole."

Kyan rolls his eyes and lightly shoves against Brandon's chest, breaking from his hold. "Fine. Now go fight. I'm putting money on you, you psychotic bastard." He laughs.

Brandon spares me the briefest of glances before he turns back to the ring. The second he steps between the ropes, the crowd goes crazy.

An announcer steps into the ring, then the bell dings.

Brandon's gaze hones in on his opponent, and they circle one another, fists up. The other guy throws the first punch, and Brandon drops his fists. The woman beside me gasps, and the guy punches Brandon square in the jaw. Brandon *never* lets the other guy get one hit in. Never. The guy hits him again, and Brandon smiles. His eyes lock on me just before he spits blood from his mouth.

Another jab lands on his face, and he stumbles back a few steps, dazed.

"What the hell is he doing?" I shout at Kyan.

He shrugs. "Ah, he likes the way it feels to get slammed in the face a few times. That's all, treacle."

But I think he's doing it to get to me—because I came when he told me not to. I watch Brandon take a few more hits until I can't stomach it any longer.

When I turn to leave, Kyan grabs my hand. "Where are you going?" he shouts over the rumble of the crowd.

"I don't want to watch any more of this."

"Brandon will have my arse if I let you leave."

"Just give me a minute."

He gives a reluctant nod, then I force my way through the sweaty men toward the exit.

There are only a few people left upstairs, playing cards at a table by the door. I take a seat at the end of the bar and bury my face in my hands. The image of Brandon taking hit after hit plays on a loop. He's always had a dark cloud looming over his head, but now it seems more like a violent storm, swirling and churning, waiting to implode. I'm afraid I don't even know who he is anymore. But then again, I'm not even sure that I know who I am anymore, either.

War and loss. Those things will destroy a person from the inside out.

"Looks like you might need this." A martini glass slides in front of me, and I glance up at the young blond standing on the other side of the counter. She drums her nails over the wood top and narrows her gaze on me. "You don't look like the kind of girl who'd be hanging 'round here."

I run a finger along the rim of the glass, not at all interested in having a sip. My stomach is already enough of a mess. A loud boom of applause comes from the floor.

"Bet Brandon just knocked the lad square on his arse," she says before walking off to serve another patron.

Minutes go by, and a few men trickle up from downstairs, counting money on their way to the front.

"Haven, get me a beer, would you?"

The legs of the barstool beside me scrape the floor before Kyan sits, folding his thick forearms over the bar. "Too much, eh?" he asks, and I give a curt nod.

Haven places a pint of beer in front of him, and he swipes the foam with his thumb. "You staying with him?"

I shrug a shoulder and finally take a sip of my drink.

"I really don't think you should go back to his flat tonight."

Annoyance tenses my muscles, and my gaze lifts, expecting a cocky smirk to be plastered to his face, but all that's there is a look of worry.

"Look, I know I come across like a ripe prick, but I know how he can get."

My defenses go up. "And I know how Brandon can get."

"Look, Poppy. I know you *knew* Brandon, but that's just it. You knew him before war ate him up and spat him out."

Lowering my gaze to my drink, I swallow. *Knew him.* Maybe Kyan is right. Maybe I've lost all grasp of who Brandon is.

"Treacle." Kyan gently takes my chin in his hand and turns my face toward his. "You've not a clue what we've seen —him and me. It ain't something you watch in a film. There's not a speck of that tragic glamour the media gives it. Honestly, there ain't a word that can touch what war is. Feckin' hell is the closest you can come to it." He releases a sigh. "And right now, I promise, you don't want to go dancing with the devil."

Even though something in my gut tells me I should listen to Kyan, I don't want to admit that I've lost Brandon, too. "It's fine," I say, pulling my face from his hold. "But I appreciate your concern." And with that, I leave my drink and make my way to the exit.

I DRIVE around London for the better part of an hour, listening to the radio and thinking. I've been so hung up on finding Brandon, I never once thought about what I would do if he didn't want to be found. Which makes me feel stupid. People only disappear when they want to be lost

I may need Brandon, but I don't think he needs me.

And I have to be okay with that.

Eventually, I pull in front of Brandon's flat and cut the engine, convincing myself on the way up the walkway that I should go in and tell him goodbye. Connor may have asked us to look after one another, but he had no way of knowing the people we would become once he was gone.

The front door is cracked open, and the repetitive thwack of Brandon taking swings at the punching bag drifts through the opening. He glances over his shoulder when the hinges creak, and I step inside. Shooting a cold stare at me, he throws one last punch to the bag, his busted knuckles leaving a bloody mark on the side. Without one word of acknowledgment, he snatches the bottle of whiskey from the coffee table, then disappears down the hall, slamming the door seconds later. I listen to the sounds of silence until the water cuts on in the shower, and suddenly, I'm not so sure I can leave.

He's lost. We're both lost without Connor.

I drop to the couch and close my eyes. We should be able to understand one another. We always have...

I WAIT for over half an hour before I start to worry that he's drunk himself into a stupor, and maybe passed out, face down in the tub.

I make my way down the hall, stopping in front of the bathroom door, and knock. "Brandon?"

He doesn't answer.

"Hey!" I grab the doorknob when he still hasn't made a noise and twist. "You okay?"

Brandon's in his boxing short, on the floor of the tub with his back against the wall, water pouring over him. He lifts the bottle of whiskey to his mouth and takes a gulp without looking at me.

"Brandon?"

When I sit on the edge of the tub, he takes another swig

from the half-empty bottle before I reach for it, but he yanks it away.

"I'm not gonna smash it this time." I hold out my hand. "Just give me the damn bottle, would you?"

His murky-green eyes slowly lift to meet my gaze before he passes me the drink. I take it, place the rim to my lips, and tilt back my head. The warm liquor heats my throat as I swallow mouthful after mouthful, only dropping the bottle long enough to catch my breath before I turn it up again.

We pass the whiskey back and forth until it's empty, then I stagger into the hallway, throwing the bottle down beside the couch because I can't be bothered to walk into the kitchen. Sighing, I fall onto the sofa, toss my head back, and try to focus my swimming vision.

Brandon stumbles down the hall in his soaked shorts and slumps against the living room wall with his eyelids half-drooped and water puddling around his feet.

His jaw is purple and swollen from the fight, and I go to the kitchen and dig through the frozen TV dinners until I find an ice pack. But when I come back to the living room and offer it to him, he simply shakes his head.

"Your face looks awful, Brandon."

"I like it," he slurs, stumbling farther into the room. "I like the pain."

Dropping onto the sofa, I throw the ice pack onto the coffee table. Most people avoid pain at all costs, yet, here he is craving it. It's his own form of punishment. *But you've been punished enough in life. We both have...*

Brandon trips over the coffee table, then falls onto the couch beside me. He lays his head on my lap with a groan. "I'm sorry, possum," he mumbles, placing my hand on his damp hair, and a tiny fissure rips through my heart. After all these years, here we are again. Him wanting comfort, and me wanting to make him feel loved, to make the pain stop.

"It's okay." I choke on my words as I brush my fingers through his thick hair.

He grips my knee. "You know it's not."

"Okay." I exhale. "It's not. But what do we do, huh?"

"We drink, and we try to fucking forget. Until we can't forget anymore." He rolls onto his back, his gaze touching mine before he focuses on the ceiling. "And then the demons will be right there. Waiting for us."

"Are they ever gone, Brandon?" I sweep a dark curl from his forehead, and his brows pinch into a frown. His jaw clenches.

"Every time I close my eyes, all I see are their faces," he says through gritted teeth. "Nothing but death and destruction." Tears creep from the corners of his eyes, rolling down to his temples.

And I can't help but think this is the part of war that's left unseen. He and I—we are the reality of what it does to people, and there is nothing romantic about it. In our cases, I don't believe there is anything salvageable from it. And I find myself questioning God again with the whys, the hows, trying to grasp the cruelty of it all. "None of this is fair," I whisper.

His eyes close, and a few more tears break free. "You should leave, poss. I destroy everything I touch. My dad always said the devil wouldn't even want me. That I was a worthless shit." He huffs a laugh. "Con found that out the hard way."

"Brandon, don't—"

"This thing inside me, I can't control it." There's a desperate sadness clinging to his voice. One that breaks me. "I'm gonna hurt you, poss."

"You already did, and I'm still here." The alcohol swims in my veins, bringing honesty bubbling to the surface. As much as I wish I hadn't said it, it's the truth—one I've tried to deny for years, but all those years ago, Brandon hurt me.

He drags a hand over his face, and I wonder if he's thinking about what he did. "I barely even know myself anymore."

I comb my fingers through his hair, fighting my urge to cry. "Neither of us are the same people. So, Brandon Blaine," I swallow when I use Connor's last name—my last name. "Who are you now?"

"I don't know."

"Well, when you figure it out, you just let me know." I lean over and press a gentle kiss to his forehead, and he trails his fingertips along my jaw in a feather-light touch. "I'm just glad I have whoever you are."

"Always, possum." He taps the tattoo on his chest. "Right here."

I cover the sob with my hand and keep sweeping my fingers through Brandon's hair until he passes out. The broken taking care of the broken. What a pitiful mess we are.

32

BRANDON

I blink open my eyes, groaning as the bright morning light scorches my retinas. My head is pounding, and my stomach clenches uncomfortably when I roll over, nearly falling off the sofa. When I glance up, Poppy is leaning against the kitchen side, a cup of coffee in her hand. Wet hair hangs in her face, and dark, makeup stains linger beneath her eyes. She looks worse than I feel, and that's saying something. I get to my feet and unsteadily rock back and forth.

"I have a headache," she mumbles.

Blurred memories surface of her drinking whiskey straight from the bottle last night.

"Whiskey will do that to you." I place my hand on the wall and make my way to the bathroom. Stumbling inside, I squint against the sunlight as I piss. Today is not going to be a good day. By the time I stagger back to the kitchen, Poppy is bent over the counter with her face resting on her outstretched arms.

I open the cupboard and grab a new bottle of whiskey. Poppy doesn't even lift her head as I pour a splash into her coffee and take a sip. This will fix my head. Poppy, on the other hand, I'm not sure there's any fixing that.

"Possum, what are you doing?"

She slowly lifts her face and stares at me, eyebrows knitted together in a frown. "Dying."

"This isn't you, Poppy. You don't do this shit."

She was the good girl. Well, unless I was involved. She was always on this pedestal, the girl that was far too good to be anything to me, but miraculously, she was my best friend.

She mumbles something before snagging my coffee and taking a swig. Her eyes water and her lips purse together, and then she turns to the sink and spits it out. "What the hell, Brandon? Whiskey? In your coffee?" Placing her palm on her forehead, she shakes her head.

I snort. "Seriously, what are you doing? You just gonna hole up in this shitty apartment, dragging my drunk arse off the couch every night and watching me fight? This isn't your world, poss, and he'd want better for you." *I* want better for her, but we both know Connor's opinion was always worth a damn sight more than mine. "Sort out your shit. Get the house back."

"I don't want it back. I don't want any of it. Surely you, of all people, can understand that..."

I drag my hand down my face. "Well, then you sell it, you...you plan. Me. This—this is not a plan, babe." I can see her spiraling right on down with me, and the truth is, in just a few days, I've come to like her being here.

Poppy was always like this shiny light, something I had to consciously stay away from. Even at the tender age of ten, I knew I'd extinguish her if I weren't careful. By the time I was eighteen, she felt like a damn addiction. Just being around her made the world a bit brighter and the shit a little easier to bear.

My world is darker and shittier than it ever was before, and here she is, her light dulled but never completely gone. Only now, Connor isn't here, and I will destroy her. The worst part is that I think I already selfishly need her too much to do the right thing.

"It's too late," she says. "I had an eviction notice on the door the day I left."

"How? The army must have paid out a war pension for Con."

Her gaze falls to the floor, and she takes a deep breath. "I spent it. Most of it, anyway, you know..."

"Don't tell me you did rent-a-crowd for his funeral." I smirk. "Got him a horse-drawn carriage and unicorns?"

She almost laughs. "No." Her eyes lift to mine, so fractured.

That familiar ache surfaces, and I find myself shuffling back to the cabinet and reaching for the bottle of whiskey to top off my coffee. "The suspense is killing me here, poss." The liquor glugs into the hot black liquid.

"Finding you. I spent it finding you."

I pause before placing the bottle down and moving closer to her. She's broke and homeless because of me. Her eyes close, and slow tears trail over her porcelain skin. I wipe them with my thumb and cup her cheek.

On a sharp breath, she leans into my touch. "*You* are all I have left in this world, Brandon."

And that's the saddest thing I've ever heard.

She wraps her arms around my waist, and I inhale the scent that is all Poppy as my lips press to her forehead. She needs me, and I need her. It's a twisted form of co-dependency, but it's all we have.

"You're better than this, Poppy. I'll help you, but I won't watch you nosedive into this shit with me."

"I'll make a deal with you then," she mumbles against my throat. "I'll get out of it when you do."

I can't agree to that because I thrive in the gutter. It's where I belong. "You always were manipulative," I say, smiling as I step away from her.

The torn look on her face tells me she knows I have no intention of getting out of here.

33

POPPY

FEBRUARY 2015

Brandon fights nearly every night. Then he drinks. And I'm just... I don't know what I'm doing anymore.

The Pit is full tonight—as always. Drunk men line the walls and every inch in between. A few women stand beside the ropes of the rings, their breasts spilling out from too-small tops. I do my best to maintain my position against the wall, not too close to the crowd or the women, but where Brandon remains in plain sight.

Larry appears from the back of the room and slips between the ropes. "Ladies. Fellas. Welcome to The Pit. Tonight, we have three fights lined up, all-new challengers for your favorite boys."

There's a loud round of applause, which prompts a deep grin to set over Larry's weathered face. "Tonight's challenger —undefeated in his last three fights—it's Dale Winters!"

A brawny man with a shaved head steps into the ring, pumping his fist in the air. A few women cheer, but their enthusiasm is drowned out by the string of low boos that follow.

"And, like I need to introduce this bastard, Finn the 'Iron Fist' West."

The entire basement rattles from the applause when one of Larry's fighters dashes through the ropes and circles the ring. The bell dings, and the two men round each other, knuckles up, gazes locked.

"Punch 'em in the face, Finn," someone behind me jeers.

Brandon stands behind the ring with his arms braced against the doorway of the changing rooms, brooding. He still hates that I come to the fights, and I don't come because I enjoy them. I come to make sure he gets home safely afterward. God knows I can't tell Brandon that.

The repetitive slap of skin on skin contact rises above the cheers of the crowd. Larry's guy gets in a good punch, and then someone's hands land on my waist. "Ain't you a purty little bird?" His warm breath sticks to my neck

I shove away from him, but his grip only tightens.

"Ah, come on now, love. Only one type of girl hangs 'round The Pit."

I jab my elbow into his gut just before he's yanked off his feet.

"Don't you fucking touch her." Brandon pins the drunk by his throat to the wall while he throws punch after punch at the man's face.

People attempt to grab Brandon and drag him away, but he won't relent. When a group of men finally manages to restrain Brandon, the man falls to his hands and knees, and Brandon kicks him in the gut while being hauled back.

I've seen him angry before, but I've never seen him so possessed by blind rage. "Brandon!" I shout, terrified.

"Blaine!" Larry charges through the crowd, carting a fire extinguisher, the fighter from earlier right behind him.

Brandon breaks free of the men, immediately grabbing the stunned man from the floor and hitting him again.

"Son of a bitch." Larry pulls the pin to the fire extinguisher, aims, and douses Brandon in foam. Much to my surprise, he freezes. Brandon's gaze falls to his blood-covered knuckles, and he flinches like he's been snapped back from an alternate universe.

"Now, get your ass on to the lockers." Larry points to the back of the room, fire extinguisher still aimed. The crowd parts, giving a wide berth as Brandon makes his way toward the exit, while I stand dazed. People swarm around the now unconscious man, and my stomach churns. Brandon's always had a temper, but that—he lost all control.

I step through the chaos of the basement, slipping unseen into the changing room just as Brandon's fist smashes into one of the metal lockers. With each hard breath he drags in, his shoulders rise and fall, and my attention strays to the jagged scar that curves around his side.

Kyan is right. I have no idea what he's been through. I have no idea who Brandon "The Breaker" Blaine is, but I do know that Brandon O'Kieffe is lost somewhere inside.

"Brandon," I whisper, lifting my hand and trailing my fingertip over his scar. The braille-like texture spells pain beneath my finger.

He spins around, grabs my shoulders, and slams me against the lockers with a bang. Fear bubbles to the surface when his eyes, void of all expression, lock on mine.

I need him to leave the warzone in his mind. "Brandon..."

His hold tightens, and his eyebrows pull together in a frown before his gaze drops to my lips.

"Brandon?"

Then his fingers wrap around my jaw, pulling my face toward his, and his lips touch mine. For a second, I can't breathe, I can't move, and I almost kiss him, but then I think of Connor, and I shove Brandon away so hard he staggers back against the lockers on the opposite wall.

He swipes his hand down his jaw, then over his mouth. Tension coils between us, tightening and constricting my chest until I feel like I can't breathe.

"We can't..." I swallow my uncertain words before turning to leave.

I LEFT THE BAR, went across to the Tesco, and grabbed a cheap bottle of wine. It didn't take me long to find my way to a random spot on the Piccadilly Circus fountain, where I sit, sipping from a brown bag, the absolute cliché of someone struggling with life. A red, double-decker bus spits out exhaust out while a band of tourist snap pictures left and right.

The last time I was here, I was with Connor and Brandon. It was one of the few times I got so drunk I couldn't walk straight, and Brandon carried me, in true possum fashion, from the pub to this exact spot. As soon as he sat me down, I started dry heaving, and he turned me around so I'd vomit in the water instead of all over my new shoes.

The few times I got to that state, Brandon was the one who took care of me. One, because it was usually his doing, and two—well, I never wanted Connor to see me like that.

I take a sip of sweet wine and wince. I wouldn't want Connor to see me like this, either... But still, I drink, and when the bottle is half empty and a blissful numbness tingles through my veins, I call Hope.

"About time you answered your phone! Where in the world are you, Poppy."

"London," I shout over the hum of traffic and laughter of people spilling from the pubs.

"London!"

"I found Brandon. He's fighting in some illegal fight ring." I give a disheartened laugh. "Not much of a surprise."

Silence falls over the line.

"Hope?"

"There's so much I want to say, but I'll save that for him." She huffs. "Where are you in London?"

I glance at the bright lights of the Piccadilly Billboard. "Westminster."

"I'm coming to get you."

"I'm fine."

"You sound drunk."

I shrug a shoulder even though she can't see me. "I just wanted to tell you I was okay. And I love you." I mute my phone when I hang up before I can tell her how confused I am, how torn. How guilty I feel that I wanted to kiss Brandon. How could I?

Placing the wine on the ledge of the fountain, I rummage through my purse for Connor's letter. I read over the words I know too well, then pause.

I ask nothing of you except this: Don't die with me. Live. Be happy. Love again because you deserve to experience as much love as this life has to give.

And I swallow.

It's almost been a year, and I have done everything possible to die right along with Connor. People move on, not because they want to, but because it's the only way they can survive. I rub at my chest, wondering if maybe I'm not as awful as I feel. But then again, Brandon was Connor's best friend, and maybe one reason the guilt is growing insurmountable is that Brandon has always, *always* felt like a betrayal when it came to Connor, for the simple fact that Connor never knew...

34

BRANDON

What the hell is wrong with me? Poppy? Of all the people. I just lost it. My mind was completely engrossed in violence, and then, there she was, like an apparition. For a second, all I wanted was to bathe in her warmth, to immerse myself in that glow she emanates. She's so beautiful and good and—*Connor's.*

She always was, and while she always will be, Connor's, she has always been my peace. She makes it all disappear; the hate and the anger and the battle raging in my mind. The second my lips touched hers, there was nothing but silence, and my mind hasn't been silent since that bomb exploded. That one, short kiss, was peace in a lifetime of war, and it terrifies me. The guilt is eating me alive, gnawing away in the pit of my stomach until I feel physically sick. I've done a lot of wrong in my life, but my best friend's widow— that's the shit that will get you a spot in the inner circle of hell.

I push and shove my way through the swarm of specta-tors, all focused on Kyan's fight. People turn and glare until they realize who I am, then they can't get out of my way quick enough.

I go straight to the fire exit on the far side of the room and shove it open. In seconds, I'm climbing up the short flight of stairs that lead into the alley at the back of the pub. I inhale the icy air deep into my lungs, allowing it to clear my mind.

A spark of light catches my eye. Finn leans against the wall of the alleyway, clinging to the shadows as he cups the flame from his lighter. Wordlessly, he holds out a packet of cigarettes, offering me one. I take the cigarette, and he lights it for me. Thick smoke lingers in my lungs before I allow it to drift past my lips.

"You're slipping," Finn says quietly.

I lean against the wall next to him. Finn fights like an animal when he's in the ring, but outside of it, he's practically a ghost. He's the guy that sits back. The one you forget is even there, but he hears and sees everything. He may not say much, but when he does, everyone listens, and, to me, his presence is a comfortable silence.

"It's just been a rough couple of weeks." I take another drag from the cigarette.

He shrugs one shoulder, throwing his fag on the ground and stomping it out. "Careful, friend. If you go up in flames with her standing too close, she's going to get burned."

I know. I know all too well. Finn pushes off the wall and saunters back inside. He has this way of putting thoughts in your head and then just leaving you to think. The hurt look on Poppy's face plays through my mind over and over. And It's not the first time I've put that look there, either. I'm an arsehole.

LATER THAT NIGHT, I linger in the hallway outside my apartment, key in hand. I've tried to think of what to say to her the entire way home, but I can't come up with a single thing. I inhale, slide the key into the keyhole, and brace myself. But when I open the door, I'm met with darkness.

"Poss?" *Nothing.*

She's not here.

I switch the light on, head straight for the kitchen, and grab a bottle of whiskey. For a moment, I feel guilty that I'm not better than this. But I'm just not, and there's no point in pretending otherwise. I yank off the top and press the glass to my lips, swallowing back a third of the bottle in several gulps. Numbness, lack of feeling; these are the things I'm constantly chasing, and Poppy—she makes everything bright and shiny. I don't want it. So, I drink, and I drink.

By the time the front door clicks open, I'm three-quarters of the way into the bottle, and rain .pounds against the windows, thunder rumbling as though the whole world is mad at me.

Poppy steps into the room, her long brown hair drenched and hanging in front of her face. She gives me a short-lived glance before making her way back to the bedroom, banging into the wall as she goes. No way she's drunk...

A few minutes later, she comes stumbling down the hall wearing one of my ratty, old Nirvana T-shirts that hits her mid-thigh. My eyes stray to her bare legs, and I try to block out the thoughts running through my mind. I'm fighting a losing battle. That kiss was like ripping off a Band-Aid. I haven't kissed Poppy for nearly ten years, not since I was seventeen years old. I blocked it all out, shoved any romantic feelings I had for her into a hole so deep, I hoped they would never surface again because I could never hurt Connor that way.

She plops down at the end of the couch, grabs the TV remote, and turns it on, surfing through the channels. I want to say something, but instead, I just tilt that bottle back.

"Gonna drink the whole bottle again?" she asks, her eyes glued to the TV.

I down the remaining whiskey and drop the empty bottle on the floor, allowing it to roll across the carpet. "Yep."

"Wanna go wander out into the street and see if you can find someone else to beat up?" She shakes her head. "Really, it's amazing. You're an angry, drunk fighter." She turns her cold gaze on me. "Way to go, Brandon. You're just like your father."

My chest tightens, but the anger I should feel is blissfully muted beneath the whiskey swimming in my veins.

The thing with Poppy, she's the sweetest person you could wish to meet until you hurt her feelings. And then she'll try to hurt you in return. I'm invincible now though; she can't reach me.

"The apple never falls far from the tree, right?"

She snorts, pushing the buttons on the remote so hard, her hand shakes. Minutes pass. She's gone through every channel at least three times before she turns and glares at me, but the effect is lost when she hiccups. "You're an asshole." Poppy's shit at being mad, but damn she's cute when she's drunk.

"I've always been an arsehole, poss. Nothing new."

There's a beat of silence before she finally speaks. "Why did you kiss me?"

And there it is, the question I don't have an answer for. All I know is that Poppy represents something good; happiness, a better time. I both love and hate her for it. I want to push her away and hold her tight at the same time. Everything about her is a double-edged sword. All I know is that for those precious few seconds that she kissed me back, I found peace.

"Why, Brandon?"

"I don't know," I whisper honestly. "It was a mistake. I was—my head was in a bad place." I stumble over my words.

"Your head's *always* in a bad place."

That little demon in me rears its ugly head. "Yeah, it is. And I 've told you a hundred times to run as far and as fast as you can." *But I don't want her to. I'm a selfish prick.* "Can't take the hits, then get the hell out of the way."

She stops the channel on some ocean documentary and flops back against the couch cushion. "I can't do that with you. Not again."

And honestly, neither can I. As much as I know I broke her heart, I broke my own, too. I wait until a commercial break, then elbow her in the ribs. "I'm sorry."

There a long pause before she huffs, "Me too." Then she scoots closer, resting her head on my shoulder with a sigh. "Everything was so much simpler when we were kids."

I kiss her damp hair, inhaling the scent of her shampoo mixed with rainwater. It was much easier when I thought the worst part of life was limited to my dad—not the entire world. "Remember when we used to climb up that oak in your garden and throw shit at Connor?"

"You mean, you climbed up and threw stuff at him."

I shrug. "Yeah."

A soft smile forms on her lips, and she swipes a hand over her cheek. That churning sensation settles in my stomach, and neither of us says another word. We watch the documentary, and eventually, she falls asleep on me. Having her small body pressed against mine is comforting, soothing in a strange way, but as much as I like it, I don't trust myself to fall asleep like this. I slip out from underneath her and carry her to bed. When I pull the duvet over her, she grabs my wrist.

"Connor?" she murmurs in her sleep, and my heart plummets.

I swallow around the lump in my throat and kiss her forehead, wishing, for her sake, that I was the man she wanted.

I sit on the edge of the bed and watch her sleep. We're two lost souls trying to save each other from unsalvageable events, and while she may be my hope, I'm surely her destruction.

35

POPPY

W eeks have passed, and Brandon and I have settled into a somewhat normal routine. Much to Hope's dismay, I've taken a job at Headley Court, helping out in their Veteran's clinic. She doesn't understand it—I don't expect her to—but I can't leave him, and going back to Ireland—there are too many memories there.

I glance over the paperwork for my new job, signing my name to the contracts before stacking them into a pile on the table.

"What's that?" Brandon asks on his way to the kitchen.

"Stuff for work."

"Yeah. What hospital did you say again?"

He knows I've taken a job as a nurse; I just haven't told him where yet. "Headley Court." I pause, and he opens a cabinet. "In the PTSD clinic."

He rolls his eyes, then swats his hand through the air and takes a mug from the cabinet. "What a bunch of bull-shit. The fighting ring is better therapy than any doctor would ever be."

Violence may temporarily grant him some relief, but, in the long run, it's ineffective. It won't help him deal with the emotions or the memories that haunt him—the trauma from his past or from war. All that ring is, is a recipe for disaster and destruction. "The ring does nothing to help you, Brandon."

"Gives me someone to hit." He spreads his arms wide. "They get paid. I get paid. Everyone's happy." Then he douses his coffee with a nip of whiskey and takes a sip.

"But you're not happy." And as much as I wish I hadn't said it, it's the truth.

The muscles in his jaw clench, and he grips the edge of the counter. "This is as good as it gets, Poppy. I don't need anything more. I don't want more."

"How can you not want more than *this*?"

At one point, Brandon would have wanted anything *but* this, because although this bleak apartment isn't the caravan, it's not much different. Everywhere I look, I see the things Brandon so desperately wanted to escape. The empty bottles, the dishes piling up. The fighting...the loneliness. He deserves so much more than this, and I just wish I could make him see it.

A strand of dark hair falls over his forehead when he drops his chin to his chest, and there's a tense moment of silence before his head lifts, his sad gaze locking with mine. "Because those are the cards I was fucking dealt," he whispers.

With a shake of my head, I push up from the couch and reach to skim my fingers over his arm. "Stop wallowing in it."

"Every time I close my eyes, I see him." His brows pull together, and he drags in a ragged breath. "Every single thing I do makes me feel guilty because Con's not getting to do it. So, I'll take the damned punches, and give them right back, because it makes me feel better." His eyes grow cold and hard, and I can almost feel the hate in the room, seeping through the air like a toxic fog. "If you want to move on—if you can just let him go, be my guest, but I can't."

Anger flares in my chest. It's not that I want to move on, but that I must. I tried wallowing in it when I lost Connor. There are days I long to die right along with him, but Connor wouldn't want that. Not for me. Not for Brandon. And if Brandon thinks this loss is harder on him than me... If he thinks I'm simply letting Connor go the way someone would a used pair of jeans. I died the day Connor did. Every part of my heart and soul crashed and burned, but Brandon wouldn't know that because he didn't see it. Because he ran, leaving me to grieve not one but two of the most important people in my life.

I grit my teeth and inch toward him, fists balled and muscles tense. "Don't you *dare* do that!" Before I realize what I'm doing, my palms smack his chest, and I shove him. "Don't you act like I'm just letting him go, Brandon."

He pushes off the kitchen counter and starts out of the room while shooting a dismissive look over his shoulder. "Don't try to fix me, Poppy. You'll be bitterly disappointed."

I step into the hallway after him, rage igniting inside me. "Like that's anything new!" I shout, regretting the words the very moment they leave my mouth.

There's the slightest hiccup in his steps before he bangs a palm against the wall and disappears into his room with a slam of the door.

Anger pulses through me, crackling and popping like a live wire as I pace the living room, then slam my fist against the heavy punching bag. The bag barely budges, so I punch it again and again, fighting tears. Fighting the sinking feeling that has weighed me down for almost a year. Fighting desperation.

I just want some sense of normal, some semblance of happiness. I long for the days when he was just Brandon, and I was his possum, the days when things were so much less complicated.

He stays in his room for over an hour before I finally give in and slowly push open the door.

The blue haze of twilight creeps in through the window, illuminating his silhouette on the edge of the bed, where his head hangs to his chest, and he's looking at a picture frame clutched in his hands.

Brandon 'The Breaker' —so indestructible, yet so utterly shattered.

Without a word, I crawl onto the bed and settle behind him. Sadness creeps in when I notice the photograph in his hands is one of him and Connor.

I peer over his shoulder at the picture of the only two men I've ever loved.

"I hated every minute of training," Brandon says. "Only stayed because I refused to leave him."

Connor only joined the army because Brandon did. They had always taken care of each other.

I take the picture frame from his hand, trying to forget the pain and remember anything else. "I bet Connor a hundred quid you wouldn't last three weeks."

"Ye of little faith." Brandon snorts, then shakes his head. "I'll give it to you; I was close to walking out when they made us sit in that muddy ditch for two days in the piss-wet rain. But Con was determined..."

I rest my chin on his shoulder, sucking in the scent of soap and sweat, the unmistakable, unchanging smell of Brandon that automatically makes me feel at ease. It's familiar—he's familiar, and I realize I still have some part of my life right here with him. "We don't have to let him go, Brandon," I say. "Just the hurt. But never him."

"I was screwed up long before Connor died. That just... It pushed me over the edge. I'm angry at everyone and everything." He turns, resting his forehead to mine while his callused fingertips brush my cheek. "Except you."

Long moments pass, and I find myself leaning into his touch. His rough fingers continue to trail over my face, and the longer they do, the more I lean into him because it's safe and as close to home as I'll ever get. "I don't want to fix you, Brandon. I just want to understand you." Tears blur my vision, so I close my eyes.

"Trust me, you don't," he whispers.

"I know you, Brandon." I trace a finger over his shoulder. "I *know* you."

There's a beat of silence before his thumb brushes my bottom lip. "God, I wish I was still that guy you knew, poss. I really do."

"You are," I whisper. "Deep down, you are."

And I believe that.

I have to believe that.

36

BRANDON

"**D**eep down, you are," she says. And there's such misplaced hope in that statement.

"That guy wouldn't have kissed you, poss."

"That guy *did* kiss me once." On an exhale, her gaze drifts to my mouth, and her eyes close. "Besides, it was just a kiss, Brandon."

"This is you and me. There is no 'just.'"

A sad smile touches her lips. "But we've always been *just* friends."

I can still picture the broken expression on her innocent, sixteen-year-old face as I uttered those exact words to her. *We're just friends.* I can practically feel my chest aching the same way it did then. The truth is, we were never just friends.

I felt things for her that I had no right to feel, because Connor loved Poppy, and I loved him. So I stepped back and watched destiny take its course, even though I wanted her more than anything else, even though I was too selfish to ever let her go completely. And every day I felt like the world's biggest prick because I was in love with my best friend's girl. Every day, I looked at her and pretended I felt nothing. In a way, nothing has changed.

Connor's ghost is more of a deterrent than he ever was in life.

In the end, we all lost. Poppy and I, we're all that's left of something so beautiful and so vital to my survival. I need her.

"No," I say. "I loved you enough to *be* your friend. Even when it hurt." I take her chin in my hand, turning her face to mine. She won't look at me. "I've always loved you, Poppy, and you know it." On instinct, I sweep a thumb over her bottom lip, hating myself when I remember how perfect her lips felt against mine all those years ago. "You bring me peace when all I know is war." My hand drops, and I move closer, an instinctive pull dragging me in. "You always have."

Our lips graze, and a calm washes over me—one only found in the quiet of snow-covered woods. Silent and utterly still. I pull her closer, needing every part of her while the voice in the back of my mind screams how wrong this is, but it's too late. Rational thought has given way to the simple need to survive.

And that's what Poppy feels like, survival.

A soft sob passes from her lips to mine before the kiss deepens. We're trapped in this swirling vortex of guilt and anger, twisted love and desperate need.

The kiss grows into something desperate, as though we're both fusing together while fracturing apart. The guilt eats away at me like a parasite.

If I were a better person, I would push her away.

If I truly loved Connor, surely I couldn't do this, to him —to her. But Poppy has always been too easy to get lost in.

Whatever sliver of my worthless soul is left, I will hand it over to her willingly, for this tiny piece of serenity and futile salvation.

Before I know it, I have my hands on her hips and shove her back onto the mattress. She's so small beneath me, so fragile, and I crave her in a way that borders on insanity. I reach for the bottom of her shirt, leaning in to kiss her again, but she slides a hand over my mouth, halting me. The trance shatters, and, once again, I feel like an arsehole.

"I'm sorry." I drag a hand down my face, shame crawling over me.

Poppy is like holy ground that I just desecrated.

The mattress dips, the silence deafening as she walks from the room and closes the door.

There are some things a man can never take back, some things that have the potential to be destructive, and this is most definitely one of them.

37

POPPY

The unmistakable taste of Brandon's lips rests on mine, and like a lovely poison, it leaves me dizzy.

The second his mouth touched mine, I lost all hope of pretending we have never been anything but friends. That kiss felt like a moment my entire life had been leading up to when it should have felt like the moment my life derailed. After all these years, I'm right back to where I started, only this time, as Brandon's best friend's widow.

My heart plummets to my stomach like a stone, sinking deep and hard until the weight of it brings me to the couch. I don't know what I'm doing.

Memories flash through my mind like the projection of old, tattered film, and I bury my head in my hands.

Brandon O'Kieffe wasn't just some guy—he wasn't just Connor's friend. For all of my life, he had been my secret. My secret first love and secret first kiss, and the only person, aside from Connor that I had ever slept with. A person I had felt so guilty for loving that I never once breathed a word of it to anyone for fear of what it may ruin.

The bedroom door creaks open, and Brandon comes

down the hall, cramming clothes into his gym bag. He doesn't even glance at me when he grabs the keys from the table and leaves me alone in his house.

"Shit," I breathe, dragging my hands through my hair and flopping back against the sofa cushions.

The muffled bickers of two people arguing come through the window, but I'm too focused on the awkward conversation I'll inevitably have this afternoon to be bothered by it until someone bangs on the door.

"Open the door, Poppy!" Hope shouts from the other side before the handle rattles. "I saw the pikey on the way out. Kicked him in the shin for being a ripe dick."

I go to the door, and the second it swings open, Hope places one designer heel over the threshold, then halts. Her gaze swings from one end of the living room to the other, and the scowl on her face deepens to a disgusted snarl. "Dear God, and I thought the caravan was questionable."

"How in the world did you find me?"

"Nice to see you, too." With a roll of her eyes, she steps inside and shuts the door. "Do you have any idea how many calls I had to make to find out where an illegal fight ring was in London?"

"How did you..."

Her arms cross her chest. "So, you were drunk when you called?"

"Yes. I got drunk and sat on the fountain at Piccadilly, then called you, which..." I love Hope, but honestly, I wish she weren't here. It's already messy enough as it is.

"I'm staying at Daddy's flat in Chelsea. If you're insistent on staying in London, at least come stay with me." She gives another disgusted glance around Brandon's apartment when I drop back to the sofa. "This place reeks of man and filth."

"It's fine."

"It's not."

"Look, as much as the pikey has pissed me off a right treat for running off like he did," she takes a deep breath and closes her eyes, "if this is what you think you need, fine. Maybe it is. A new start, someplace different. But Brandon... I can tell you from dealing with Silas, this is not a road you need to go down right now."

Silas. She's comparing Brandon to Silas? Surely he's not that bad.

"You need to—"

"I don't need to do anything," I almost shout.

There is no doubt this is a disaster waiting to happen. All the swirling tension, the grief and anger, and what-ifs. Nothing about it is a good idea, but at the same time, I think I want to drown right along with him. "I'll think about it."

"Think about it. Fine. But we aren't sitting in here today, so come on."

I glare at her. "I don't want to go anywhere, Hope."

She gives an adamant shake of her head. "Not hearing it. I'm hungry, and I'm sure as shit not eating anything he has in his freezer."

We eat lunch at the Giggling Squid, then Hope drags me to a nail salon and over half of London before we end up at the Dog's Bell.

Sunlight filters through the lead-glass windows, spilling over the vacant tables. At four in the afternoon, the normal hustle and bustle of the pub is missing. It's only Kyan and Brandon at the bar, and my heart does an uneven tap dance in my chest because I can still feel that kiss bleeding through my veins.

Hope leans in, nodding toward Brandon. "Always so broody. Just look at him."

But I wouldn't call the slump in his shoulders or the way he's scrubbing a hand over his jaw brooding. To me, that's broken.

Kyan's gaze strays to the doorway when he tips back his pint glass, and a slick smirk kicks up the corner of his lips. "Ah, look what that cat drug in. Who's the pretty redhead with you?"

Brandon gives the doorway a fleeting glance, then goes back to his drink.

"Brooding..." Hope sings in my ear.

"My friend Hope."

Hope nods. "I'm her best friend."

Brandon snorts into his glass, and Hope walks up behind him, whacking him on the back before she settles into the seat beside Kyan. "I'm still pissed at you, pikey."

Brandon looks at me. "Why is she here?"

"She's staying at her Dad's in Chelsea."

"Jesus, she's staying?" He takes a hefty swig of his drink.

Hope narrows her gaze on Brandon, eyes blazing. "Yes, and Poppy's staying with me since your apartment is deplorable."

With that, Brandon slams his drink onto the counter and pushes up, grabbing my arm and leading me to the corner of the bar out of the other's view. He turns and folds his arms over his chest. "Talk."

"I'm going to stay with her—"

"No."

The tension presses in on me from all sides, and whatever is going on between us is toxic. "Brandon, I'm just imposing. And after this morning—"

"No, possum." He takes a deep breath, unfolds his arms,

and then slowly closes the space between us. Towering over me, he grips my chin and lifts my face until my eyes meet his, then his gaze falls to my lips. "No," he says quietly, sternly.

My staying with him shouldn't be a question. Hope is right; we're both too much of a mess. But, like always, I can't help myself when it comes to Brandon. He's the imploded remains of a destroyed planet, and I'm his lone moon, bound by a simple gravitational pull I can't seem to escape.

"I can't stay with you because..." I chew at my lip, finding it too hard to hold his gaze. I look down, and he ducks, forcing me to look at him again.

"It won't happen again," he says.

A mixture of relief and disappointment bleed through me. I hated that unsettled feeling that I was left with, wanting him when I shouldn't. God, I shouldn't...

"I can't lose you," I whisper, knowing that statement holds so many meanings.

"I literally disappeared, and you still found me. You *can't* lose me." There's just a hint of desperation in his voice, his eyes pleading with me. "Stay."

I place my palm against his chest, not sure whether to pull him closer or push him away. We're both so vulnerable. "I..."

My gaze quickly lifts to the perfect dip in the middle of his lip. With Brandon, there should be no "us." We're two people whose lives are infinitely intertwined but were never meant to touch. I want him to need me just as much as I need him. I loved Connor more than anything in this world, but he's gone, and I don't think I can survive any of this fallout without Brandon.

"No matter *what* happens." He places his hand over mine and squeezes. "You'll always be my best friend.

Always." Then he leans in, kissing my forehead, and I wrap my arms around his broad waist, inhaling the scent of his whiskey tainted cologne.

We're both lost in the middle of a tumultuous storm, and the only way out is together.

38

BRANDON

APRIL 2015

I t's been a week since I kissed Poppy, and we're both trying to pretend this is normal, but the guilt is still very real. So real, I find myself walking into the gym just to rid myself of it.

Finn stands in the corner, his vest soaked with sweat while he pummels away at the speed bag. I'm spared a brief glance before he goes back to his workout.

With little thought, I tape my hands and then make my way to a corner to hammer my fists against one of the bags over and over. The violence consumes me, and I allow my mind to slip until it's blinking through the images that plague me. The rhythmic sound of my fists hitting the bag morphs into the steady *pop, pop, pop* of gunfire. My legs become unsteady at the memory of explosions vibrating the ground beneath my feet, and Connor's haunting death stare provides the grand finale. It's an image that has been branded into my mind in vivid detail, and it's there, waiting for me every time I close my eyes. I focus on it, allowing the pain to engulf me because I deserve it. I've wronged him.

Poppy is not just some chick. Hell, she isn't even one of those girls that you think could be a keeper. She's Poppy Blaine. She's family.

"Brandon?"

I lash out when someone touches my shoulder, then I slam my hand around Finn's throat. He easily twists out of my hold, and his brows pinch together in a deep frown. He should know better. I'm here for a reason. This bag takes punches so people don't have to. But it takes me a second to regain my bearings as my pulse thrums in my ears, blocking out the noise around me.

I stumble back, breaking away from the memories and focusing on what's in front of me. "Sorry," I mumble.

He folds his arms over his chest, watching me like a hawk. "You slept with her, didn't you?"

"What? No!"

"Only the guilty torture themselves."

Pacing, I drag a hand through my hair. "I kissed her. I didn't mean to."

"And now you feel bad?"

My heavy hands fell to my sides as my shoulders slumped. What was left of my heart was as downtrodden as my thoughts. "I can't even explain to you how Connor was with her." I shake my head but not with much thought. "She was everything to him, and I betrayed that." Twice now.

"Brandon." There's something sad in his gaze when I meet his eyes. "He's dead." He says it as though it's justification, and Connor's death eliminates my loyalty to him.

I don't want justification or to be relieved of guilt. "He was my brother. Death doesn't change that."

"No, but death can't feel betrayal." He turns back to his speed bag. "He'd want you to live."

Live, not desecrate his memory.

———

THE LAST THING I expected when I got home was for Poppy to be dressed in a pair of tight jeans—she had no business wearing—and telling me, we were going out.

She insisted it would be good for us to get out of the apartment and away from the bar, but I hate people. I never used to. Hell, there's a lot of things I never used to do or dislike. Now though, crowds are an issue.

Poppy sits next to me, throwing nervous glances my way as the tube fires along the tracks. I squeeze my eyes shut and try to regulate my breathing. It feels like the walls of the train are pressing in on me, no doubt because it's buried beneath the weight of an entire damn city.

"You all right?" she asks.

"Yep." My fists clench so hard that my knuckles ache.

Poppy grabs my hand, prying my fingers apart. "It's all right." Slowly, she rubs her thumb over the crease of my sweat-slicked palm to ease away the stress and strain she clearly sees in my body language.

This shouldn't even be an issue. People ride the tube every day, but I'm on high alert. Every instinct I have forces me to scan my surroundings for threats, needing an escape route at all times. The human drive to survive is all-consuming, and when you've been in the kind of places I have, that instinct goes into overdrive.

The most normal situations pose the ability to become hostile in an instant. Only this isn't war. And it doesn't matter how many times I tell myself that, my mind can't over-ride primal drive. My body can't forget the trauma.

The second the tube stops at Knightsbridge, I push to

my feet, tearing my hand away from Poppy and shouldering through the crowd. People shout and curse, but I don't care. I don't stop until I reach the street. The smog of the city air has never felt so enticing.

By the time Poppy catches up to me, she's out of breath.

I don't give her a second's reprieve. "Okay, so you dragged me into the center of this shit-hole city. Now what?"

"Don't know. Just thought it would be nice to get some fresh air." She says this just as a double-decker bus sputters past, the thick smell of exhaust filling the air—irony at its finest.

"So fresh," I grumble. "Carbon monoxide poisoning, just what I always wanted."

I plop my arse on a metal bench beside the railings down to the subway. "I'm just going to sit here until you make up your mind."

A wry smile works over her lips. "You really want to leave that decision up to me?"

"Tell you what, you make a decision and I'll tell you whether I'm coming with or going home."

"Tower of London, then Madame Tussaud's, and The London Eye."

"I'm going home." I stand up, and Poppy grabs my arm with a laugh.

"You can't leave me here." She pouts, and that always did get to me.

"I'm not doing the tourist shit. Do I look like a small Japanese man?" I point at her while she laughs. "And I'm not carrying you around."

"I didn't ask you to, now did I?" She takes my hand and tugs me down the congested sidewalk.

"I've heard that shit before." I swear, I spent half my childhood carrying Poppy around. *My feet hurt. My legs are tired...* She was annoying, but damn, I could never tell her no, and I was always twice the size of Connor...and he was fat. Maybe I should have made him carry her; he'd have lost a few pounds. But then she wouldn't be my possum.

"Come on," she says. "We haven't done this stuff since we were kids in school."

We stop at a crosswalk, and I exhale a defeated breath. "Fine. But not the wax shit. No one needs to see a still life of Britney Spears."

The light changes, and I go one way while she tries to tug me another.

Her brows wrinkle, and she points to the opposite side of the street than I'm headed. "The Tower of London is that way."

"I'm not going to the Tower of London and doing the scenic bullshit. I'll do the Natural History Museum."

"*You* want to go to a museum."

"I like the dinosaur," I grumble.

She laughs and loops her arm through mine. "Okay. Dinosaurs it is."

By the time we walk the mile or so to the museum, her cheeks have flushed a rosy red from the cold, autumn wind. I pay the admission to get in, and then we're standing in front of the massive Brontosaurus skeleton, its neck stretching toward the high ceiling.

We once came here on a school trip, and another time, Connor's parents visited London for a long weekend and brought me along to keep him company. There was always something so grand about it. I can't really explain it, but when I'm standing in front of the remnants of a creature that is millions of years old and probably five times the size of an elephant, I suddenly feel small. So incredibly inconsequential.

Poppy smiles as she watches a screaming child goes hurtling past me, a balloon trailing in his wake as a stressed-looking guy runs after him. The kid runs circles around the poor man, and I wonder what she's thinking—if she's thinking about the children she never had with Connor.

"I miss being that little sometimes, you know?" Her gaze is still glued to the kid.

"Yep. No responsibilities, free food, and you can even shit yourself and someone else will clean it up for you."

She drags her attention from the child and scrunches her nose at me. "You're such a boy."

I cock a brow. "All man, sweetheart."

"Oh my God, come on." She marches away from me, and I follow, laughing—and staring at her arse. I need to stop doing that.

She wanders around the room, finally stopping in front of the butterfly display.

"Kind of harsh," I say, looking at their lifeless bodies pinned to a board encased behind glass, hundreds of them all lined up in rows. All so people can admire their pretty wings.

Poppy studies the insects behind the glass and then turns to meet me with sympathetic eyes. "It is, but then again, life is harsh, isn't it?"

"Yeah, but it's not supposed to be for a butterfly. Damn." I lean closer, studying the iridescent color of their wings. "Don't they only get a few months anyway?"

"Maybe months are years to butterflies, who knows." Poppy shrugs. "Quality of life, not quantity, right?"

I stare at the butterflies for a moment longer, then tentatively thread my fingers through hers. It feels strange, and yet, the simple touch grounds me.

The museum crowd seems a little less threatening, the noises quieter. Poppy brings me back to the here and now, physically forcing everything else from my mind. It seems impossible, and yet, here *we* are.

39

POPPY

After dinner in a small pub, we take a cab back to Brandon's house. It sputters to a stop, and I check the meter before pulling money from my purse, but Brandon grabs my shoulder and passes cash to the driver.

"You know, we could have taken the tube," he says, climbing out and stopping to hold the door for me.

He acts like it's no big deal, but I wasn't blind to how uncomfortable the train made him. The smallest movement from someone beside him and his eyes went wild. His muscles remained tense the entire time we were out, and I could tell it took everything in him just to focus on me when I would speak. There was no way I'd force him back on that tube, but I also didn't want him to think I knew how uneasy he was.

"I wanted to take a cab," I say as we step inside.

He falls onto the couch and rubs a hand over the back of his neck. "Want to watch a film?"

"Sure." I sit beside him, ignoring the awkward tension that shouldn't be there—the desire that wants nothing more than his lips on mine again. I subtly lean away, putting a little space between us.

"Pick something." He drops his phone onto my lap on his way to the kitchen, and I scroll through Netflix. *Stardust, Pirates of the Caribbean, Charlie and the Chocolate Factory and...*

"Hey, Brandon?"

"Yeah."

"How do you feel about a classic?"

He comes back with two sodas, handing me one before he takes his seat again, leaving no space between us as he kicks up his heels onto the edge of the coffee table. "Yeah, sure."

With a smirk, I press play and drop the phone to the cushion. The soft notes of "My Heart Will Go On" hums from the TV before the sepia-colored picture of the boat flashes on the screen.

"Oh. Hell, no. Anything but this."

"Oh, come on, Brandon. You never would watch this when we were younger."

"Yeah, because I'd rather spend intimate time with a ghost pepper on my ball sack than watch this."

"Really?" I scowl at him. "It's an epic love story; who doesn't love an epic love story? And it's this or *The Notebook* because I am not watching *Die Hard*. Ever. Again." I watched that more times than I want to admit when I was younger— all just to be around Brandon.

"Leonardo-fucking-Dicaprio or Bruce Willis. No comparison."

"You told me I could pick," I argue.

"You picked this because you know I hate it."

"I went to see the dinosaurs for you."

Dragging a hand down his face, he groans. "Fine, but if I

fall asleep halfway through, it's because you want to watch an entire film about a boat sinking. A. Boat. Sinking. It's not even like it gets blown up. Some guy just drives into an iceberg." He shakes his head. "So stupid."

I smile as I pat him on the knee. "It's a tragic part of history."

"Tragic waste of my time," he grumbles, slurping back his cola.

And here we sit, watching a movie I've seen fifty times. It's not unlike anything we've done before, but it is different because everything has changed.

Every so often, Brandon's hand brushes my thigh, and I inch a little closer than I should. There's a mixture of excitement and fear and guilt. As a kid, I'd spent countless nights watching movies wrapped up in Connor's platonic embrace and never thought anything of it. Somehow I'd missed how truly special that was until now. And I only recognize it now because I miss it—that easiness of just being with someone, of being held and touched. Brandon makes me want that —*crave* that—just like he always has. The heat of his body bleeds into mine while I try to focus on the movie when Jack and Rose wade through the rising waters.

"She says his name too much," I say.

"We can watch *Die Hard*."

"Nope. I consider forcing you to watch this an accomplishment," I whisper, my eyes locked on the screen.

"Fine." He grabs me beneath my arms and yanks me across the couch like I'm nothing but a child, and settles me between his thighs, resting his chin on my head. For a moment, I remain tense, but he's so warm and safe and just, Brandon. Then I relax against his solid chest, and even though I'm looking at the TV, my entire focus is on him. Every breath. Each steady beat of his heart against my back.

I give in until it feels like nothing outside of this can touch me. Brandon is my personal cocoon from the hurt and the grief, and I want him to turn me into something beautiful and free.

BY THE END of the movie, I'm sobbing.

He leans into my line of vision with a smirk. "You're *actually* crying over that?"

I sniffle and swipe at my cheeks to clear the tears. "It's sad."

"And yet, you *wanted* to watch it?" That smirks morphs into a grin. "She could have given him half of that door, you know. Kinda dumb if you ask me." Brandon moves me away and stands from the couch to stretch.

"It would have been too much weight and sunk them both."

"He *dies*."

I glare at him. "He sacrificed his life for her." Leave it to Brandon to try and degrade my favorite movie. "Someone always dies in epic love stories, Brandon. Don't question it."

He holds up his hands in surrender. "Fine, poss. Whatever you want to believe." Then he starts toward the bathroom.

I go into the bedroom, leaving the door open while I change into a T-shirt. I listen for the sounds of Brandon's progress as the toilet flushes and the taps turn. Before he opens the door, I climb into the bed, nerves twisting my gut. My palms grow sweaty when the hinges to the bathroom door creak and Brandon's shadow stretches across the wall of the hallway.

My mouth goes dry, and I barely eke out his name. "Brandon?"

The light silhouettes his frame when he steps to the doorway. "Yeah?"

"Can you... " I hesitate. It's not wrong, I tell myself. I have to live. "Come lay in here for a little while?"

He inhales—hard—like he's contemplating, then he tilts his head back. I expect a groan to follow, but it never does. Just silence.

His head lowers. "*What* are we doing, Poppy?"

I wish I had an answer for that. "I don't know." My words are barely a whisper and more like a plea.

He props his arms against the frame, and the movement pulls his shirt tight across his thick chest. Despite how hard I try, I can't seem to drag my eyes away from him.

"You don't want me sleeping with you, poss."

"Please?"

There's a beat of silence before he steps into the room. A fissure of unease crawls through my stomach when he strips out of his shirt, the lies on top of the comforter. Spreading his arms wide, he pulls me against his chest, and I go willingly, breathing in everything that is Brandon.

"Just for a little while," he whispers into my hair.

"Just for a little while."

This isn't complicated. It's simple need—the need to have someone. To be loved, even in the most complicated of ways.

40

BRANDON

All I can hear around me is the thunder of gunfire, the snap of bullets cracking through the air and a hoarse cry beside me. I glance to my left just as another soldier hits the ground, clutching his thigh. Blood wells around the soldier's fingers as he grits his teeth, throwing his head back against the mound of mud we're using for cover. I drop my weapon and try to quiet my pounding heart as I struggle to breathe. As my focus returns, I hear someone nearby radioing for air support, and I manage to tie a tourniquet around the top of Serg's thigh. Once it's secure, I pop up with my gun in tow, staring down the sights of my rifle. A small cluster of buildings sits about a hundred yards away, and it's there that the enemy is taking cover. We're firing blind and hoping something hits.

The rumble of the jet on the horizon can be heard long before I see it. And it's then that I see a woman dart out of a house, a child clutched in her arms. She ducks behind a building, but I already know it's too late for her.

The sound of the pilot's voice crackles over the radio, and then the jet splits the air overhead at the exact time as the entire area erupts into a ball of fire. I drop down beside Serg just as the heatwave ripples overhead. And then there's nothing—just the sound of fire and destruction...and the screaming inside my own mind.

I gasp awake, sitting bolt upright as I drag air into my lungs. It takes me a second to focus my vision, but when I do, I find Poppy, sitting up, huddled on the edge of the mattress, staring at me. My pulse clangs against my eardrums, my muscles tremble under false stress, and a shiver works over my damp skin.

"You okay?"

I give a jerky nod, then swipe a hand through my sweat-dampened hair. And I wait, terrified to ask, "Did I hurt you?" I finally manage, my voice barely above a whisper. All I can think about is the first night she found me when I woke up with my arm across her throat.

"No." She pauses. "But, you scared me." A stray piece of hair falls in front of her face when her head tips forward, and I catch myself wanting to push the strand behind her ear.

We sit in silence, and I squeeze my eyes shut as I try to shake away the last remnants of the dream.

"Brandon." Her fingertips brush my jaw, and I open my eyes to find her in front of me on her knees. The street light outside streams through the window, casting an orange glow over her face. A small line sinks between her brows as her eyes search mine. "Come here."

She lies back on the bed, taking me with her until my head is resting on her stomach. "It's okay," she whispers, and the softness of her voice makes me want to believe her.

I want to believe that there will be an end to this, that eventually, I will be able to stop reliving the same thing every night.

"Do you remember that time when we went shrimping in the harbor and I fell in?"

I laugh. "Yeah."

She fell off the old jetty because the wood was rotted. Honestly, it was past midnight and dangerous as hell, but we were fourteen. We didn't care. The water was pitch black, and Jesus, she screamed when she went in. I thought she was hurt until she started shrieking that the shrimp were going to get her. Connor and I laughed so hard we couldn't even help her out of the water, and my God was she savage.

"You always rescued me when I needed it." Her fingers rake through my hair, that familiar touch so soothing it forces my eyes closed.

This is what Poppy does, she comforts and soothes. She takes in little birds with broken wings and tries to fix them, and when she can't, she cries.

And I hate it when she cries, so for a moment, I'll pretend that she can fix me, that she can make me fly again, even though we both know she can't.

41

POPPY

MAY 2015

The warmth of Connor's fingers skims my waist, dancing underneath my shirt as real as if they were really there, caressing my skin. I smile. I've missed him. This touch. The way this feels. His warm lips kiss the crook of my neck, and his arm wraps around my waist, tugging my body flush with his. Halfway between awake and asleep, I recognize it's a dream, but as my eyes flutter, I fight to remain asleep—to stay in the dream and his embrace. I don't want to let go when it feels so real, so right, so needed. I can still feel his hands on me, his lips...

But even as my eyes pop open, I still feel his hands on me, his lips—then Brandon groans against my throat. And I realize why it was so real. Brandon shifts in the bed, his hold on me tightening.

"Don't," he mumbles, his breathing deep and uneven with sleep. "Don't leave me," he whispers before his lips press against the top of my shoulders.

Nothing has happened between us since the day we kissed, although the tension has been unbearable. He and I both know what it's like to cross that line, and sometimes it's better to wonder what something would be like than to know.

But I long for that connection.

I'm starved of it. Sex and attraction and primal need. A heavy breath escapes Brandon's lips, the heat of it blowing across my skin, and sending chill bumps over my body while that undeniable urge settles between my thighs just before the guilt perches on my chest. Only, I don't know who I am betraying more, Connor for lying in Brandon's arms, or Brandon for dreaming of Connor while I'm in his bed.

I love them both—separately—I always have.

Despite the fact that I keep telling myself Connor is gone and he wants me to live, I can't seem to convince myself that it somehow justifies my feelings for Brandon or alleviate the guilt. If anything, death simply immortalizes Connor's place in my life. It took everything he was and preserved it in stone, leaving him untouchable and incomparable for eternity. But Brandon and I aren't frozen in stone.

We're here, living, breathing.

We're what's left.

I bite at my lip and turn in the bed to face him, watching the way the streetlight plays across his face while he sleeps. His eyelids flutter. His chest peaks and dips unevenly. I can literally see him fighting those dreams that seem to haunt him more nights than not, and all I want to do is take that away from him.

Leaning over his face, I trail my fingertips over his warm arm and along his side, and I whisper, "I love you, Brandon." And I touch my lips to his. One quick kiss, it's all I need for fear to rise in my chest.

I go to pull away, but his hand flies to the back of my neck. His fingers tangle in my hair, and his lips part beneath mine. One of his arms winds around my waist, then he pulls me flush against his solid body. My mind and body go to war, rationality battling against a basic primal need.

But Brandon doesn't hesitate. His fingers slide beneath my shirt and splay across the small of my back, igniting something raw, something that has been glaringly absent since the last time he kissed me. Only Brandon can heal my broken soul with the splintered remnants of his. He kisses me until I don't know where he starts and I begin, and just when I'm convinced he'll never let me go, he does.

We're both breathless, staring through the darkness at one another.

"Brandon—"

"Shush, poss." He doesn't give me time to protest and instead drags me onto his chest, placing his palm against my cheek. His lips brush my hair, and his arm tightens around my waist before he relaxes beneath me. Minutes later, his breathing evens out. He's fallen asleep, leaving me very much awake—and on top of him.

I BARELY SLEPT LAST NIGHT, which has made for a taxing day at work. But even though I'm exhausted, I'm glad to be working again, thankful for the sense of purpose. I finish making notes on Mr. Brighton's chart before filing it away. So much of his story reminds me of Brandon. Mr. Brighton lost his best friend to a roadside bomb. He was the one survivor in the convoy, and he's every bit as angry at life as Brandon. Today, he shouted at Doris, the charge nurse who looks like a true-life version of Cinderella's Fairy Godmother because she "glared" at him.

Doris slaps a patient file on the counter before checking her watch. "Past time for you to go, dear." She fluffs her graying hair, and a slow grin works over her lips. "Unless you want to go play Bingo with Mary and me tonight?"

I log off the computer and grab my purse from behind the desk. "I've got dinner plans with a friend."

Her face lights up, and she wiggles her eyebrows. "Oh. A guy friend?"

"No, but I'll take a raincheck."

"Raincheck. Pfft." She waves me off. "You're young. You don't want to play bingo with a lot of old birds. Although..." She grabs her handbag and rummages through it before pulling out a shiny, silver flask. "I do like to hit the bottle hard on a Friday night."

Laughing, I push open the door. "I'll see you later, Doris."

I try to call Brandon on the way home to see if he wants to go to dinner with Hope and me—although I know he'll say no—but he doesn't answer.

The second I set foot in the apartment, I know why he didn't answer.

The staple bottle of whiskey sits on the coffee table, and Brandon's on the sofa, legs spread and elbows resting on his thighs while he stares at the ground. He doesn't spare me a glance, not when I close the door or when I drop my keys loudly on the counter. I clear my throat, and still nothing.

"Brandon."

His cold, flat gaze to lifts mine, and I notice a fresh cut on his face. "Hey, poss." He takes the bottle from the table, cracks the seal on the lid, and brings it to his lips to swallow back several heavy gulps.

Some days Brandon's up, and I think maybe, maybe it will be the day he snaps out of it, but then he goes down. Hard. And this is down. Way down. Every time he comes back from a fight, he's angry and he drinks. When he gets like this, there is nothing that can shake that darkness and rage that hangs around his shoulders like a wool cloak. At times I believe he basks in it.

I've tiptoed around this topic as long as I can. Those fights do nothing but make his situation, whatever that is, worse.

I snag the bottle of whiskey from him on my way into the kitchen and toss the glass into the trash. When I return to the living room, his eyes narrow. "That's real fucking help-ful," he says with a humorless laugh.

"Brandon, please tell me you realize you have a problem?"

"Jesus, Poppy." He throws his head back and drags a hand over his face. "All you do is bitch."

"No. It's not bitching. It's me caring about you, Brandon. And this—this has got to stop."

"This is a one-way road, possum." He pushes off the sofa, walking straight past me without as much as a backward glance.

From here, I can just make out the grin sneaking over his face when he opens the kitchen drawer—the one where he keeps his weed.

I storm into the kitchen, grab the collar of his shirt, and yank him away from the counter. Then slam my hip against the drawer, nearly closing his hand in it. "You don't need it."

There's a spark of anger in his eyes a second too late. He grabs me by the waist and slams me against the fridge with such force it rocks back, rattling everything inside before it settles on the floor again with a bang. I brace my palm against his chest, and his quickened heartbeats pound against my hand.

I can feel the tension ingraining itself into every one of his muscles.

"Brandon," I whisper. "Let me go. Please." I swallow. There's a dark voice muttering in the back of my mind that this is the part of Brandon I don't know. The part of him I can't fully trust. A part of him that scares me.

A wry smile touches his lips. For a split moment, he's almost the Brandon I recognize, but he's buried beneath so much anger and hatred that it's hard to see the boy I grew up with—the one I love.

His grip tightens when he inches toward me. My skin prickles when the warm air that escapes his mouth fans across my throat. In seconds, his lips brush my earlobe. "Isn't this what you want, Poppy?" There's a cruel edge to his words that I hate, and although I don't want to believe for a second that he would hurt me, he's making me nervous.

"You're scaring me, Brandon."

His gaze narrows and his eyes swirl with a storm of emotions just waiting to hit—one I have no idea of when or where it will strike. But as quickly as it came, the storm passes. Brandon huffs out a hard breath through his nose, lessens his grip, and then touches his forehead to mine. His palms capture my cheeks, and he breathes me in like oxygen he needs for survival. Then, he kisses me. But where I expect violence and anger, hate and fury to transfer with his lips, instead, all I find is reverence.

"I'm sorry," he whispers against my lips, his hands trembling as they stroke my cheeks and down the column of my throat.

I search his eyes for answers, for the whys of how life is such a mess. I want Brandon to make me forget everything that isn't this exact moment. Just him and me. And then he kisses me again, long and hard.

His fingers dig into my waist, and he lifts me, wrapping my legs around his hips before he moves me away from the fridge and down the hall. I land on his bed, and he comes after me, caging me in with solid arms. Before his lips meet mine again, I tug at his shirt while his hands roam my body, and then he stills.

"Not like this," he breathes against my mouth.

And those words are enough to snap me out of the moment, and I stare at him bewildered.

But Brandon barely budges when he closes his eyes and places his lips to mine again. "I want you more than I've ever wanted anything or anyone in my life. But you deserve better. Not like this."

A flicker of anger spikes in my chest. That has always been Brandon's excuse, that I deserve better, and while that may be how he feels, I want better for him, too. I want to be his sanctuary, the place he goes when the demons get too close.

"I don't want *better*, Brandon. I want *this*." I sweep a hand over his face. "I want you."

There's a slight tic in his jaw, and he grips the bottom of my shirt. "Say it again."

"I want you."

And then the dam between us breaks.

With each passing second, with each touch, we slip farther. And when Brandon finally strips the last piece of clothing from my body, he draws in a deep breath. We're right back here, on the front lines of the moral war that has waged between the two of us for as long as I can remember.

My eyes lock with his, and I let my legs fall open in invitation. It's then that the incredible weight and warmth of his body covers mine—skin to skin. I'm desperate for this connection, and at the same time, I'm terrified.

The emotion, the raw need to belong to him, consumes us both, and the way we tumble and fall is heartbreakingly beautiful. Two people who shouldn't belong together but can't belong to anyone else.

Each breath and touch and kiss ingrains itself within me until there is nothing more than Brandon and me, drowning in our own tragic bliss—expressing the inexpressible through the movements of our bodies.

I want to linger right here, immortalize us in the dark of night because right now, we're both whole, and I know it will never stay this way.

42

BRANDON

I lie in the dark, listening to Poppy's soft breaths. Her cheek is pressed to my chest, her small body nestled against my side, every naked inch of her touching me. I have slept with countless women and drunk enough whiskey to drown a small town—all in a bid to forget. And the irony is, she is the only thing that shelters me from my own memories. Yet she's the very thing that should haunt me the most.

At times, she's the only thing that keeps me grounded, the only thing that makes sense. But she's also my biggest source of conflict. The second I step back, the second I get some perspective, I remember that fact.

I crave the calm that she brings, even when I have no right to. I close my eyes, and the image of her and Connor on their wedding day flashes through my mind. They were so happy, and she looked at him like he was her entire world. He was, to both of us, and now we're living in some post-apocalyptic replica of a time when Connor made everything seamlessly better.

I wake up to sunlight pouring through the cream

curtains. It's morning. I slept through the whole night. No nightmares. No sweating. I can't remember the last time I made it through the night without a serious dose of whiskey or weed.

Poppy is lying next to me on her side, the duvet skimming her hips and exposing her naked back. And in the cold light of day, it's all too real. This is Poppy, my possum, Connor's wife. It feels...wrong to see her like this.

The guilt is warring with my basic instinct to survive because I'm no longer deluded enough to think that I can do this without her. It's too dark, too bottomless. She is my only source of hope, my light at the end of the tunnel. And as awful as I feel about betraying Connor, as much as I loved him, I can't quite make myself let go of that light.

I silently climb out of bed and go to the bathroom. Perspective; that's all I need, just a moment.

My battered and bruised reflection stares back at me from the bathroom mirror. I can barely look at myself, and it has nothing to do with my exterior injuries.

I climb into the shower and allow the hot water to soothe my aching muscles. Bracing my forearms against the tile, I drop my head forward and rest it against the cold surface. This is a mess of epic proportions. I don't even know what I think or feel anymore, but the ever-present band of panic is tightening around my chest, squeezing me. The thought of facing Poppy is too much.

I need air.

I finish my shower and dry off before grabbing some gym clothes from the bathroom floor. Praying Poppy doesn't wake up, I head to the living room, shove on my shoes, and walk straight out the front door like my arse is on fire.

43

POPPY

W hen I woke this morning, Brandon was gone. And he's never awake before midday. When I left to meet Hope for lunch, he still hadn't come home or returned my call.

I've barely touched my sandwich, and every few minutes, I check my phone, which is enough to tip Hope off that something is going on.

"Was it any good?" she asks.

I finish my text to Brandon, asking if he's okay before I look up. "What? Was what any good?"

She stares at me from across the table, clasping her coffee cup while a smirk settles on her lips. "Don't lie to me. I know you slept with the pikey. It's all over your face."

My cheeks sting with heat. Feigning a laugh, I reach for a packet of sugar, then dump it into my coffee. "Don't be ridiculous, Hope."

"Liar!" She points at me. "You are lying. I know you, and you slept with him." One eyebrow arches. "Stand up then."

"What?"

"Stand up. If you didn't sleep with him, stand up." A wry

smile works its way across her lips when I don't budge. "Just what I thought."

"Hope," I sigh. "What are you talking about?"

"Just stand up, and I'll drop it."

"Fine!" I push my cup to the side and get to my feet, tossing my hands in the air as I glare at her. "I'm standing."

Shrugging, she lifts her cup to her mouth and takes a sip. "Fine."

But when I sit back down, I can't bite back the wince.

"Guilty!" she shouts, slamming her palm on the table like a judge with a gavel before she leans over, closing the space separating us. "The wince. You screwed him."

I prop my elbows on the table and cover my face with my hands.

My phone dings with a text, and I glance through the slit between my fingers, reading Brandon's one-word response: **Yep.**

"Look at it this way, it's not like you're a first-time offender." She reaches across the table and yanks my hand away from my face. "Shit happens."

Shit happens. It sure does, I think, while I send another text.

Me: We need to talk.

Brandon: Yep.

Brandon hates when people send him one-word responses, so the fact that all he can manage is *yep* is not a good sign.

I stare into my coffee cup, unable to shake the tingling in my stomach when I think of how it felt when he touched me; of how much he is something I need and crave.

Another ding from my phone. **Brandon: It was a mistake.** And the reality of it all comes crashing down.

LATER THAT EVENING, I sit on the patio of Hope's apartment, staring across at the rows of identical, white townhomes.

I never texted to tell him I wasn't coming back tonight, and although I should, he hasn't sent another text after he said last night was a mistake. And what happens if I go back?

We fight. Maybe kiss, maybe end up in bed together again?

It's as though all rationale disappears, and I'm unable to weed through my emotions. But most of all, I'm hurt and disappointed. In myself. In him...

Hope bustles onto the patio and takes a seat on the lounge beside me. "You like the flat?"

"Yeah, it's nice."

It's extravagantly nice. A three-bedroom flat in a neighborhood most people only dream of living and Hope's father signed it over to her simply because she'd wanted it. That's how her life has always gone. Whatever Hope wants, if money can possibly buy it, it's hers.

I gaze off, watching a man across the street jog up to a door, roses in hand. He knocks, and when a woman answers the door, he wraps his arms around her waist and kisses her the way I only see in movies—the way Brandon kisses. A knot forms in the pit of my stomach, slipping like a snake coiled around itself, and I reach for the wine but stop.

"Go ahead. Drink it." Hope's attention is also locked on the couple across the street. "Trust me, sometimes you just need it."

"I don't *want* to need anything."

"Ah, but that's a problem. We all need *something*, don't we?" Hope releases a long sigh. "Poppy, I know you're confused about the whole Brandon thing, but stop beating yourself up."

"I can't lose him."

"You'll never lose Brandon O'Kieffe," Hope says. "Since the day I met you, that boy's been as lovesick for you as you have been for him. He may be a pikey, but if he makes you happy..." She studies me for a moment. "What are you scared of, Poppy?"

While I am worried about losing Brandon, I think what I'm most afraid of is losing the memory of Connor. "Forgetting Connor," I whisper.

Hope's face crumples, and she reaches for my hand. "Poppy, you won't forget him, but he's gone, and nothing is going to bring him back."

I close my eyes and lean back in the seat, wishing things never had to change. After a few minutes, Hope exhales. "I can't believe I'm about to say this, but sometimes, the regret of not doing something is far worse than the regret of what you did."

And that's just the thing, either way, I know I will regret something.

———

"B-4." The announcer coughs into the microphone. "B-4."

Hope has about ten bingo cards spread out in front of her, the little stamper hovering over them as she searches for the place on her board. Smiling, she pounds it over one of the cards. "That's right. I just made B-4 my bitch."

Doris glances over at me, grinning as she lifts her flask to her mouth. "I like her."

I nod. "Hope's something, that's for sure."

"Aw, I'm a little fond of you, too, Doris." Hope eyes the flask. "What's in there?"

"Whiskey," Doris says, then passes the flask to Hope.

"Spirit animals, Doris, we are spirit animals." She tips the flask back just as the announcer calls out another space.

"G-45. G-45."

I stamp the spot on my card. And the next thing I know, the silver flask is shaking right in front of my face. I glance over at Hope. "You're sad," she says. "Whiskey makes people happy."

"So, basically, you want me to be a drunk?"

"No. Just be like an Irishman."

"Again, a drunk?"

"Look, I'm pretty sure the Irish have the lowest rate of depression in the world."

"They do not."

"Sure, they do. You can't be sad when you're drunk."

I stare at Hope, shaking my head. "You're crazy, you know that?"

"The next space is N-12. N-12."

Hope jumps up from the table, knocking over her chair and scaring awake the elderly woman who nodded off on the other side of her. "Bingo!" She waves one of her cards around before placing a foot on the metal folding chair and grinding the air as she sings out: "Bingo. B-I-N-fucking-G-O."

Everyone stares, Doris claps, and I just sink into my chair and cover my face with my hands.

"Damn, that was the last game," Doris says, tipping the flask back again.

"All right." I gather the bingo cards and stack them together. "Well, thanks for inviting us, Doris."

She nods.

Hope grins. "Yep, I think I've found a new hobby."

"Great, so your list is drinking, screwing, and bingo?"

"Basically. Sounds legit."

My phone dings with a text. I pull it from my purse

while Hope walks to the front of the room to collect her prize: A heated neck massager.

I stare at the text, my chest going all tight. **I told you you'd hate me. Sorry, poss.**

Like a child, he's ignored my texts and calls for the past day. And then he sends me this crap. Brandon is an emotional rollercoaster, one storm after another, and even though that should be enough to make me run in the opposite direction, it hasn't.

"A heated neck massager. Amazing!" Hope holds the bright pink object up and smiles. "Perfect for a rainy day, huh?"

"Yep."

Hope's phone blares from her purse, and her lips pull into a wry smile. "Well, I know what *that* one wants." She digs her phone from her purse, touches the screen, and places it to her ear. "Hey, hot stuff." She pauses for a second, and her smile slowly fades. "Fine. Fine. I'll send her over." She disconnects the call and shoots an annoyed look in my direction.

"Brandon got shitfaced and evidently needs you. Kyan said he's done babysitting him."

THE SECOND I walk into Brandon's flat, I roll my eyes. Clothes and empty beer cans scatter the living room, and Kyan's sitting at the end of the sofa with a beer in his hand while Brandon hangs halfway off the couch, swatting at a bottle of whiskey on the table.

Kyan's gaze locks on me when he grabs the liquor and hands it to Brandon. "Well, 'bout time you came back. He's been like this for twenty-four hours. Missed his fight."

Brandon looks over, squinting his bloodshot eyes. "Possum. You're here." He lifts the bottle to me. "Come have a drink."

"Possum?" Kyan says, laughing as he slaps a hand over his forehead. "Fuck me."

I glare at Kyan, and he shrinks back a step. "What the hell are you doing, Brandon?"

Brandon's eyebrows pull together in a frown. "Drinking."

"Yes, that I can clearly see. But *why* have you been drunk for twenty-four hours."

The frown deepens, and he lifts the bottle to his lips, turning it up, and taking a glug before he drops it to his side.

"For the love of..." Huffing, I cross the room, pointing at Kyan when I reach the couch. "And really? You've been sitting here feeding him alcohol?"

Kyan shrugs.

"God, you are an idiot," I mumble. "Just get out of here."

Holding up his hands, Kyan gets to his feet. "He's got a fight in eight hours, you may want to try to sober him up a bit."

"He's not fighting."

"Oh, like hell he's not. He missed his fight last night. Larry'll have him by the balls if he no shows again."

My face heats, and I push onto the tips of my toes, inching toward Kyan's face. "Tell Larry if he thinks Brandon's fighting, I'll have *him* by the balls."

"You got a bit of feist in you yet, don't you?"

I shove him one good time, and he stumbles toward the door.

"All right then, I'll see you later, Brandon." The door closes behind him, and I turn back to Brandon, who's attempting to take off his shirt but failing miserably.

"God, you are like a child sometimes," I say as I lean down and tug his shirt over his head.

His chin drops, and I grab it, raising his head back up. "Thanks."

"Why are you drunk—I mean, you're drunk a lot, but *this?*" I let go of his chin, and his face falls forward.

"You left, poss," he slurs.

"I went to Hope's. I didn't leave."

Without lifting his head, he mumbles, "Left me."

Sighing, I flop onto the couch next to him and comb my fingers through his hair. When he looks up, I notice his cheekbone is swollen and bruised. "So, if you didn't fight, why is your cheek all banged up?"

He rubs a hand over his cheek. "My cheek?"

I toss my head against the cushion on a hard exhale. "You wear me out."

"I can wear you out if you like?" He grins, even though he can barely open his eyes.

He's on point tonight, and it takes everything inside me not to laugh. "Wow."

He lifts his hand, trying to stroke my hair, but instead, he ends up petting my cheek. "I'm sorry."

How many times will I hear that if I stay with him? I'm terrified that I'm setting myself up for a lifetime of apologies, a constant Tilt a 'Whirl of emotions, and while I know there's so very little about this that's ideal, I crave it. "You have to take better care of yourself."

"No." He halfway shakes his head. "I'm sorry I fucked you."

A stuttered breath catches in my lungs. He regrets what I long for. *This* is why I shouldn't have crossed that line because, just like the first time, I took it to mean something more.

"And now you hate me," he mumbles. "Please don't hate me. Just forget it happened. Then we can be Brandon and

possum again." He nods to himself. "Brandon and possum."
His brow wrinkles, and he looks so distressed that I have the
urge to smooth out the deep-set lines.

"I don't hate you," I whisper. "And we'll always be
Brandon and possum. Nothing can change that."

A flicker of a smile touches his lips but quickly fades, his
eyes going distant. "He would hate me."

"Damn it." I feel my chest tighten, not from anger, but
from how pathetic the two of us are. "Stop it. Just stop it. If
he were alive, we wouldn't be here, but we are. Connor's
gone." My words catch in my throat. My chest aches. "So
just..." I exhale and drop my chin to my chest. "*Stop.*"

"You know, he made me promise? We were in this shithole hut in the middle of the desert. There was a goat. And
bullets, lots of bullets. He made me promise him that if he
karked it, I'd look after you." He draws circles on my arm
with his fingers. "That goat was cool as shit."

"A goat..." I shake my head, and we sit in silence, each
staring off into nothing for a moment. "In his grave letter he
asked me to look after you. So, here we are, looking after
each other." I trail my fingertips along his jawline, and he
huffs a laugh.

"Of course he did. And that's exactly why Connor was
always so worthy of you."

Worthy of me like I'm some prize. I narrow my gaze.
"*Don't* say things like that."

"Okay."

I turn on the TV, and Brandon's head lands in my lap,
and we sit, me combing through his hair while we watch a
rerun. Just when I think Brandon's passed out, his fingers
grip at my shirt.

"Please don't leave me."

I lean over, placing my face right in front of his. "I'm not leaving you." I take a breath, warring with myself because I want to kiss him, but I can't manage the fallout. "Friends no matter what, remember? I promised."

"But I don't want to just be your friend." His finger brushes my bottom lip. "And I feel like a fucking arsehole for it."

44

BRANDON

My head is pounding, and my mouth tastes like something curled up and died in it. When the bed shifts beside me, I open my eyes and glance across at Poppy. Her back is to me, her small body covered in one of my over-sized T-shirts. Dark hair spills across the pillow, and the scent of her shampoo just manages to cut through the stench of whiskey on my breath.

I can't remember a thing past the fact that I came home and she was gone. I thought she had left, and I started drinking. Whatever this is between us, it's dangerous to me because it's so damn vital. I crawl out of bed and stumble into the shower. It feels like a marching band has taken up residence inside my head, and it hurts to think, which is... inconvenient given the tornado of thoughts whirling through my brain.

By the time I get out of the shower, Poppy's up and moving around the kitchen. I throw on a pair of tracksuit bottoms and brace myself before I go into the kitchen. As soon as her eyes crash into mine, a painful squeeze takes over my chest.

"Hey," I mumble.

Clasping a mug of coffee in both hands, she asks, "How's your head?"

"Been better."

She pours me a cup and grabs the whiskey from the cupboard, dumping in a shot. She's learning.

"Ah, the hair of the dog."

Her brow wrinkles. "Hair of what?"

I snort. "And you call yourself Irish, woman." I pick up the mug and swallow a mouthful of hot liquid.

She rolls her eyes. "I'm not Irish."

"Oh, I know." I smirk. "Measch."

She narrows her eyes at me, tossing out some playful banter. "At least I'm not a pikey."

"Don't pretend you don't have a thing for pikey lads," I say, cocking an eyebrow. "You were always hanging around the camp."

A soft smile touches her lips, and she ducks her head. "Did you never realize I was in love with you for all those years, Brandon?" Her question takes me by surprise, and what feels like a lead weight settles on my chest.

"Don't say that," I whisper, squeezing my eyes shut and gripping the edge of the kitchen island.

"Answer me."

"He loved you. And that was all that mattered."

"And I loved you first. And for years, that was all that mattered to me."

I slam my palm over the worktop. "Fuck, Poppy. What do you want me to say? Yes, I knew you had a crush on me. Yes, I wanted you, but we were kids. I was no good. I *am* no good. Connor...he deserved you."

This has lingered between us for years, unspoken but ever-present. Connor buffered it because I would always put his happiness before my own. Every damn time. He was my brother, and I would have given him the world. This is the first time we've put a voice to the great, pink elephant that has always been just in the periphery.

"Is that what it was about?" Her face crumples for the briefest of moments. "What you thought we *deserved*?" Her jaw tics, and she pulls in a breath. "Because I'll tell you what I think I deserved. And that was to be loved by the boy I was in love with. To have him acknowledge that he took my virginity, for him to treat me like I was more than just a friend."

She makes me want something I shouldn't. She is hope, and hope is fatal to a guy like me. When it's gone, there's nothing left. And if we do this, one day she will leave, because I will break her the way I do everything and everyone. I'm just trying to prolong the inevitable, keep her at arm's length for as long as I possibly can. I drag a hand through my hair. "I would have destroyed you, Poppy."

"Do you not realize that you did anyway?" She shakes her head. "You did anyway."

"And Connor was there to wipe away the tears, to love you. Don't—" I clench my fists, a wave of anger gripping me in its clutches. "Don't diminish what you two had."

Her eyes quickly fill with tears, her cheeks turning a deep red. "Brandon, I loved him. I—"

"Doesn't sound like it." I know I'm a dick, but I can't stand the idea that Connor was nothing more than a stand-in, a band-aid to her heartbreak.

I barely see her move before her palm collides with my cheek. "Don't you dare. I loved you both!"

I move closer to her until I can feel her rapid breaths over my face. "You were supposed to love Connor more."

"Fuck you!" She shoves me away, then moves around me.

I grab her by the wrist, and she halts. "I won't watch you spiral down with me. You're all I have left." I speak the words, a broken confession.

She takes a step toward me, her expression angry. "You don't have a choice."

"Is that so?"

She grabs my shirt, jerking me toward her. "I love you. So no, there is no choice, Brandon."

My heart thuds unevenly in my chest, and that age-old longing creeps up. It's selfish and shitty, but I'm starting to lose sight of all the reasons I should stay away from Poppy. I cup her cheek, touching my forehead to hers. "There are only so many times I can do the selfless thing when it comes to you." I tilt my chin, brushing my lips across hers. I crave her like my own personal brand of crack. "It's always been you," I breathe the words I can't fight any longer.

I'm already trapped in my own personal war, and I need her beside me, not standing across the battle lines. I can't help but feel as though this was always inevitable—her and me. No matter how many women I screwed or how perfect Connor was for Poppy, this has always been a twisted form of fate. And I hate that.

For Connor, I hate that.

Poppy presses her small body against mine. My arms come around her waist, and damn, she feels like home.

———

IT'S A BIG FIGHT TONIGHT, and the pub is packed. The roar from the crowd is a constant in the background, and adrenaline fires though my veins. There's nothing quite like the fervor of a big fight. It's infectious.

Poppy sits on the metal bench to the side of the room, her leg bouncing and her arms folded over her chest.

I stare at her as I yank my shorts over my hips. Her bouncing stops, as those grey eyes linger on my bare torso. She slowly lifts her gaze to my face, and a blush touches her cheeks. It's so damn cute.

"You know I hate that you do this," she says, standing and walking over to me.

I smirk. "Easiest money I ever made, poss."

"Yeah, I'm pretty sure drug dealers make 'easy' money, too. Doesn't mean you should do it." She glares at me, and I can't help but see that little girl she once was, sulking because she didn't get her way. "I mean, if he beats your ass, fine, but don't let him hit you just because you like it. Don't be a Neanderthal, Brandon."

"It's manly. I'm just making him feel better about himself anyway."

"It's idiotic."

I grab her waist and pull her against me. "You concerned about the preservation of my dashing good looks?" I brush my lips across her jaw, placing a kiss below her ear.

It's strange being able to touch her. I've always loved her from afar. She was like the sun, beautiful and so unattainable. Now she's right in front of me, and I can't quite believe she won't burn me.

"I won't let him 'beat my ass,'" I say in a poor imitation of her American twang.

"Dick."

"Stay here." I kiss her forehead and walk away, heading to the exit. The second I open the door, the noise from outside becomes deafening: *Breaker, Breaker, Breaker.*

"You let him hit you, I'm flushing your weed down the

toilet," she shouts, her soft voice just carrying over the cries from the crowd.

I glance over my shoulder and wink at her before stepping through the door. I don't want her watching, out here amongst this lot. It's too distracting.

The audience presses all around me. The shouts and cheers rise like a crescendo, beer sloshing everywhere as they jostle against one another.

I slide between the ropes lining the ring. Larry is standing in the middle, microphone in hand as he riles up the crowd, encouraging them to bet more of their money.

"It's Brandon 'The Breaker' Blaine!"

The roar is insane, and I remain in the corner, my hands loose at my sides.

"He is undefeated, ladies and gents. A legend in this here ring." More cheers. "And fighting him tonight is a monster, a rebel, the undisputed bad boy of the professional middle-weight world, Ronnie 'Wreckage' Sanders!"

My opponent climbs through the ropes with his head held so high it makes me smile. The crowd boos him the way they do every outside contestant. The thing about The Pit, they support their own. And given that Larry loves to big up the whole ex-military shit, they're all about supporting Larry's guys. Of course, that means they bet on us, and that's no good, so Larry keeps trying to bring in bigger and badder fighters in an attempt to make some money.

Ronnie Sanders is just such a guy, banned from professional boxing because he half ripped a guy's ear off with his teeth. The guy clearly has no morals, and truthfully, that's how I like it.

Larry steps out, and then the bell rings. Ronnie grins as if he's about to slaughter me. When I'm here in this ring, everything outside of it ceases to exist. Something in me shifts, and I morph into nothing but raw aggression and lethal instinct, because, to be a fighter—a good fighter—you have to stop thinking and simply react.

I take the few steps towards him. His smile drops a fraction, eyes narrowing as he studies my approach. I feign left, and he lifts his guard, defending his face. I drive my fist into his gut hard enough that I know he'll be winded, but he takes the opportunity to swing at me. Usually, I'd stand here and take it; hell, I'd even be excited at the prospect of being smacked by a guy with his kind of reputation, but I force myself to think through the simple blood lust and remember Poppy's request.

I duck and pop up, pulling my fist back and using all the strength I have when I drive my fist into his temple. My knuckles crack under the pressure, and a dull ache explodes over my hand. He staggers back on his feet for a second before he goes to his knees in front of me and then falls like a felled tree.

The shouting and clapping explode around me. I glance to the side of the ring where Larry stands flanked by Finn and Kyan, and Larry looks pissed. Finn has a small smile on his face, and Kyan, well, he's got his arm around some blonde in a tight dress, staring at her cleavage.

When I step out of the ring, people part like I'm Moses and they're the Red Sea, scampering away as I make my way to the door in the corner. I grip the door handle, pause, and take a deep breath. It doesn't matter how calm I try to be, fighting does something to me, forces something primal and aggressive to the surface. My blood burns through my veins. I close my eyes for a second and try to force the rage back to that place where it sits, waiting to break free at the slightest provocation.

No sooner do I step into the small corridor than Poppy

appears in the doorway of the storeroom. Her eyes search my face, and I know she sees the bomb waiting to go off. It's here, when I'm in this place, that the line between reality and nightmare becomes so very thin. Being in that ring is a dulled down version of war. There are no bullets, and I'm not going to die, but it still brings out that reflexive survival instinct.

Poppy watches me for a moment as though she's unsure what to do next. "You okay?"

I nod stiffly. "Just...give me a second."

Her brows draw together as concern fills her eyes. She calls to the lost fragments of my soul that are buried in shadows so thick and black, I can barely see out.

I try to resist her, I do, but it's futile. Before I know it, I'm storming across the space that separates us. Her eyes widen, and she takes a trembling step back before my hands land on her waist, and my lips slam over hers. For a moment, her body stiffens, and then almost immediately softens. She's so trusting. Small hands wind around my neck as she submits to me completely. Everything about her washes over me, calming everything in its wake. She bridles the rage and calms the storm. When I lift her she parts her thighs, wrapping them around my hips as I press her to the wall. I trace my nose down the side of her throat, breathing her in like pure oxygen.

The door to the locker room cracks against the breeze-block wall, as Larry shoves his way inside. Poppy squirms away from me, and I drop her back onto the ground.

"What the hell was that shit out there, huh?" Larry's face is red, his eyes wild as he rounds the corner into the small room. "Shit like that ain't gonna win me no money, son. You pull stunts like that one, and no jackass is gonna fight you. Jesus."

I move Poppy behind me, blocking Larry's view of her. "I've told you before, old man, I fight the way I fight, and I win."

"And I've told you before that if you can't at least make it entertaining, I ain't got no need for you." His left eye twitches a little. "Shit-fire, I mean, I like you and all, but a business is a business." Rubbing his hand over the back of his neck, he sighs.

"I'm your best fighter, Larry. You know it. I know it. Half this crowd only came here for me, so take it or leave it."

"You may be my best fighter, only 'cause you're half looney as a fucking schizophrenic wombat, but shit, no one wants to watch you knock the bastard out first go."

"Plenty of illegal fight rings in London, Larry. I can walk into any one of them tomorrow. You just say the word." I don't want to be an arsehole. I like Larry. He gave me a means of making money and, to a degree, a sense of belonging that I hadn't felt in a long time, but I'm not a puppet. I'm not about to go in there and fight to orders. They may be illegal, but they sure as hell don't need to be fixed.

His expression falls blank. "None of those other places are gonna put up with your shit, boy. How many times have I had to drag your drunk ass outta your apartment and sober you up? How many times have I pulled you outta some bullshit bar fight before the cops got called and your AWOL ass really gets into trouble? You think anyone else is gonna put up with that mess?" His gaze falls behind me onto Poppy. "Besides her, huh?"

I take half a step forward and open my mouth to respond when Poppy shoulders past me and practically squares up to Larry. He stares down at her tiny frame, brows raised.

She glares at him. "*You* are part of his problem. Have you ever paid attention to how angry he is when he leaves? Maybe instead of dragging his drunk ass out of his flat to fight, you should have tried to send him to get help. Don't act like a martyr because you're not."

I stand here, unable to move or interfere.

"A martyr? Who said any—"

"If you cared about him, you would get him help."

"That's what the fighting's for to—"

"Oh, shut it with that bullshit, would you? Look at him." She points at me. "Does he look like you've helped him?"

"Poss, let me handle it," I pull her to my side.

She crosses her arms in front of her chest and taps her foot over the floor. "Oh, yes, by all means, go ahead, *Brandon*. Handle it."

"Take it or leave it, Larry," I say. "You want me to take a punch? Get better fighters." I pick up my bag and place an arm around Poppy's shoulders, basically dragging her from the room.

Damn, she's like a dog with a bone when she's mad. I haven't seen that side of her in so long, I'd almost forgotten it existed.

45

BRANDON

It's been months of being with Poppy, months where I've found some semblance of calm within my own personal anarchy, and although I've accepted the fact that life goes on and all you can do is try to slog your way through the shit the best you can, I still feel guilty.

Not a single morning goes by where I don't wake up next to her, knowing that it should be Connor.

I'm also painfully aware of the circumstances that I live in, and the fact that she's *willingly* joined me in it. She works during the day, and I fight at night. Every time I fight, that little switch inside me flips. Sometimes I like it. It serves as an outlet for the rage. Other times I loathe it. Poppy hates it. She hates the fighting, and she hates Larry simply because he owns the fight ring. But what she doesn't see is that without it, I really am good for nothing. It's the only thing I excel at anymore, and it pays the bills. It's not the fight that's the problem, it's the aftermath, the long moments where my mind dives into the violence and the blood lust. And it's in those times that I can't see Poppy clearly anymore. She slips into the background for a while, a secondary consideration to my desperate primal urges.

I'm sitting on the couch, holding a bag of frozen peas to my jaw when I hear her key in the lock. *Shit.* I shove the peas behind a sofa cushion just in time for her to walk in, two plastic bags stuffed with food in her hands.

"Hey." I get up and take the sacks from her, dumping them on the kitchen counter.

"Brandon?"

I don't turn around. "Yeah?" I take shit out of bags, shoving it in cupboards. Hell, I have no idea where this crap even goes.

She grabs my shoulder and turns me around, her gaze narrowing on my throbbing cheek. "Why Is your face red?"

"Fight," I say as a way of an explanation. I mean, shit, I *do* fight for a living.

Rolling her eyes, she opens the cabinet I just closed, takes the milk out, and then puts it in the fridge. "I don't know why you let Larry bully you into getting hit."

"I don't," I say defensively. The truth is, I *like* getting hit, and although things are so much better with Poppy in my life, I will *always* seek out that small punishment. I will *always* like the pain, which makes me a prick since I know it upsets her. "He took my advice, got a better fighter." I shrug.

She glares at me, those grey eyes of hers stormy as hell. "No one is a better fighter than you. Try again."

I take a step toward her, smiling as I wrap my arms around her waist. "Your faith in me is cute, but there is always *someone* better."

"Okay, so, he hit you? *You* let some other guy get the upper hand?"

I lift my shirt, showcasing the blossoming purple bruise where I *let* the fucker nail me in the kidney.

"Doubled me over and went for the face. The kid's got skills." I trail my fingers over her cheek, and her expression softens slightly. "You're sexy when you're mad." I smirk, leaning in to kiss her.

She covers my mouth with her hand. "You're lying to me, Brandon O'Kieffe."

"I'm not..." I mumble beneath her palm.

"You're not a skilled liar." She presses her hand harder over my mouth as she inches her face toward mine. "Your left eye is twitching. It *always* does that when you lie."

I tug her hand from my mouth. "Oh, I'm skilled at a lot of useful things." I cock a brow and kiss her neck—she lets me for all of two seconds.

"That's up for debate." She turns away, and I pick up the dishcloth, twisting it around in the air and flicking it at her arse. She yelps and backs away before taking off across the living room and down the hall toward the bedroom.

When I catch her, I grab her waist and toss her onto the bed. I brace my weight over her small body, feeling the warm rush of her breath over my jaw. Her face is flushed, a wide smile on her lips as she stares up at me.

"You're an ass," she says slightly winded.

"Don't pretend you don't like a little spanking." I grip her thighs, pulling them apart and settling between them.

I press my mouth to hers the way I've wanted to all day. And there it is, the calm, that feeling of something being so right it soothes your very soul. I just need my daily hit of Poppy, and I'll be okay. I kiss her until she's breathless, and then I sit up, pulling her with me until she's cradled in my lap. Her fingertips absentmindedly draw circles over my back, sweeping along the numb area where my scar starts.

"I have a surprise for you."

A smile inches over her lips. "I can only imagine."

"Sorry to say, it doesn't involve me naked."

I lean over, pushing her back as I reach for the bedside table. "Close your eyes. Open your hand."

She hesitates, arching one brow. "I swear to God, if it is a small animal or insect, I will have a heart attack and die."

"This is not primary school, and I'm not keeping a frog in the bedside table." I smirk. "Close your eyes."

She takes a deep breath, closes her eyes, and holds out her hand. I place the key in her palm. "Okay. Open your eyes."

She picks up the miniature stuffed-possum keychain, the key dangling. "Aww, a tiny stuffed rat to match your tattoo." She smiles. "What's the key for?"

"First, it's a possum. In both instances." I point at the keyring and then my chest.

Her eyes narrow with a glimmer of excitement hidden behind her lids. "Uh-huh."

"And the key is for our new flat."

The smile fades just a touch as her eyes fly back down to her palm. "New flat? "

"Don't pretend this place isn't a shithole." I watch her expression intently.

Honestly, I'm nervous. Poppy living here is, well, a friend helping a friend, I guess. Only we're not just friends anymore. Still, I'm basically making it official without even asking her.

Her eyes haven't moved away from the key in her hand. "*Our* flat?"

"Yep." I go for casual, attempting to hide my anxiety. "Unless you....you know, if you were planning on getting your own place." I shrug. "I could do with a new place anyway."

"No, it's great. It's really sweet of you."

I hiss a breath through my teeth. "Sweet?"

"My only place is with you, Brandon, and you know it."

"Good." I press my lips to the side of her neck "We move tomorrow."

She pulls back, eyes locking with mine. "How much deposit did you have to put down?"

"Six months' rent," I say, warily.

"How much is the rent?"

"Poss, I make more money off one fight than most people make in a month. Don't worry."

"It's not the money, well, I mean it is, but it's not that." Closing her eyes, she shakes her head. "You're not the same person after a fight. And I don't know how much longer you can..." she trails off, dropping her gaze to the worn carpet.

"How much longer I can what?" My heart rate ticks up. "Deal with your fucked-up fella?" I clench my fists as a wave of anger washes over me. Anyone but her. It can come out around anyone, but not Poppy.

She hesitates, and I can tell there's something she is tiptoeing around. "I just don't want anything to happen to you."

"What do you expect me to do, Poppy? I fight, and I make money. How is it any worse than getting paid to shoot people in a war zone?" It's the only thing I'm good for, the only thing I'm good *at*. I still have enough pride to earn money and pay my way, even if it *is* the pikey way.

"You're still *in* a warzone. And that's what scares me."

"I know. Trust me, I damn well know. But there's not a lot of opportunities for an AWOL soldier now, is there?"

Her head drops forward, sending hair spilling over her face. "I hate that you ever went into the army. Hate it."

"Can't change it. All I can do is survive." I get up and walk out of the room because I need a minute. This was supposed to be a good day. This was supposed to be a moment for us, something that would cement Poppy in my life more permanently. Now, it just feels like she'll up and leave at any moment. That she doesn't want to be permanent.

I go to the kitchen, and my hand lingers over the handle of the whiskey cupboard. After a solid thirty seconds of going back and forth in my head, I finally drop my hand and walk away, picking up my fingerless gloves. I take to the bag that's hanging in the corner. The heavy chain creaks against the ceiling hook each time my fist connects with the worn, bloodstained canvas.

"Brandon."

I pause and feel Poppy's finger graze my sides. Her palms slide over my bare stomach before her cheek presses against my back. I grip the bag and rest my forehead against it, breathing heavily.

"I'm sorry," she whispers. "And thank you."

I cover her hand with my own before turning to face her. Her arms fall to her sides. "I just want you to be happy." I sweep her hair behind her ear.

"And that's the sweetest thing you've ever said."

"How about, I love you?"

She smiles. "That goes without saying, now, doesn't it?"

"Getting cocky." I pull her close before kissing her to show just how much.

46

POPPY

JUNE 2015

Brandon lies sprawled out on the couch in our new apartment, glaring at Hope.

"What?" she says as she nudges an unpacked moving box out of the way with her foot. "It's bad luck not to have a housewarming party."

He cocks a brow at her, and she glances at me.

"I stick by the fact that he's a prick, Poppy." She points her finger at Brandon. "I mean, look at him. All sulking over a party."

He drags both hands down his face, tossing back his head on an exasperated groan. Hope mumbles something under her breath on her way to the kitchen, and Brandon looks up at me.

I shrug. "You know how she is."

"A pain in my arse."

I smile. "It's just some of the guys from The Pit. It'll be fun."

He grumbles and flops back on the couch, covering his face with a throw pillow. Hope pops a bottle of champagne, and Brandon jumps. Seconds later, she's shoving champagne flutes in our faces.

I take mine, but Brandon stumbles into the kitchen, coming back with his bottle of whiskey.

"Oh, Moet's not good enough for you, eh?" Hope says. "And, you know, I'm offended you drink that shite whiskey. What's wrong with McGrath Whiskey?"

"It's connected to you." He winks as he twists the cap from his bottle and takes a swig.

There's a knock on the door. Brandon mumbles a few swear words as he sets down the bottle and goes to open it.

Kyan and Finn are all huddled on the threshold. Brandon extends his arm, motioning them in. The second Kyann steps inside, he shoves a bottle of whiskey and a pink blob into Brandon's arm.

"From Larry." Kyan laughs, "Lars said there's no better gift than whiskey and a bald pussy." He snickers again, and Finn just shakes his head.

"A cat?" Brandon turns around, holding a little pink kitten with the tiniest tuft of orange hair in the middle of his head. His big yellow eyes dart around the room. He's the ugliest thing I've ever seen.

Hope steps forward and points at the cat. "What is that?"

"It's a pussy cat with no hair," Kyan says.

She gives Kyan an unimpressed expression. "It looks like it got into a fight with a lawnmower."

"Yeah, well, Madame Wrinkles got it on with one of the pikey cats out the back alley." He shrugs. "Poor little bastard is like a hairy, bald mix."

Brandon shakes his head. "I'm not keeping a cat." He places the kitten on the floor, and it backs up against his legs.

"Aw, it's well cute, what with its little patch of hair." Hope crouches down, clicking her tongue to call it over. The kitten unwarily makes its way over to her, and she scoops it up in her arms, then turns to me. "What are you going to name it?"

"It's not getting a name," Brandon says, grabbing his bottle of whiskey from the table.

She holds up the kitten, touching her nose to its face. "He who shall not be named. Ah, bless it."

Finn pats Brandon's back as he walks past him, pulling a vape pen from his pocket as he takes a seat on the edge of the couch.

"Okay, now everyone's here, along with newcomer, Voldemort." Hope hugs the kitten to her cheek.

"Oh, good," Brandon says with a clap. "She's attached to it. She can take it home."

"Get a drink; we're going to play a game." Hope grins, ignoring Brandon.

Brandon throws his head back against the sofa cushions. "We best have more whiskey in the house."

"Well, as always, he's a delight," Hope glares at Brandon and pulls out a long, black box from her purse.

I perch myself on Brandon's lap and run my fingers over the stubble on his jaw. "Be nice."

He scowls at me. "Fine. But we aren't keeping the cat."

"You know," Kyan says, "People pay like two grand for those hairless cats. Larry said they sold the other kittens for eight-hundred quid each, and they're not even purebreds."

"Well, shit. Somebody hand the little bastard his balls and get him on it," Brandon mumbles.

Hope opens the box and glances at Brandon with a smile. "It's called the game for horrible people. Right up your alley."

"Well, you are a soulless ginger. And you did bring it."

"You do realize if it's just pure fact, it's not an insult, you twat."

"The two of you are about to do my head in," I mumble. "Can we just play the game and have you two shut up?" I head to the kitchen and open the fridge while Hope explains the rules. I pop a few pizzas into the oven and pour myself another glass of champagne. By the time I get back into the living room, everyone is in a laughing fit.

"Okay." Brandon holds up a card with a smile. "'And the Academy Award for firing a rifle into the air while balls deep in a squealing hog goes to Mr. Clean, right behind you.'" He tosses the cards onto the table. "That one *has* to be the winner."

"Thank you," Kyan says, feigning a bow.

Brandon pats Finn on the shoulder. "Finn, 'Being a motherfucking sorcerer and mouth herpes' was a close second."

"What kind of game is this? Jesus."

Brandon glances up, smiling with Voldemort in his lap. "The game for horrible people, poss."

AUGUST 2015

"**I**'ll see you tomorrow, Doris."

Doris glances over the top of a patient file, her gaze drifting to Mr. Brighton, who is sitting on the other side of the room.

"I'm walking him down on my way out, don't worry."

"Mr. Grumpy."

"He's not that bad," I whisper, swatting her on the shoulder.

By the time I get on my coat, Mr. Brighton is holding the door open for me. "After you, love," he says with a smile before he glances at Doris. "Have a lovely weekend, you old winch."

"Same affection to you, you wanker."

He chuckles, and we head toward the front entrance.

"Any big plans for the weekend?" he asks.

"Not really."

"Ah, come on now. Lover boy's not got plans for you?"

I shrug. "Maybe." I'm the only nurse Mr. Brighton will see, and I don't mind.

Over the past few months, I've come to look forward to

his appointments. He tells me about his ex-wife and estranged children, about the war, and I tell him about Brandon. Sometimes I think I just want to have someone tell me Brandon's going to be okay.

Mr. Brighton pulls a cigarette from his coat pocket and lights it. "He's still fighting?"

"He says it's all he's good at."

He nods knowingly as he takes another drag from the cigarette. "You know, Poppy, Hollywood is a crock of shit." Smoke billows from his lips. "They paint this picture of war where it's all black and white, it's not. There are a million shades of gray in there." Another swift drag. "I've not met many soldiers who actually wanted to kill someone."

He's no longer looking at me, more like through me. It's the same fogged-over look Brandon gets when he talks about the war like it drags them right back to that desert and holds them hostage in their own head. So, I stand, waiting for Mr. Brighton to come back.

Squeezing his eyes closed, he lifts the cigarette to his lips, his hand shaking as he puffs away. "Killing a person, it screws with your head. It's not like in the movies, Poppy. Most of us aren't running out there in a battle cry with guns raised, bullets flying. Most of us, whether we'll admit it or not, are scared shitless. And those horrors we live day in and day out, they don't ever go away. They haunt you. They whisper to you in your sleep." He hesitates for a moment. "Sometimes, I think the guys who died were the lucky ones because they have peace, and that's a damn sight more than I can say for myself."

The hum of traffic on the road swirls around me. I know I should say something, but I'm at a loss.

He frowns. "I think the fighting doesn't matter much because the fighting's not the root cause of it, you know? He stops fighting, that war, those horrors," he taps his forefinger over his temple, "They'll still be there. Until he can learn how to ignore those ghosts clinging to his back, well..."

It feels like a stone just sank to the bottom of my stomach because it all sounds so hopeless.

"Hey, poss."

Mr. Brighton glances over my shoulder, and I turn around to find Brandon a few steps behind me, his hands shoved in his pockets.

I introduce the two men, and they shake hands, followed by an awkward silence.

Mr. Brighton clears his throat, locking his gaze on Brandon as he nods toward me. "Your Poppy is the ray of sunshine around here, you know it?"

Brandon smiles, and a cab pulls over to the curb. Mr. Brighton tosses the cigarette down before he clasps a hand over Brandon's shoulder. "You take care of her." Then he turns to me. "You've got a good heart, love. And I thank you for that."

"See you next week, Mr. Brighton," I say.

He waves as he climbs into the cab.

"He's my favorite," I tell Brandon as we walk down the sidewalk. "He reminds me of you."

48

BRANDON

We watch her patient take off in the cab, and then I take Poppy's hand and lead her down the steps to the subway.

"You know I can drive?" Poppy says.

I shake my head. "We're going into the city." London at rush hour...we'll be on the road for hours.

I can feel her eyes on me. The underground this time of day is a personal brand of hell for me, but I want to do this for her. I want to show her some kind of normalcy and be able to give her a life. That involves doing shit outside of the apartment. So, I grip her hand as we fight our way through the commuters and squeeze onto a packed tube.

I hate having people at my back, and tension grips my body as sweat trickles down my neck. Poppy subtly shifts, moving behind me and wrapping her arms around my waist. My gaze darts around at the people pressing in on us, and the second we reach our stop, I'm dragging her through the open doors. She never complains, simply jogs to keep up with me. When I reach the top of the steps, I take a deep breath as the tightness in my chest evaporates.

"Okay?" she asks.

I nod. "Yeah, come on. We'll be late."

"You still haven't told me what we're doing."

"That's generally what a surprise entails, you not knowing." I smirk at her.

We move through the crowded streets of central London until we're right by the river. The smell of silt, oil, and shit hang heavy in the air.

Poppy shoots me a funny look when I lead her toward the London Eye. "You, the guy who *refuses* to do, in your own words, touristy shit, are going to the London Eye?" She puts a palm to my forehead. "Have you fallen ill, babe?"

"Don't say I don't do romantic stuff for you." I lead her into the small ticket building and hand the guy behind the desk a piece of paper.

He glances over it and smiles wide. "Mr. West, follow me."

"Mr. West. So..." She suspiciously arches her brow at me. "Now you're Finn?"

"If the credit card fits."

The guy lifts a little rope that I think is supposed to make this look a bit VIP. We wait a moment as pods pass us one at a time. An empty pod pulls up, and he opens the door, sweeping his arm to the side. "All yours."

We step inside, and Poppy's eyes dart to the ice bucket and box of chocolates resting on the wooden bench in the center.

"Okay, now I know you must be ill."

I shrug. "You like this kind of shit."

"Well, aren't you romantic, *Mr. West*?"

"I'll be sure to pass that on to Finn." The pod starts to move, cruising at a snail's pace. I kind of wish the thing would pick up some g-force. It would make it more interesting.

She lifts the bottle of champagne from the ice and reads the label. "Going overboard a bit?" she says under her breath. The top comes out with a pop, and instead of pouring it into a glass, Poppy shrugs and drinks straight from the bottle.

"You always were a classy chick."

She eyes me. "Says the pikey because he knows what class is?"

"Hey, my ma had scatter cushions in that caravan. That's like a luxury, I'll have you know. The dog that was chained to it had a proper collar and everything. No bailing twine for Sean."

"I did love that dog." She laughs. "And I think your dog was the only one who actually had a name. If that's not high-class pikey, I don't know what is."

"Yeah, Ma loved Sean Connery." I grin.

She smiles. "This was sweet of you." She pushes up on her tiptoes to give me a kiss. A short kiss—after I just dropped over three hundred quid on this pod—and then she walks over to the glass, looking out over the dirty city as the sun drops behind the horizon.

I'm not one for a view, but then again, I could push her up against that glass and make this date really memorable. I place my hands on her hips, pulling her back against me. When I brush my lips over her neck, she tilts her head to the side. And I smile against her skin. My hand slips beneath the material of her top.

And then, she yanks away from me. "Really? This thing is nothing but windows."

"You just look so pretty standing there in the sunset." I smirk. "You'd look better naked though..."

"No." She draws away from me, and I step after her. "Brandon," she warns.

She backs up to the glass, and I cage her in, pressing my hands on either side of her head. "Possum," I breathe against her lips, waiting.

"You're an asshole."

"I'm just standing here, poss."

Her chin tips up a fraction, and she presses her lips against mine. I lift her onto the handrail that runs around the pod and step between her thighs.

She kisses me. "God, I hate you."

"Nah, babe. You love me. I mean, I did get you champagne."

"I love you, but I still hate you."

"Oh, you're mean today." I kiss her again, and she moans into my mouth.

"I want you," she whispers. "That's why I hate you."

"Done." I grab the bottom of my shirt and yank it over my head in two seconds flat. Getting it on, on the London Eye. I'm down.

Her eyes pop wide. "Put your shirt back on!"

"You sure about that, poss?" I whisper in her ear.

Her teeth tear at her bottom lip. "We'll go to jail."

"Or end up on PornHub..."

She buries her head in her hands, laughing. "We don't have enough time."

"You give me too much credit; you really do." I pull her off the railing and turn, laying her on the bench. I trail my fingers up her thigh, her breath hitching as I slowly lift the skirt of her dress.

"Brandon..."

So much for her "we don't have time."

WHEN WE'RE DONE, I check my watch. "Eight minutes to spare." I take the box of chocolates, remove the lid, and shovel a few truffles into my mouth. "You and chocolate make a good mix." I wink at her. "Want one?" I ask, holding out the box.

Sighing, she reaches in and grabs one, taking a small bite. "You're sweet, Brandon. Perverted, but sweet. I think I'll keep you."

"Is that your way of saying I'm good in the sack? Because you're welcome." I smirk and go to take another handful of chocolates, but they're all gone. "What the hell? Who puts only five chocolates in a box?"

"Dear God...it's not a box of Celebrations." She snatches the box away, staring inside before she chucks it to the floor. "I hope you throw up from that."

"That's not nice."

49

POPPY

Boats drift down the Thames, their lights shining from atop their mast. "I can't believe I let you do that to me on the London Eye." I tip back the bottle of cheap cider.

"*Let*?" He huffs a laugh. "I think you'll find my smooth moves were just too much for you." He takes a bite of his kebab, spreading garlic mayo and chili sauce all over his face.

"I can't believe you like those disgusting things. It's most likely some plague-riddled sewer rat they've skewered and fed to you for a few quid."

"It's man food."

"And it will give you man shits."

He bobs his head to the side. "Worth it. Anyway, that shit," he points at the bottle in my hand, "will give you the hangover from hell in the morning. How about I shotgun the toilet, you can hurl in the bath."

"Wow, and people swear chivalry is dead."

"Keep telling you I'm a class act."

I sigh because, sometimes, with Brandon, that's all I can

do. I shouldn't find his immaturity as endearing as I do, but I can't help myself.

He grabs a piece of meat and holds it up to my face. " Here. Try it."

I shrink away from the food he's dangling between his fingers. "I don't want any."

He shoves it in my face again. "Take a bite."

"Look, I don't want your nasty meat."

A slow grin works over his face. "Really?" he says, wiggling his eyebrows.

"Asshole."

"Seriously, though, you're missing out." He swipes the bottle of cider from me and takes a swig, shaking his head and squinting one eye like he's having a stroke. "Oh, God. That shit is like vinegar."

"Compliment the taste of rat, hmm?"

"No." He inhales and leans back on the bench. "You remember that time Connor drank a whole two-liter bottle of that on a dare?" He starts laughing, barely able to get the words out. "I thought he'd actually died. And *you* dared him."

"Look, I don't remember daring him..."

"If it had been anyone else, he would have said no, but he'd have walked on hot coals if you said it." He shakes his head, smiling.

"Bless him. Poor thing had to have his stomach pumped and everything."

"God did he bitch about it." Brandon rolls his eyes, but I can see the warm smile on his lips, the softness in his expression. I think he likes to remember the three of us growing up, the way we were before life became hard and cruel.

"*Why* were we all friends, anyway?" I ask. "All we ever

did was harass each other and get each other drunk."

"Eh, you were the half-breed, I was the pikey, and Connor was fat. Who else was going to hang out with us?"

"True." I smile and lean my head against his shoulder. "Who'd have ever thought me and you would end up in London?"

"If there's one thing I've learned, poss, it's that no matter where you go in the world, the places don't mean shit. It's the people. I'm glad you found me. I'm just sorry you had to lose everything to do it." He closes the plastic kebab tub and gets up, tossing it in the trash. He turns to me and holds out his hand. "Ready to go home?"

I nod and take his hand.

Little things like tonight, they're what make everything seem worth it. It's the way he makes me feel. The way he loves me, the "us" that has always swirled somewhere beneath the surface, that makes me know I would never let him walk away from me. No matter what.

———

WHEN I WAKE the next morning, the sun is much brighter than it should be for—I glance at the clock and sit straight up, then jump out of bed. "Shit!"

Brandon bolts up. "What!" He swipes his hand over his face before holding it to his chest. "Shit. Don't do that."

"I'm going to be late."

"So? No need to give me a coronary over it."

I dig through the piles of clean laundry I've yet to put away while Brandon rolls out of bed and staggers into the living room.

Once I've managed to make myself look halfway put together, I go to the kitchen. Brandon's standing at the counter, staring down at the box of two-day-old pizza. "Okay, you've got two choices here. Pizza or Coco Pops."

"I'm fine. Thanks, though."

He steps around the counter with a cup of coffee in his hand. "Coffee. No whiskey." He flashes a smile, and I push up on my tiptoes to kiss him.

His hand snakes around my neck as he sweeps his tongue over my bottom lip. I fight the urge to part my lips, and I somehow manage to pull away from him. "I'm late."

"And I'm horny, babe. We all got our issues." He scrapes his teeth over his bottom lip in a way that just shouldn't be allowed.

"Well. Save it, and I'll handle you when I get back."

"Possum..."

He takes a step toward me, and I hold a finger up. "Don't."

His smile is full of dirty promises as he takes my hand and yanks me closer. His lips skim just below my ear. "Just call in sick," he whispers, his hot breath tickling my neck. "We'll have a sex day. It's like a snow day, only better."

I melt into him for a second, nearly caving. He nips at my ear, and I playfully shove him away.

"I have to go. I'm already late." I snatch up my coat and rush to the door. "Love you."

When I turn around, he's leaning against the kitchen counter with Mort scooped up in his arms. I don't believe there can be a cuter sight than Brandon O'Kieffe clutching a tiny, bald kitten in his arms. "Love you, possum."

By the time I get to the clinic, I'm half an hour late, and I cringe when I walk through the doors. Doris is bent over, shoving patient charts into the filing cabinet.

"Sorry I'm late. I overslept." I throw my purse under the counter, drop my lunch by the mini-fridge, and I check the schedule. "I'll go get Mr. Brighton," I call out on my way to the waiting room.

But the only person out here is Mr. Williams. He smiles at me over his newspaper, and I smile back before shutting the door and heading back to the nurse's station.

I plop into the seat beside Doris. "Did you already take Mr. Brighton back?

"Mr. Brighton passed away last night." She stands and wraps her arms around me in a comforting embrace. "They just called."

A familiar sadness settles over me. "What? What happened, he was just..." He was just fine.

"He took his own life, dear."

I clutch at my tightening chest.

"It's a terrible thing when your own mind is your worst enemy. He's at peace now. At peace..."

The rest of the day is a blur. Patients come in and out, and all I can think about is Mr. Brighton and how he waved when I told him I would see him later. Did he know then?

After my shift, I sit on the tube, deep in thought, and by the time I get home, anxiety is crawling across my skin because what if. *What* if?

The apartment is quiet with no trace of Brandon or Mort when I drop my keys onto the kitchen counter.

"Hello?" My voice echoes around the empty apartment.

Nothing. I walk to the bedroom door and push it open to find Brandon and the cat both in the bed. One of Brandon's muscular arms is thrown over his face. The other is cradling the Mort against his side.

"Brandon?"

"Hmm?"

I sit on the edge of the mattress and rub his arm. "You feeling okay, babe?"

"Yeah." Mort struggles to free himself from beneath the weight of Brandon's arm, then walks over his stomach, purring like a little engine.

I place my hand against Brandon's forehead, but he's not warm. "Want to go get Chinese? I know how you love your crispy seaweed." I smile.

He moves his arm and drags his hand down his face, then rolls onto his side, turning his back to me. "No, I'm good."

The Brandon I left this morning and this Brandon are so vastly different. Mort bites my finger because I'm not petting him, so I swipe my hand over his head a few times before placing him on the floor. I do the only thing I know to do when Brandon is like this—lie down next to him, wrap my arms around his broad frame, and hold him.

"I love you," I whisper.

He remains silent, but reaches for me, placing my palm against his chest.

His heart beats steady under my hand, but there's a sadness radiating from him, and it tears me in two because there is nothing I can do to take this away.

We are never more alone than we are when we're trapped in our own minds. And Brandon—the place he's trapped, it's a place I could never begin to understand. He's not angry, he's drowning in sorrow, and I don't know which emotion is harder to witness. So, I just hold him, and he clings to my arm, not allowing me to let go.

We lie in silence, and eventually, his breaths grow shallow from sleep. I've almost lulled off when he violently tosses, throwing his arm. His head thrashes from side to side, and his face twists into a grimace.

I want to wake him, but I'm afraid to. "Brandon," I whisper.

His arm flies out to the side, swiping the lamp and the glass of water to the floor. Mort hisses, his bell tinkling as he runs from the room.

Brandon mumbles Connor's name in his sleep, and chill bumps scatter my skin.

He sits bolt upright in the bed, chest heaving as he pulls in deep breaths. His head whips to the side, and when his eyes fix on me, he relaxes. "Did I hurt you?"

Shaking my head, I rub a hand over his clammy chest, and he falls back against the mattress, his chest still heaving, and his skin clammy with sweat. "Bad dream?"

He nods.

"Tell me."

Inhaling, he turns to face me. "I can't." His eyes squeeze shut, and he swallows. "It's not the kind of shit you talk about."

I don't say anything, but when his eyes open and meet my gaze, he exhales again before he wraps an arm around my waist and pulls me down against his chest, placing a kiss on my forehead. "Go to sleep, poss."

I think of Mr. Brighton, of how he called the memories of the war ghosts. And I just want to know. "Tell me, Brandon. *Please.*"

"You don't want to know the details of how he died. It will run through your mind on repeat. Trust me."

I lay my head on his chest, listening to his heartbeat, like a caged animal desperate to get out. "I am stronger than you think," I say. "I accepted long ago that it was brutal." I pause, my gaze veering up to him for the briefest of moments. I feel like I'm invading some personal space of his, but I can't help it. "Did he suffer?"

"No. It was an IED. I don't even remember the bomb going off. I just remember waking up. The foxhound was on its side, everyone else was dead. I tried to save him, I tried, but he was already gone." His voice is a distant hum, disconnected as though he recalled a story he read in the paper. "The truck was leaking diesel, and, for a moment, I thought that if I just stayed there, just kept pressing on his chest, the whole thing would blow, and I wouldn't have to crawl out of that fucking truck and leave my best friend behind."

For a second, I feel like I'm suffocating with him. There are so many things I selfishly want to force out of him, but I won't. I just want the undue guilt he carries day in and day out to vanish. For all Connor meant to me, I know he meant so much more to Brandon. Connor was my love, but to Brandon, Connor was his salvation. "You did the right thing," I whisper. "You know that."

"There were four of us in that truck. Connor was the best person I knew, and he died while I survived. *How* is that right?" He inhales a ragged breath. "It's not fucking right."

"Some people, Brandon..." I fight the tears and the hurt, even though I want nothing more than to collapse and crumble. I want to wallow in this hurt with Brandon, but I can't allow myself. "Some people are too bright for this world."

He squeezes me tighter. "Yeah. He always was the golden boy."

50

POPPY

Every time I closed my eyes last night, my mind drifted to thoughts of Mr. Brighton, of how he smiled and called Doris a wench the last time I saw him. I wondered what dark place he must have been in for to death to seem enticing. For most people, life is a series of ups and downs, peaks and valleys—but when the valley is so damn bleak and dark, how long can a person survive there?

I'm afraid one day Brandon may get so low he'll never be able to come up again, like Mr. Brighton...because while Brandon wouldn't do something like that, that darkness would.

The coffee maker beeps, and I fill my cup to the brim just as the bedroom door creaks and Brandon shuffles out. Dark circles loom beneath his eyes, and I question how he can look so exhausted even though he slept most of the day yesterday.

"Morning," he mumbles as he steps in front of me and grabs a mug from the cabinet.

"Sleep good?"

"Yeah." He cups my cheek and presses a kiss against my hair before moving to the coffee machine. He pours creamer into his cup, followed, of course, with whiskey before he moves to the couch. "You sleep okay?"

"Yeah..."

Mort claws his way up the side of the sofa, crawls into Brandon's lap, and nudges his hand. Brandon sips his coffee, stroking the tiny tuft of fur on Mort's head while he stares off into the nothing, with a vacant glaze to his eyes. And I wonder, how would I know. How would I possibly know if Brandon had reached the point of no return? Anxiety creeps up my throat.

I sit on the edge of the sofa, petting Mort's back. "Brandon." I hesitate. I've always been able to talk to him, but something about this feels invasive, like I'm accusing him or degrading him. "I worry about you."

His eyes narrow, and he shoos Mort away. "There's nothing to worry about."

"The doctors at the clinic are really good with PTSD, and I just thought..."

He rubs a hand over his face, places his coffee on the table, then takes my mug from my hand, and sets it beside his. "Poss"—he drags me into his lap and tucks a loose strand of hair behind my ear—"You're everything I need."

"Brandon, stop." I move his hand away from my cheek, and he glares at me.

"I'm serious."

"You're the only one who can help me, poss. I don't know what you want from me."

But I can't help. I can't make things better for him, because sometimes, I'm just as lost as he is, and sometimes, I fear our sorrow threatens to drown us both. "Brandon, don't you see I can't fix you. I can't—"

"Fix me?" His eyes narrow, and his jaw clenches before he carefully shifts me off his lap and stands.

That came out differently than I meant it, and I stumble for words to backtrack, but he's already pacing.

"Is that what I am to you?" His body bristles with agitation, and his fists clench. "Something broken? Defective?"

"I didn't mean it like that." My heart pounds against my ribs. "I just meant—"

"I don't need you to fix *shit!*" He storms out of the room, and I drop my chin to my chest on a hard exhale.

I know that sounded like I think he's a broken toy that can be pieced back together, but that's not at all what I think. I'm terrified, worried that nothing will make this better and that all he'll do is continue to sink in the muck and mire of depression, and it makes me angry. It makes me angry that this is the life he's been given—*we've* been given. Nothing about it seems fair. I follow him into the hallway. "You don't need to be fixed; you need help. *We* need help."

"There is *no* helping this!" His voice booms off the walls, and I flinch. "There is no fucking cure. No *fix*. This is survival, one day at a time. You knew what you were getting, Poppy." He spreads his arms wide as a mocking laugh slips from his lips. "Is it everything you hoped it would be?"

That dig stings, and it brings angry blood rushing to my cheeks. From the age of ten, I had hoped for so much more for us, for Connor. "Nothing in my life has ever been everything I hoped it would be. But the way you were yesterday—"

"It was Connor's fucking birthday yesterday!" he shouts, then slaps a palm over the wall, and my thoughts come to an abrupt halt, my lungs seizing.

I forgot him. I was so consumed with running late and Brandon and Mr. Brighton, so worried about my life as it is now, that I forgot someone I promised I never would, and this is where my strength gives out.

Burying my face in my hands, I sink to the floor. This time, I don't try to stop the tears from falling.

"I'm sorry," I whisper. To Brandon and Connor. "I forgot." A fresh wave of pain grips my heart in its clutches.

Brandon crouches in front of me, swiping his thumbs below my eyes to dry my tears before he pulls me to his chest, cocooning me in his warmth. "It's all right."

But it's not. I want to throw things and punch things. I want to destroy something until it's as ugly and battered as I feel—but, instead, I cling to him.

"I love you," he mumbles against my hair.

When I fall to pieces, he is the only thing that keeps me from completely breaking.

51

BRANDON

OCTOBER 2015

I step into the ring and crack my neck from side to side. Josh Harmon grins before he blows me a kiss.

"I'm gonna break that pretty little face of yours," he says. His eyes are blown wide, pupils nothing more than pinpricks, and his hands twitch in agitation as he bounces on his feet.

Brilliant. I tell Larry to step it up, and he brings me some gear-jacked thug.

I don't respond to his jeers, but I do allow the rage to swirl and build like a thick cloud until it swamps me, wrapping me in its tendrils.

The sound of Larry's voice becomes a distant hum, as if I'm underwater, removed from the situation rather than at the center of it. And then, the bell dings and everything snaps back into place in an instant: the roar of the crowd, the smell of sweat, beer, and cigarettes. And the rage—it punches against my skin like a rabid animal waiting to get out.

Harmon comes at me like a train, fists swinging. He instantly tries to step inside and block my leg with his. It's a dirty move, and in any normal fight, an illegal one. I swerve to avoid his trip and catch the end of his swing, only a glancing blow, but enough to split my lip.

I pause, swiping my fingertips over the tiny cut and smiling when my hand comes away bloody. He comes at me again. Whatever he's on must be some good shit because he's lightning-fast, but even with his speed, I still nail him twice in the face. It doesn't faze him.

He takes another swing. His fist barely brushes past my side, but I wince at the sting that breaks out over my skin. When I glance down, I notice three bright red lines stretching across my ribs. Blood wells up and spills down my side, and the crowd erupts. Some booing, some cheering.

Larry shoves his way into the ring, closely followed by Kyan. "Time!" he shouts. "Disqualified for breach of conduct."

Harmon throws his head back and laughs as he lifts his hand. The light glints from the razor blades the bastard has in his wraps.

Larry and Kyan step in front of him.

"Protecting your boy?" Harmon says. "I would have destroyed him."

I snarl and step forward, but Finn is in front of me in a second. Harmon grins, spits on the floor, and steps out of the ring.

"We both know you would have had the fucking junkie," Finn says.

He never swears, and I can practically feel the tension hammering off him. His anger may be controlled, but all it does is feed my own. I shove away from him and pace the ring a few times, clenching and releasing my fists. My ribs sting. Blood trickles down my side, mixing with sweat.

Larry stops me, placing his hand on my side as he inspects the damage. "Go get cleaned up," he says, studying my face closely. "Finn, go with him. Get him some first aid, and do *not* let him out."

By the time I'm back in the storeroom, I'm murderous. My skin itches and anger crawls over me like ants. Finn sits on the metal bench in the middle of the room with a small first aid kit in his lap. Although seemingly calm, his knee jerks repeatedly in my peripheral, and his agitation makes me nervous. Too much time in a battle zone will get you like that. When you live, work, and kill beside other guys, you feed off their emotions. If one of them suddenly becomes tense, you best assume you're about to get a bullet in your arse. In a way, you become like a pack of animals, each looking at the others for behavioral cues, and his anger is only setting light to my own, stoking it and stirring the flames higher.

"Finn, you need to go," I say through clenched teeth.

"Larry told me—"

"Look, you're pissed, and it's not helping me." I clench my fists and squeeze my eyes closed. I hate feeling this out of control, a slave to this aggression.

He hesitates for a second, then nods, gets up, and leaves the room. The second he does, I slam my fist into one of the metal lockers. The skin at my ribs pulls with the movement, and I place my hand over it. Blood slicks my palm. "Fuck!" I roar, jumping when the door to the storeroom slams against the wall.

Poppy's gaze skims my side, and she shakes her head. Inhaling, she takes the first aid kit from the bench and begins rummaging through it.

"I'm fine," I say.

"You're bleeding." She kneels in front of me, swatting my

arm away from my side so she can inspect the cut. "I don't think you need stitches, at least." A line sinks between her brows, and her lips press into an angry little line. "You should have knocked his teeth down his throat."

It's so cute that the anger in me ebbs slightly.

"I would have if Larry weren't such a pussy about it."

She fiddles with a bandage. "I mean, what did he hope to accomplish by swiping you with a razor?"

I concentrate on a spot on the wall while she tapes the dressing in place. I count to a hundred in my head and focus on breathing. In and out. I allow the pleasant scent of Poppy's perfume to drown out the smell of blood and sweat and violence.

Her fingers trail over my cheek, and I blink, staring down at her. The little frown line is still there.

"Stop worrying, Poppy."

She scowls at me. "I didn't realize that you getting shanked by some filthy asshole—in an underground, illegal fight pit—was something I shouldn't be worried about."

"Babe, it's a scratch. I did not get shanked." I can't help but smile at that.

"Don't try to downplay this, Brandon."

I lift my hand and sweep the hair from her face, tucking it behind her ear.

Her eyes flutter closed, and she swallows. "I hate this," she whispers.

I press my lips against her forehead, then throw on my shirt and hoodie. "Let's go."

As soon as we step outside the storeroom, I spot Finn lingering against the back wall. Hope is with him, no doubt chewing off his ear about some pointless bullshit. The second he spots me, he crosses the room, Hope trailing behind.

The crowd in The Pit is still thick, and if anything, the blood has only riled them even more for Kyan's fight. I throw my arm around Poppy's shoulder and pull her tight to my side as we all make our way to the exit and into the alley. The door bangs shut behind us, wrapping the cold air and the smell of rotting food and piss wraps around me

"Let's go play some Bingo," Hope says.

I swear that girl is completely oblivious to anything that goes on.

Poppy exhales, obviously still agitated. "I'm not in the mood for Bingo, Hope."

"Suit yourself. Finn, you want to go with me? It's great. You win neck massagers and—" Hope snaps her fingers beside Finn's ear. "Hello?"

But his eyes are aimed at a point in the alley, his posture tense. It's when he tugs Hope behind him that every instinct I have jumps to attention.

I step in front of Poppy and stand beside him just as a group of guys step out from the shadows and underneath the dim, orange glow of the streetlight. Josh Harmon stands in the center of his friends, who all look every bit as thuggish as him. Harmon's lip is split, and although his right eye is swelling shut, I can still see the rage swimming in his expression. I crack my neck to the side and tighten my fists.

"Poppy, go back inside," I say, through clenched teeth, fighting to keep control of myself until she leaves.

"No." Harmon leers, attempting to peek around me. "Stay, sweetheart."

"Don't talk to her." I'm shaking as I attempt to hold back the wall of pain I'm ready to inflict on him. I can feel the tension bristling from Finn at my side.

Harmon laughs, and his friends join in like a pack of

well-trained dogs. "I'm going to beat your arse in front of your little whore girlfriend."

That's it. I fall on him like a damn building.

My fist slams the side of his face three times before one of his friends jabs me in the kidney. Something in me delights at the challenge of taking on every one of them, and my little demon rises to the occasion, basking in the raw violence.

I beat the shit out of the pair of them, nailing my knuckles against flesh and bone over and over until blood coats my hands. I'm so consumed, so blinded by the sole purpose of destroying the guy in front of me, that I'm only vaguely aware of the other two, out cold on the floor—courtesy of Finn.

Now it's just Harmon and me. My fist and his face.

"Brandon," Poppy shouts. "Stop it! Brandon." I hear her, but nothing registers. "Finn, make him stop. He's going to kill him!"

"Nothing he doesn't deserve," Finn's voice is laced with the same kind of darkness that's roaring through my head.

I hit Harmon until my arm aches and his face is a bloody mess.

"Brandon, please," Poppy's voice hitches on a sob, and I wish I could go to her, but I can't make myself stop.

Something brushes over my arm, hands grabbing at me, and I swing, and at the last second, I realize that it's Poppy. I pull back the force of my punch, but it's too late. My fist collides with her jaw. She crashes against the concrete, and time stands still. The anger vanishes, and all that's left is the horror of what I've just done.

She's sprawled out on the filthy ground with her hand to her mouth, blood trickling from her lip. Finn and Hope rush over to help her.

"Poppy..." I start, and Hope charges me.

Her hand meets my cheek with a resounding clap. "You're a head case." She points a finger in my face. "You stay the hell away from her."

"Poppy, I'm so sorry," I whisper.

She won't look at me, and that breaks me. I feel like all I ever do is apologize to her.

Hope stands like a guard dog, her expression fierce when I take a step forward. "Don't you dare."

Usually, I'd argue with her, but I'm too ashamed of myself right now. I drag both hands through my hair and tilt my head back. "Please, look after her."

Hope turns on her heel with a flick of her red hair and leads Poppy out of sight. Finn lingers, tentatively casting glances at me.

I look at the unconscious bodies littering the alleyway. This is what I do. This is what I'm capable of, and I've never given a care—until Poppy stepped into the middle of it.

———

MY MIND and body have gone completely numb, and, by the time I arrive at Finn's place, I can't even remember getting here.

"Here." Finn comes from the kitchen, a beer in one hand and an ice pack in the other. He tosses me the ice pack and points at my hand. I glance down at my ripped and bloody knuckles, and all I see is them coming into contact with Poppy's beautiful face.

"I need to go to her." I start to get up, but he places a hand on my shoulder.

"Just let Hope deal with her for now." He places an

unopened beer on the coffee table, then takes a seat next to me.

"They were just there, and she was there, and I lost my shit. I would never hurt her." But I did. I did hurt her.

Finn sips his beer. "I know. It was an accident."

My mind races in a whirlwind of guilt and horror while I stare numbly at the wall.

Eventually, Finn goes to bed, and I grab my phone, staring at the blank screen before I pull up Poppy's name. It goes straight to voicemail, so I text her:

Me: Possum, I'm so sorry. Please forgive me. I love you.

I wait and wait but get no response. My heart pounds in my chest as a very real fear eats away at me. *She's going to leave me.* She's going to leave, and then what? She's everything, and without her, it's all completely pointless. She's the one person I cannot bear to hurt.

I finish one beer, then another. I go from not wanting Poppy to leave to realizing, maybe she *should*. I think about the times I've hurt her—from things as stupid as the Barbie doll to parading girls in front of her when I was a teenager, thinking it would make her realize she deserved better. I took her virginity, then avoided her for months, not to mention, that was a secret we both kept from Connor...I left Connor. I left her, and now this—bringing her right down with me. I'm a disaster waiting to happen, a ticking bomb, and she's strapped right in with me just, awaiting the inevitable bang.

She is my peace, but I just saw that even she can't quiet this demon inside me, which is why I decide to do the selfless thing for once in my shitty life. I don't want her forgiveness, I just want her to be happy and loved and safe. I will only hurt her, and that's not what love should be. So, I'll let her go.

    Me: I don't deserve your forgiveness, and I can't live with myself, knowing I've hurt you. Just know that I love you, always.

52

POPPY

H ope takes away the icepack that's been on my face for the past thirty minutes, then tosses it into the sink. "This is what I was talking about. He's messed up, Poppy."

"That wasn't Brandon," I mumble.

"No, Poppy, it *was* Brandon." With a shake of her head, she pushes away from the counter and comes to sit next to me on the sofa. "He's..."

"He didn't know what he was doing." And that, I believe. "It was a reaction. I shouldn't have tried to stop him. I should have just..." My mind jumbles with excuses, but I can't help but wonder, am I justifying this too much? I love him, but am I trying to make something work that has no business working?

"Did he mean to hit you? No, but did he? Yes." Hope places her hand on my knee. "He needs help, and you know it. Poppy, you work with these blokes day in and day out. You know what war can do to someone."

What war can do to someone. War is death on so many levels, a poison that seeps through a person's veins and never lets them go. It took Connor's life, and, on some days, Brandon is like a zombie, always haunted by the memories; the cruelty and gore. War sentenced him to hell, and so it sentenced me right along with him.

"Poppy, I know you want to help him, but at what cost to yourself? You can't just—"

"I can do whatever I want. It's my life." And it's a mess. One I don't want to discuss.

Hope gives a curt nod before she pushes off the couch and goes back to the kitchen.

I drag a hand over my face. I shouldn't be mad at her, but my emotions are so on edge. I'm still confused. "I'm sorry," I say on my way to the hall. "I just. I think I need sleep."

"I understand, Poppy. I do."

I close the door to Hope's spare room, dragging in an uneasy breath as I pass by the dresser and make a conscious effort to avoid my reflection. I'm in love with a man I've known my entire life, who houses darkness no light will ever find its way into. That part of him was created to survive, but now, I worry about how he will survive himself.

———

THE NEXT MORNING, I wake with a sore face and a mind full of questions: Do I go home and pretend everything is okay? Do I leave him? But what kind of person would leave someone they love when they are at their darkest?

Hope and I go to The Cozy Club for breakfast, and much to her displeasure, I decide to go home.

The second I step into the bedroom, Brandon's gaze snaps to mine, then falls to my cheek, his jaw tightening before his head drops forward. "I'm so sorry."

There's a gym bag on the bed with piles of folded clothes around it. "Where are you going?"

"Away."

"Away where?"

When he finally lifts his gaze to mine, there's a distance in his eyes that I don't like. "We're done, Poppy." He shoves clothes into the bag. "The flat is paid up for the next six months, and all the bills are covered."

Shock ripples through me. He's leaving me?

With each passing second, every new article of clothing he packs away, the worry and fear and confusion are swallowed by anger and hurt.

My fists clench, my jaw tightens, then I grab a stack of T-shirts and hurl them across the room. "Fuck you!" I take a pair of jeans and chuck them at him, then the bag. "You don't get to give up that easy!"

He hasn't budged or said a word, he won't even look me in the eye, so I shove my hands against his chest and push him as hard as I can.

"Did you hear me, Brandon? You don't get to give up that easy!"

Seconds tick by before he closes the space between us and pulls me against him. I fight his grip, but his thick arms pin me in place, making me feel unbearably broken in his arms.

"I hate you," I breathe against his chest.

"You should."

My fingers fist his shirt. The thought of letting him go terrifies me. There is so much that's wrong between us, an ocean of loss and heartbreak, anger and sorrow, but I need him. I've needed him since I was ten years old. "Please," I beg. "Don't do this."

A small frown line sinks between his brows while he

cups my face, tilting my head back until our eyes meet. "I love you, Poppy. But I hurt you, and sooner or later, I'll do it again. Sometimes love is about sacrifice."

But it's my heart that's being put on an altar, and that doesn't seem fair.

"I told you once that I would destroy you." His thumb brushes my bruised cheek, sending a twinge of pain across my jaw. "I'll give everything I have not to."

He kisses my forehead before grabbing the bag from the floor and zipping it, then he walks out of the room without a backward glance.

After everything we've been through, he thinks he gets to just walk out? All of my life, Brandon has tried to decide what I do and don't deserve, and I'm not letting him this time. He thinks his leaving will somehow save me when all it will do is inevitably destroy me. Rage bubbles to the surface, sending my pulse into overdrive.

"You quit. *Everything*!" I storm after him, swiping at tears. "You quit the army, and Connor, and now me."

He stops midstride and whirls around with clenched fists, to face me. "How can you want this, Poppy?"

"I don't want *this*." I take his hand, fighting the sob lodged in my throat. "I just want you."

"Last night." He yanks his hand from mine. "That *is* what I am. A ticking fucking time bomb, and babe, you can hate me all you like, I don't care." He reaches for the door again.

"You don't just walk away from something like we have."

"I'm doing it for you."

"Don't you *dare* say you are doing this for me." I fight the emotions crawling and scratching their way up my throat. "You're doing it for yourself."

His chin drops to his chest, and he rests his forehead against the back of the door.

"You could get help, Brandon."

His palm slams onto the door, and he spins around, dropping his bag before he storms toward me. "This can't be fixed! It will always be there. I'm trapped in my own damn head. Day in day out, and when I close my eyes, do you know what I see?" His face morphs into something hard and vicious, his voice rising with each word. "I see Connor's dead eyes staring at me. I try so damn hard to bring him back. And every. Fucking. Night. He dies. Tell me, can they delete that memory? Pull it out of my head?" He taps at his temple, jaw set, and tears welling in his eyes, and I'm left speechless because no amount of my loving him will ever erase that from his mind.

"No, they can't take that away," I say. "But there's so much more to life than that piece of hell you constantly live in."

His eyes shut on a hard breath. "There *is* more, Poppy. It's you. And I want more for you—" he gestures between us —"than this."

And with that, he opens the door, and he leaves me.

53

BRANDON

I lean back in the office chair, staring across the desk at Dr. Watson. She's in her late thirties with a sharp, blond bob that screams, "speak to the manager." Propping her elbows on the desk, she stares down the length of her nose at the paperwork in front of her.

I sigh impatiently and fold my arms over my chest, wishing I hadn't turned myself in. This is proving to be bullshit.

Finally, she looks up at me, a small smile touching her lips. "It's been almost two years since you deserted, Mr. O'Kieffe."

"Well done. You read my file," I say through clenched teeth. I don't like the word desert. It implies that I left people who were relying on me, and I didn't.

"Well, that's my job." Her fingers drum over the table. "Why did you leave your post?"

"My post was at my best friend's side." My chest tightens with a pain so old and engrained you'd think I would be used to it by now. "He died. Job done," I grate out.

"I understand it must have been hard to witness your

friend pass away, but your job was with the military. Again, why did you leave?"

I snort, plastering a smirk on my face as I lean forward. "I have no loyalty to the army. It's never done shit for me." I watch her watch me.

"Why have you turned yourself in?"

"I have my reasons."

"You're good at avoiding questions, aren't you?"

"Honestly, I'm just going through the motions. So why don't you just sign whatever you need to sign, and I can get out of this shithole."

"It's not that easy, Mr. O'Kieffe. You need to understand, you committed a crime, and while I'm here to help you, I need to understand why you left, why you've turned yourself in."

"I don't know why I left." I shrug one shoulder. "Vehicle blew up, everyone died except me. I got out, and I started walking, and I didn't stop." *Until now, until her.*

She jots down something on her notepad. "Do you have trouble sleeping—nightmares, flashbacks?"

I frown as I remember waking up with my arm pinned across Poppy's throat. I nod.

"How do you handle those?"

I huff a laugh. "You tell me."

She nods. My leg keeps bouncing. I just want to get this shit over with and get out of here. I don't need her psycho-analyzing everything—things no bloody degree can give you a clue about. She can't help me. There's only one person who can help me, and I left her to come here. I swipe my hands down my face.

The doctor opens her desk drawer and pulls out a sheet of paper. She hands it to me along with a pen. "I want you to answer these questions based on your feelings over the past three months as best you can."

I don't take it; instead, I just glare at her.

"Brandon, I need you to answer these so I can help you."

I take the piece of paper and pen, glancing over the questions. *Do you feel on edge? Do you feel worthless?* Sighing, I toss the paper back onto her desk. "This is a waste of time."

"Not many people willingly walk in here two *years* after they've deserted, so why, if you aren't going to cooperate, are you here?"

I drag both hands through my hair and sigh. My heart thumps heavily in my chest, and I almost don't want to talk about Poppy, as though she's my crippling weakness. "I'm tired of running. Tired of flying under the radar."

"Okay." She leans over her desk and pushes the paper back toward me. "Then fill this out."

Fuck my life. I take her paper and tick no to every single one of her questions, then push it back across the desk. "See, I'm fine."

"Being a smartass will get you nowhere, Mr. O'Kieffe." She sighs. Again. She does an awful lot of that.

"Look, I turned myself in. Willingly walked through the damn gates. What more do you people want from me?"

"I understand that, but what I'm afraid you don't understand is that unless I can document what your reason for leaving your post was, you may very well end up in jail. Depending on whether you were someone who was tired of being at war or someone who has suffered severe mental trauma, the punishment the military sees fit varies." She arches a brow. "Greatly."

I place my palms flat on her desk, clenching my jaw so hard it hurts. "With all due respect, *doctor*, until you have been in a war zone, until you have watched the only brother you ever had die, you can't help me. Your books don't even come close. The only person who can help me is beyond these walls, so just do whatever you need to do. Let me serve my time, so I can get back to her."

"I'm doing what I need to do." She opens the drawer again, pulling out another one of those damn questionnaires. "You do what I need you to do, and I'll make sure you get back to her as soon as possible."

"Fine." I go over her questions, answering them *almost* truthfully.

———

IT'S BEEN over a week since I've seen Poppy, and the second I lay eyes on her, it's like I can breathe properly again.

She sits at a small table next to the window in the visiting room, her gaze trained on the world outside. Her teeth gnaw at her bottom lip, and I can practically feel the anxiety rolling off her from here.

"Hey," I say, taking a seat opposite her.

"Why didn't you tell me?" Her voice is shaking, her eyes turbulent.

Taking one of her balled up fists into my hand, I smooth her fingers out and brush my lips over her knuckles.

She snatches her hand away and glares at me. "Don't try to charm me, Brandon. Answer my fucking question."

I have to stifle a laugh because damn she has a dirty mouth when she's pissed. "Didn't Finn explain this?" It was shitty of me to leave it to Finn to tell her, but I knew she'd fight me.

"Are you serious right now? I didn't want *Finn* to explain it to me." She stands and snatches her purse from the table.

Pushing to my feet, I grab her wrist and yank her

towards me. We collide before my lips slam over hers. Her body goes rigid, and then she softens and becomes pliant in my arms.

When my heartbeat slows and my mind calms, I pull away, resting my forehead against hers. "Please don't go," I breathe, stroking over her cheek.

"Sometimes, I hate you." She sighs. "You should've told me."

"You wouldn't have let me do it, and I needed to, poss. For us." I force myself to step away from her and sit down. "This might be the only time in my life that I actually made the right decision. Don't hate me for it."

She falls into the chair across from me, her shoulders sagging with defeat. "How long do you have to stay here?"

"No idea. It all depends on what the shrink says."

"Oh God, I'm sure the doctor is having a field day with you."

"I don't think she likes me."

"You better not be an asshole to her." Poppy gives me a stern look. "You've been an asshole, haven't you?"

"I'm a delight!"

"Great, they'll never let you out in that case. You know..." Her gaze falls to her lap, and she begins fidgeting with a loose string on her sweater. "I talked to Fergus, one of the military guys at work. He said that since you have PTSD, they should let you go as long as you agree to treatment."

"Who the hell is Fergus?" I scowl across the table. What kind of stupid name is Fergus? "He sounds like a prick."

Throwing her head back, she groans and drags a hand down her face. "That's all you heard? He's one of the guys that rotate through Headley Court. He gave me some books on PTSD to help me—"

"Yeah, I'm sure that's what he was doing, *helping* you."

She rolls her eyes. "Stop. Focus on the issue at hand. PTSD."

"I don't have PTSD. The army just wants to stamp my forehead and move along."

Poppy looks at me like an abandoned puppy on one of those TV adverts. "It's not a bad thing to have," she says. "You can't help it, Brandon."

I tilt my head back, focusing on the harsh fluorescent lights above me. "Possum..."

"For me. Just be honest with her; let her help you. *Please*."

I swear to God, I should just hand her my balls for safe-keeping. I've almost finished growing my vagina anyway. "Fine," I huff, meeting her gaze.

A smile lights up her face, and she leans across the table, placing a chaste kiss on my lips. I reach for her, but she backs up quickly. Letting out a groan, I grip the edge of the table. A week without her, and I'm feeling particularly uptight.

"I have to go, or I'll miss my train, but I love you."

We both stand, and I pull her close. I inhale the scent of her perfume deep into my lungs. "I love you."

54

BRANDON

NOVEMBER 2015

I turned myself in, fully expecting to spend months, if not years locked up for going AWOL.

I didn't go to prison, though, because I was diagnosed with post-traumatic stress disorder. There, I admitted it to myself. It feels cliché and whiny, a blanket diagnosis for every guy who has demons. But whatever it is, it is real.

The rage is real, and according to the doctor, it always will be. This is permanent, an altered aspect of my personality that I now have to live with. It seems daunting and damn right depressing, but I have Poppy. I have a reason to fight this, a reason to be better.

I scowl at the reflection in the full-length mirror. This is what normal life looks like apparently, a twat in grey polyester trousers that clearly were not made for a guy of my build. I'm going to have thigh chaff within the hour. I leave the bedroom, and Mort runs over, his bell tinkling with every step. I scoop him up, stroking the little ginger tuft on his head and I think how he looks like one of those troll toys that Poppy used to collect when she was a kid.

In the kitchen, I find Poppy singing along to a song on the radio. Her tiny body is swamped by one of my T-shirts.

"Good morning." Her gaze sweeps over me, and her smile deepens. "You look really hot in that uniform." She bites down on her lip before grabbing my tie and yanking me down for a quick kiss.

"You're a bad liar," I say with a glare.

"Are you excited about your first day?"

She looks so hopeful, but seriously, who the hell sits down and thinks: My grand ambition in life is to be a security guard? No one. "Sure."

"Your work isn't far from mine, maybe we could do lunch?"

"Sure, poss."

Since I got home, I can see this sense of hope in her eyes. As if everything will be okay, and maybe, just maybe I'm fixed. Hope is such a tenuous, yet powerful emotion, and I haven't felt it in a long time. So, I smile. I allow her hope to infect me because perhaps this will all work out. This job could be just what I need—what *we* need.

I eat breakfast and down my coffee. It's not the same without whiskey in it, but normal people don't drink Irish coffee before they go to work. I'm told I should be living rather than surviving, and some twat told me alcohol is simply a mask... Well, right now, this doesn't feel like living; it just feels like shit.

———

I GLANCE at my watch for what feels like the hundredth time. How the hell can anyone get paid to just sit and watch a door? The lobby is filled with classical music that repeats on a loop. I throw back my head and stare at the ceiling, ready to go and jump off the nearest bridge. For the first hour or so, I struggled to deal with all the people, the crowds. But after a time, I guess I got desensitized. Now, I'm desensitized to everything. I want to bash my head on the desk.

"Brandon."

I blink and look up at Poppy. "Hey," I say.

"How's your day going?" She glances around the lobby then back at me.

The truth: It makes me want to stab myself in the eye with a paperclip. "Great," I lie and hope she didn't see my eye twitch.

She holds up a paper bag with a little panda on it. "Got you that crispy seaweed you love."

There is a God. The highlight of my day is going to be that seaweed. "See, this is how I know this is true love."

55

POPPY

FEBRUARY 2016

Hope lies on the couch, her head hanging off the edge, her feet on the wall. "Come to Auntie Hope, Mort." She clicks her tongue, and the cat goes prancing over to her. "Where's the pikey?"

"The gym."

"So..." Hope waits for a second before blowing a hard breath through her nose. "How's he doing?"

"Fine."

"No, really?" Her legs drop from the wall to the couch, and she sits up, static causing her red hair to shoot out in all directions. "Brandon O'Kieffe has never been fine as long as I've known him."

"Hope..." I sigh.

Every once in a while, she does this. She thinks I'm hiding something from her or lying to her. She refuses to believe that Brandon's doing okay, even though there's no more fight ring, no more rage. He still has his ups and his downs, but he's much better. *We're* much better.

"Look, I'm just saying, something's going to give at some point."

"Why does something just *have* to give at some point?"

"You do realize he has done a complete one-eighty, right?" She stares at me, chewing at her lip the way she does when she wants to say something she thinks may piss me off. "People relapse. It's part of life, Poppy, and I just don't want you blindsided when it happens."

"He. Is. Fine."

"Brandon was beating the shit out of lads twice his size when he was fourteen. By sixteen, he was winning money, and by seventeen, he was a bare-knuckle boxing champion. He joined the army where his job was to kill people." She stares wide-eyed at me for a moment, as though those state-ments should bring me to an epiphany. "That boy is a hot-blooded male through and through. He lives to fight, and he's damn good at it, and now, he's a security guard?" She shakes her head. "I don't buy it."

I take a breath, then grab the remote from the cushion beside me and turn on the TV, pressing the button hard when I flip through channels. I know she's trying to help, but she's not, so I hope she'll just drop it if I don't respond.

"All I'm saying is, don't be naïve."

That strikes a nerve, and I toss the remote onto the coffee table before shooting her a glare. "Who the hell are you to give me any kind of life advice? Your dad gives you money whenever you want it. You get to flounce around and do whatever suits your fancy. Just..." My face grows hot. "You have no idea what real life is like, Hope."

She flinches like I just slapped her, and in a way, I guess I did.

"You can hate me for it, but I will always tell you the shit you don't want to hear." She scoots Mort out of her lap, shoves her feet into her heels, and slings her Hermes handbag over her shoulder before she crosses the room with a huff. "Because God knows, someone needs to." Then the door slams behind her.

I stare at the wall, my skin tingling with adrenaline. And guilt. Guilt because a small part of me knows Hope is right, but I don't want to believe it. So I pretend I don't see the way Brandon glances at the alcohol behind the bar when we go to a restaurant or the way his leg bounces under the table. I tell myself it's nothing to worry about when I feel his body tense beside mine anytime we ride the subway or go to a museum or movie.

Because things are better. They have to be.

56

BRANDON

People meander through the park, smiling and laughing while I sit on the bench and watch a woman throw a ball for her dog. I fiddle with my phone and skip my music to a different song just as a text appears on the screen.

Finn: U around today?

I chuck my phone back inside my pocket without responding. As far as Poppy is concerned, I'm with Finn now, training at the gym. I've been doing this normal, everyday bullshit for three months—the stuff every other person on the planet seems to cope with just fine, but all it does is bring me down.

When I first came out of therapy, I used to hang out with Finn a lot, go to the gym and work the bag. Hell, I even used to spar with him just to feed that desire for a bit of violence, but as the months have gone by, I find myself feeling more and more alone, and instead of reaching out, I recoil.

I pretend to Poppy that everything is fine, but I just don't have the energy to pretend for anyone else. I can't let her know that I hate this because a normal life is what she deserves. She deserves a guy who has a stable job, who doesn't fly into a rage all the time because he's fighting, exasperating the very thing that threatens to consume him. But that job is unfulfilling in every way, and to make matters worse, the pay is awful. I could make more in one fight than I make in a month as a guard, which means Poppy had to take a different job at a private hospital to make up for it. Sure, it's a promotion for her and her pay is better, but it means she works nights. Because I'm not good enough. Because I can't provide for her.

When I see Poppy, I smile, I kiss her, I want her, but I'm ashamed of the man she's stuck with. I'm terrified that one day she will look at me and realize I'm not worthy of her love, and I never really was.

That sense of worthlessness is a constant, weighing me down until each and every moment feels utterly inconsequential. Fighting is all I've ever been good at, all I was ever good for. Without Brandon "The Breaker" Blaine, I'm just a guy with no prospects, no dreams.

Sometimes, I think about going back to The Pit. Just a few fights here and there couldn't hurt, right? But Poppy would work every hour God gives and sacrifice everything to keep me out of that ring, and doesn't that make me a selfish bastard for wanting it back?

A little girl runs over, crouching beside the bench to pick a dandelion. She closes her eyes, then huffs a breath like she's blowing out birthday candles. The seeds catch on the breeze and scatter in all directions before she runs off. Maybe that's how life is—short with a hundred little wishes, a hundred moments...I remember the time Poppy gave me that dandelion; how special it made me feel, and I think, maybe that was the moment I fell in love with her—maybe that was the beginning of everything between us.

With a sigh, I get up to make my way home.

POPPY IS LYING on the couch, wrapped in a blanket with some program blaring from the TV when I walk in and drop my gym bag to the floor. Her face breaks into a smile when she sees me, and she manages to make me feel like the most important person in the world for just a few seconds.

"Hey, poss." I quickly kiss her before heading to the kitchen.

"How was the gym?"

"Good." I grab a plastic tub out of the fridge and peer inside, inspecting the contents. Something with tomato sauce. I shrug and pop it into the microwave. When I turn around, she's leaning against the door frame, her arms folded over her chest.

"How was Hope?" I ask.

"Fine…"

I can tell something is off by Poppy's tone, and by the way she shifts her weight from side to side. A small line sinks between her brows before she moves forward and wraps her arms around my waist. "I love you."

Something in those three words sounds so desperate, and there's a hint of sadness in her eyes, but I don't ask why. Maybe I don't want to know. "I love you, too."

"Tonight's my last shift this week, which means I get four nights of sleeping with you." She tightens her hold on me and looks up with a smirk. "Naked. We're sleeping naked."

"Are you trying to corrupt me? I'm a full pajamas guy these days, you know? A steady job, normal life. If you're not careful, I'll start scheduling you in for Friday night missionary."

"Brandon O'Kieffe, you could never be normal."

Isn't that the sad truth? "I'm telling you, stripey pajamas and slippers. Give me a few months, and there will be slippers."

"You start wearing slippers, and we're going to have problems."

The microwave beeps, but I ignore it. These moments of happiness are what I live for with Poppy. "You'd still want me."

"True." She grabs the waist to my tracksuit bottoms and tugs me to the bedroom, undressing me as we go.

"Didn't even need the slippers," I mumble.

———

GUNFIRE ECHOES around me like the crackling of fireworks. I don't even know which way the bullets are flying. Shell casings tinker against the hard, desert ground, skittering over the toe of my boot. I aim, fire. Aim, fire. Methodical, precise, robotic. Faces of men appear in the rifle sights, but I pull the trigger before I can lock on, and then I'm onto the next. Refusing to look at them. Refusing to commit them to memory, the second I do, they become more than a target. They become a person with a family, a wife, kids.

I swing my gun to the next target, and Connor's face stares back at me through the sights. I try to move away, take my finger off the trigger, but I can't. My limbs feel like lead. A sad smile crosses his face, and then...I'm pulling the trigger. Bang! He drops to the ground.

In the blink of an eye, the scene changes. I'm on my knees in the back of that truck, my hands pumping over his chest; cold, dead eyes staring at me, mocking me, accusing me. I feel like I can hear his voice in my head: *You should have died, and I should have lived. You're living my life. You stole her, and you aren't good enough for her. You'll never be me, Brandon.*

"I'm sorry. I'm sorry." I say the words over and over, needing his forgiveness, willing him to wake up even though I know he never will. I need him. She needs him.

I JOLT AWAKE, gulping air into my lungs while the dream clings to me. I've had these same dreams ever since Connor died, reliving that moment over and over, but this is different. This is more. It's mixed in with the fighting and the shooting, the nameless faces, and the guilt. And for the last few days, I've heard him. He's there, in my head, taunting me, his presence in my mind like a soft caress.

I don't want Poppy to know I'm still having the dreams. I don't want her to know that I'm still messed up in the head. That what she's left with a shitty stand-in for the guy she married.

I stupidly clung to that futile hope that the therapy would make everything better, never even realizing how much I needed that possibility.

But this is it.

This *is* better. As good as it gets, and while I don't want this life, I have no choice, but she does.

She does...

POPPY

APRIL 2016

"What the fuck!" Brandon shouts, waking me from a restless sleep. Something in the living room crashes, and I glance at the clock flashing: 1:08 in red.

Glass tinkers like it's being swept into a pile, and I climb out of bed, warily making my way to the living room.

The blue haze from the TV puts off just enough light that I can make out Brandon's body, huddled over, sweeping up the remnants of whatever he broke into the dustpan.

Mort jumps down from his spot on the couch, kneading his claws on the rug. "Stop it, Mort." I snap my fingers at the cat, and Brandon freezes.

"Hey, poss."

"What happened?"

"It's nothing; I just knocked over the lamp. Go back to bed." He dumps the shattered glass into the trash, then flops back onto the sofa.

"Come with me," I say, wanting nothing more than him to curl up beside me and hold me. Lately, it seems more times than not that he falls asleep watching TV, and I miss the intimacy. The closeness of waking up with him right there.

"No."

My heart crumples. "Please." I sound desperate, but I don't care. I've spent half my life feeling desperate when it comes to him.

"Just go back to bed, Poppy." He drags a hand through his hair, then fists a handful of it like I'm working his last nerve. "Please."

I study him, the furrow of his brow, the bounce in his knee, and I know why he's out here and why the lamp is broken. "Did you have a nightmare?"

"No. Leave it alone."

A commercial comes on the TV. The pale light dances across his face and I catch his jaw tense, and I know he's lying.

"It's okay if you did."

A cynical laugh rumbles from his chest. "Good to know I have your permission to be a fuck up."

"You're not a fuck up. It's just a dream—"

"Really?" He sits up and swings his legs off the sofa, resting his elbows on his spread knees while his head drops forward. "Is that what you tell yourself? That I'm not screwed up? That I just have bad dreams?" There's a cold cruelty lacing his voice. "Do you think I'm all *fixed*, Poppy?"

That jab was low, and it hurt. "All I want is to understand."

He balls one fist tight and rests it against his forehead, gritting his teeth as he presses his knuckles into his skin. "You will never understand me!" The hate that fills his voice causes me to flinch. "Why the fuck would you want to understand this?" He slaps his palm against his bare chest, while his shoulders rise and fall in uneven swells.

Moments like this make me feel completely helpless like I'm just watching him drown while I'm holding onto a life raft. Like he's Jack and I'm Rose.

When I step forward and try to take his hand, he jerks away.

"God, he's right." He grips his head, his fingers winding through his hair in agitation. "I'll never be good enough for you."

"Brandon." I hesitate to ask. "What are you talking about?"

"Why don't you just leave, Poppy? I'll never be what you want me to be! I hate this. I hate that job. I hate this bullshit life."

He paces the length of the floor, his fists constantly clenching. I don't know where any of this came from, but it's here, and it's been here, looming beneath the surface.

"Stop it. Just..." I cover my face with my hands.

"I hate that I don't fit in your perfect fucking box."

"Stop it," I shout.

He laughs, his expression turning cruel and unrecognizable. "Why? So we can go back to pretending I'm Connor?"

That is an arrow through the chest, hard and swift, and one that leaves my jaw dropped. Out of all the things Brandon has said, that is the cruelest and the most depressing because what he'll never see is that it has always been him—always, Brandon, who owned my heart. I fight the tightening sensation in my chest, my brow wrinkling. "Why?" I exhale and swallow, trying to manage my emotions. "Why would you say that?"

"I stole his life. Took his girl. Hell, I even have the shitty nine-to-five he would have happily worked for you." Brandon kicks the coffee table over with a string of obscenities, and Mort goes dashing across the living room.

"I swear to God!" Brandon's fist goes through the sheetrock, sending dust into the air. Then he grabs a vase from the side table and smashes it, and I find myself moving away from him until my back hits a wall. And just like that, he freezes. His eyes lock on mine, and all that rage rippling over his face melts into despair and grief.

Without a word, he takes his jacket from the hook by the door and storms out, leaving me standing in the middle of so much destruction; the remnants of love and war.

58

BRANDON

I found the first shitty bar I could and ducked in for a drink, but now there's a bottle of whiskey on the bar top in front of me, a short glass beside it that I keep filling up and necking in a few gulps.

Finally, that numbness and quiet I've missed sets in, and my mind stills. Today, tomorrow, they don't matter, just this exact moment, and to a guy like me, that's sheer bliss.

What was I thinking, trying to work a normal job, trying not to drink? I didn't get rid of the monster, I just threw it in a cellar and prayed it wouldn't come back out, but eventually it was roaring so loud the floorboards were shaking, and when it got loose...

I wish Poppy would get out of this shit because God knows I'm too damn weak to leave her.

———

It's past three when I stumble out of the bar and into the drizzly London night. Traffic zooms past, the lull of tires over the wet tarmac almost has me in a trance when I step off the curb. I close my eyes and keep putting one foot in front of the other until I'm in the middle of the road. Waiting, thinking that if I stand here long enough, perhaps fate will fix everything for me.

A horn blares, followed by the breeze of a vehicle passing close by, then someone grabs onto my shirt and yanks me back several feet. "Hey mate, what are you doing?"

I turn, focusing my blurred vision on the stranger. "You all right?" He glances back at the traffic and thumbs to the bus, now taking the corner. "That double-decker nearly flattened you out."

Adrenaline floods my veins as I watch the cars whizz past, then shake my head as my senses return. "Thanks."

He pats me on the shoulder and gives me one last, concerned look before walking off.

I WANDER THROUGH LONDON; down alleys and across parks, until I end up at Finn's door, asking if I can crash for the night. I skip work the next morning, and when my manager calls wanting to know where I am, I tell him he can shove the job, then hang up.

"Smooth," Finn says from the kitchen doorway.

"Looks like I'm in the market for a job, huh?"

"Your skill set is pretty limited." He rounds the coffee table. "But, you can always fight."

I know he's joking, but the idea is oh so tempting. Such easy money, and that feeling... I miss the energy of it, the bloodlust in the air, but most of all, I miss the respect that everyone used to look at me with. I miss being the best at something. And maybe I miss the continuity of it.

Fighting was something I did before everything went to

shit, a constant point in my life that has never changed. The ability to fight. The ability to win.

I dial Larry's number, imagining the disappointment on Poppy's face, and while I wait for him to answer, I tell myself I need this in ways she can't understand.

The line clicks. "Well, there you are, you son of a bitch." Larry laughs. "What'cha want?"

"I want a fight."

59

POPPY

"**P**oppy." Hope shouts through the door, and I groan. She has no idea about what's happened over the past twenty-four hours: that I didn't go to sleep until four this morning when Finn called to let me know Brandon was safe, or that, when I called his work, I was informed he'd been fired.

"I know you're home." The knob rattles before she bangs on the door. "Open up, or I'll be forced to smash your bedroom window and climb in."

I get up and flip the lock, and the second the door opens, she's shoving one of her jackets at me.

"Here. Put this on." She grabs my arm and pulls me into the walkway before I have a chance to blink. "Let's go. Chop-chop." She snaps her fingers.

"I'm not going anywhere, I—"

She drags me toward the parking lot. "Oh, yes, you are. We're going to The Pit." She stops midstride and places a stern hand on her hip. "And you want to know why? Because Brandon, like the prick that he is, is due to fight in about twenty minutes."

"What?" My blood pressure ticks up, and within seconds, my entire body is on fire. "Oh, I'm going to kill him."

————

BREAKER. *Breaker. Breaker.*

I've never seen this place so crowded. People are shoulder to shoulder, yelling and shouting and toasting their beers while I duck underneath their sweaty arms and weave between heckling men.

The microphone crackles before the jarring screech of feedback kicks in. "Gone from the ring for four months, he's back with a vengeance." Larry pauses for dramatic effect, and everyone goes nuts. "Brandon 'The Breaker' Blaine!"

Brandon steps out from the back, hands taped, and hair messy. He paces the pen like a tiger hungry for blood, and with each agitated movement, I catch a glimpse of his monster, willing and ready to claw its way out.

I finish shoving my way through The Pit, losing Hope as I go. I pass Finn before I climb between the worn ropes.

Men whistle, and Brandon whips around, his nostrils flaring like an angry bull when his eyes land on me. I march between him and his opponent, only stopping when my face is inches from Brandon's chest. "Get out of this ring, Brandon."

The crowd boos, then a crumpled beer can lands at my feet. "Get the pretty out of the ring," someone yells.

"Brandon, please. Get out," I repeat because there is a very real fear gripping my throat. I'm terrified of the setback, the inevitable downward spiral.

"Get your bitch out of the ring," the opponent shouts over the boos bouncing from the concrete walls.

Brandon's jaw sets, then his neck cracks to the side. I've

seen that look in his eye once before, the night he nearly killed two guys—the night he hit me.

Brandon moves around me, and his gaze strays to the side. "Finn," he says in a low voice before his attention swings to his opponent, then he charges. A hard punch lands on the other fighter's face, the spray of blood splattering the front of my shirt.

"The fuck did you just say to her?" Brandon fists the guy's hair and slams his head back against the concrete with a loud crack.

The opponent manages to block his face from another blow, but Brandon just goes to his torso, battering it with ruthless jabs.

Someone's arms wrap around my waist, lifting me up and over the ropes. "You all right?" Finn asks as he drags me away from the ring.

The crowd is going ballistic, but even with their cheers, the sickening whack of the guy's skull against the concrete rises above the noise.

I thought I was helping him. I thought that getting him away from this violence would allow his wounds to heal, but I know nothing. All getting him out of this ring did was place a Band-Aid over a knife wound. It didn't even stop the bleeding, much less heal him.

Finn escorts Hope and me upstairs while Larry and Kyan attempt to subdue Brandon. Finn seats us at one of the empty tables, then disappears through the doorway beside the bar.

Hope tries to talk to me, but her words are nothing more than background noise, I'm focused on the fact that I caused this. I stepped into that ring when I shouldn't have. I can't help but think that maybe I'm part of Brandon's problem; all I seem to do is make things worse. When we were sixteen, I showed up at his caravan and kissed him. I was the one who grabbed his hips and pulled him inside of me. And nearly ten years later, I was the one who tracked him down when all he wanted to do was disappear. I am part of his problem...

Hope must sense the thoughts running amuck through my mind because she rubs a soothing hand over my shoulder. "You can't feel guilty about any of this."

But the thing she'll never understand is—I can.

And I do.

———

HOPE FOUGHT me about coming back home, but she lost, and now, as I make my way to the door, my stomach kinking and twisting, I wish I hadn't. I have no idea what to expect when I go inside, so I take a breath before shoving my key into the lock and turning it. The door swings open and I stop mid-stride, keys still in my hand while my heart beats out a rhythm of heartbreak like it's been tethered and quartered and pulled in four opposing directions

It's not the sight of Brandon on the floor with his back against the sofa, his bloodied fingers clutching a bottle of whiskey, or the dark red smudge staining his cheek that breaks my heart. What pulls my soul apart are the tears pouring down his face while his chest heaves.

I've seen Brandon angry and quiet, and I've watched him cry, but outside of when his Ma died, I can't ever remember seeing him sob, and it terrifies me.

I close the door behind me, fidgeting with the keys in my palm before I take cautious steps toward him.

He tips the bottle back and swallows several heavy gulps before I drop to my knees in front of him.

"Brandon," I whisper, knowing he's not here right now, afraid I'll startle him.

His empty eyes meet mine, his wounded soul begging me for help that I have no idea how to give.

"Poss," he murmurs. "I just want it to stop." The utter brokenness that resonates in his voice drags me down a bit deeper. And deeper.

The memories that plague Brandon day and night may as well be a terminal illness because I fear he will die with them still clinging to his mind. They're as much a part of him as he is a part of me.

"I know." I cup his cheek, and he closes his eyes before leaning into my touch. "I wish I could make it stop."

"I'm sorry." He tips back that bottle again, and God, how I hate that he feels the need to apologize to me for something he has no control over, for the awful cards he has been dealt.

"Nothing to be sorry for." I grab his sweat-slicked hand, and he allows me to pull him to his feet. All I want to do is pretend this isn't as bad as it is, that it's just another rough night when I know it's anything but. "Let's get ready for bed."

He stumbles into the wall several times before we reach the bathroom, and I help him out of his bloodstained clothes.

"I'm sorry," he whispers when I turn the taps to the shower, and again when I help him onto the edge of the tub.

Unable to manage the tears still lingering in his eyes, I run a washcloth under the scalding water, then rinse the blood and sweat from his face, his neck and chest. His hands.

He doesn't say a word the entire time, just stares at me like the world ends right here with him and me.

After I dry him off, we go to lie in bed. Like so many

other nights of my life, he rests his head on my chest, and I place my palm against his cheek while running the fingers of my free hand through his thick hair. But this time, the silence is blaringly quiet.

I focus on each of his ragged breaths, understanding for the first time that some pain, some ghosts—well, they're just too much.

"You know you should get out of this, Poppy," he says, his broken words cutting through the silence. "Save yourself. For me."

I sweep my hand through his hair again, pressing my chin against the top of his head. Just needing to feel him. "We're not talking about this right now."

His arms wrap around my stomach, holding me so tight that he shakes like he's scared if he lets go, I'll disappear. "I turn everything I touch to shit," he says. "I'm poison."

And that is what Brandon has been told his whole life, what he's been conditioned to believe. How can I possibly explain love to someone who can't love themselves, who can't manage to see their own worth—*How* do I explain to Brandon that he is my world?

In this silence, I realize I can't. Those words can leave my lips ten thousand times, but Brandon will never hear them. Some things just won't break through that darkness.

I continue to sweep my fingers through his hair until his breaths even out and his tense muscles relax. And when he's asleep, I cling to him a little tighter because I'm so afraid I'm going to lose him.

———

LATER IN THE NIGHT, I wake to a dark room, gasping. My lungs burn and ache for a breath I can't seem to catch.

Someone's grip tightens around my throat, and I claw at the hands crushing my windpipe. Arching my back from the bed, I kick and swat the person pressing down on my throat.

Spots dot my vision, and the last thing I think about is Brandon before the pressure disappears. Dragging in lungful after lungful of air, I throw myself from the bed and stumble to the floor.

"Oh, God."

Brandon is on his knees on the bed, staring at his hands. "I..." He thrusts both hands into his hair and doubles over, a broken cry leaving his lips. "Fuck!"

My legs are shaking, and when I try to stand, I collapse before I crawl across the floor and grab the jeans from earlier, pulling them on while I fight the tears. Fighting everything inside of me that tells me to run away from him.

"Poppy?"

I force myself to look at him. "I'm okay. I'm just going to..." Mort slinks out from underneath the bed, coiling around my leg. "It's fine, Brandon. It was a dream." I rub at my neck. "I'm okay," I say before closing the door and step-ping into the living room.

I grab the blanket and curl up on the sofa, silently breaking apart in the dark. I want to be strong for him like I always have, but everyone has their breaking point. And I'm terrified where mine will be.

60

BRANDON

P oppy comes in before the sun rises. She gets dressed for work, then kisses me and leaves, like nothing ever happened. Like this is normal.

I nearly killed her.

She's the only good in my life, and what happens when I extinguish her?

That dream was so vivid, and it was Connor. Only Connor was the enemy, and I was choking him—choking her. I bite back the strangled sound slipping from my throat. I would never hurt them. They are the two people in this world I would never hurt, and yet, I did. I'm no longer living *with* a monster. I *am* the monster.

She'll never let me go because she's Poppy, and she loves too hard. She'll shred little bits of her soul if she thinks she's saving mine, but there is no saving me. It's up to me to set us both free.

I rummage through the junk drawer, past spare keys and nail polish, and an old birthday card. My fingers brush the smooth glass of my pipe, and I grab it along with the little baggie rubber-banded to it, then I go to the couch and light up.

Mort perches on the arm of the couch, watching in silent judgment while I stroke his arched back. There's a certain simplicity in lounging on the sofa with a smoke, and I need the calm to find my resolve, so I smoke until the afternoon sun creeps through the living room window. Then on a deep breath, I finally get up and take the pen and notepad from the kitchen.

I flip past the note Poppy wrote a few days ago when she went in early for her shift.

I love you, Brandon O'Kieffe. It's always, always *been you. X*

I swallow and turn the page over. The crisp, untouched paper stares back at me until I start writing, bleeding ink onto the page.

Possum,

I'm sorry.

I've loved you for as long as I can remember, and as time has gone on, I've only fallen more in love with you. You are my world, and I know you love me, which is why you'll forgive me for anything.

But, poss, some things shouldn't be forgiven.

I don't know how to walk away from you because I can't survive without you, and I'd sacrifice everything to keep you safe. I've been fighting this war for so long, and I just want it to stop. I just want that sense of peace I find when I kiss you, the serenity your touch brings... I live for those single moments. But you can't survive this thing that lives inside me, and I won't let it have you.

I love you. It's always been you. Never forget that.

This isn't goodbye, only see you later.

Brandon.

I inhale another drag off the pipe, allowing the smoke to burn my lungs. When I know Poppy will be on lunch, I call her, I just want to hear her voice before I let her go.

The phone rings once, then the line clicks. "Hey."

I swallow around the lump threatening to choke me. "Hey, possum."

"You okay?"

"Yeah, you?" I'm so far from okay, but right now, I don't want to hash over everything. "I'm so sorry."

"I know." She takes a deep breath. "I was thinking about making tacos tonight."

This is why I have to do this because she's just so good and pure, and she'll take it and take it until there is nothing left. She's pretending nothing happened and why—Because she was unlucky enough to fall in love with me. "That sounds great," I whisper.

"Brandon... I love you."

"And I love you, poss. Always."

"I'll see you when I get home."

"Okay." I swallow hard, and then she hangs up.

I close my eyes, clenching the phone in my hand for a few seconds before I send a text to Finn.

Me: Hey, fancy going to the gym? Meet me at my place?

Finn: Be there in half an hour.

And there it is: half an hour. It has to be now. It has to be Finn and not Poppy.

I tidy away the few dishes in the kitchen. Mort hops up on the counter and meows. "Oh, Mort, come on." I pick him up and take him to the bedroom, along with his litter box and water bowl, closing the door so he can't get out. Then I fumble along the hallway and into the spare bedroom where my work out equipment is.

I wrap my arms around the punching bag in the corner, lifting it off the hook and laying it on the floor. Then I remember the door and go back to the living to leave it cracked for Finn. The next few seconds are just a series of motions: I grab the chair and the TRX strap, tying and fastening everything where it belongs.

When I sit, the strap tightens. Every instinct in my body tells me to stand back up, to survive. But I don't. I just want this turmoil to stop; all the images and thoughts that plague my mind, I want them to quiet. But most of all, I want Poppy to find peace. So I stay here until my lungs burn and scream until my head spins and my heart pounds in my chest. I push my body's frantic pleas away, and I remember the first time I saw her, just ten years old, and even then, I knew she was going to turn my world upside down.

The beats of my heart grow erratic, and I wait for that nothingness that holds the promise of so much peace. I gasp for air that won't come, and still, I think of her. Poppy Turner will forever be the girl that ruined me for all others. If it's possible, I know I'll love her even in death, and I find my peace in that when the cold numbness falls over me like a veil. And just as everything fades, I see Poppy's face, her smile, and that peace I've been chasing for so long envelops me in its warm, soothing embrace.

61

POPPY

NOVEMBER 2016

D ry grass crunches beneath my shoes as I weave between the tombstones. The cloudless sky is blue, the world inconsiderate of how dark it should feel without him.

I've avoided coming here. It's too hard, but I just needed somewhere to go, thinking that he may hear me.

Patrick wiggles in my arms, whimpering before I wrap the tiny blanket around him and kneel beside Brandon's grave. Grass clippings scatter his headstone, and I brush them away, tracing my finger over the plaque; over the name I wrote so many times on notebooks and diaries while swooning and wishing Brandon would love me.

The world presses in on me, like the universe is on the verge of imploding, like I'm right back to the moment Finn told me Brandon was gone, and I'm dying all over again.

"He looks just like you, Brandon." I take a deep breath and stare down at our son, so peaceful with his eyes closed and tiny fists clenched in sleep. "He really does."

Eight months later, and it's still not real because Brandon was always there. And maybe that's why I'm in such denial because a vital part of my heart has always belonged to him, and my soul refuses to acknowledge he's gone. They both are.

"Brandon," I take an unsteady breath. "This is Patrick." My throat burns, and I close my eyes for a moment. "Our little boy that I hope is *just* like you."

I sweep a finger over his soft cheek, hating that he will never know the sound of Brandon's voice. I hate that the life I had imagined since I was ten years old is now impossible, but I remind myself that for a moment, for a flicker in time, we had it. We *almost* had that dream.

"I wish you were still here," I whisper. "But, I know you set yourself free."

Brandon was in such a dark place, already half-dead, and I tried to understand him, help him, love him; but unlike I had been lead to believe, love does not conquer all.

I cradle Patrick against my shoulder, and he grunts, nuzzling his soft head against the crook of my neck. "Brandon, if death was the only place you could find that quiet you needed—"I choke back sobs and take deep breaths—"I hope you found your peace, but I will forever miss you." Tears fall, constricting my throat. "*We* will forever miss you."

Brandon Patrick O'Kieffe was a once in a lifetime experience, and there is nothing—nothing that would ever make me walk away from that. I'll still hold him in my heart when I'm ninety years old, knowing that I was lucky enough to have experienced a love most people will never have.

The astounding and beautiful truth about love is, it doesn't matter how long you had the person, just *that* you did. So, I'll cling to the belief that I'll find Brandon in the next life, after all, our love is one that spans eternity, one that deserves more time. In another life—one without the demons.

Shifting our son in my arms, I bring my fingers to my lips, press a kiss to them, then I place my hand on his grave while pain riddles my insides.

My breath catches in my lungs as an all too familiar grief captures my heart. "This isn't goodbye, only see you later."

the end

ARE you in need of a warm, heart felt love story with a happy ending? Read The Sun by Stevie J Cole.

THE TRUTH

20. That is the estimated number of veterans who take their own lives every single day in the United States alone. (US Department of Veteran's Affairs, 2016).

Those are not simply numbers; those are 20 people who are loved and needed. 20 people who are lost each day, forever changing the lives of those they leave behind.

To the men and women who have so selflessly defended our countries, thank you. We will always remember.